D0667126

THE MURALS

THE MURALS

William Bayer

This first world edition published 2019
in Great Britain and the USA by
SEVERN HOUSE PUBLISHERS LTD of
Eardley House, 4 Uxbridge Street, London W8 7SY.
Trade paperback edition first published
in Great Britain and the USA 2020 by
SEVERN HOUSE PUBLISHERS LTD.

British Library Cataloguing in Publication Data
A CIP catalogue record for this title is available from the British Library.

ISBN-13: 978-0-7278-8973-7 (cased)
ISBN-13: 978-1-78029-634-0 (trade paper)
ISBN-13: 978-1-4483-0333-5 (e-book)

All Severn House titles are printed on acid-free paper.

Severn House Publishers support the Forest Stewardship Council™ [FSC™],
the leading international forest certification organisation. All our titles that
are printed on FSC certified paper carry the FSC logo.

Typeset by Palimpsest Book Production Ltd.,
Falkirk, Stirlingshire, Scotland.
Printed and bound in Great Britain by
TJ International, Padstow, Cornwall.

Preface

The following account of the discovery of and investigation into the creation and meaning of the so-called Locust Street Murals is told in the voices of its participants. Their testimonies were recorded, compiled, arranged and edited by one of them . . . whose identity will be revealed in due course.

In order to enhance readability, recounted conversations are presented in dialogue form and occasionally condensed. Names and features of several of the characters have been changed to disguise their identities. Certain fictional techniques have also been employed in the tradition of the 'non-fiction novel.'

Some of the participants have dramatized their participation while others have flatly presented theirs. These variations in style are due to the individual personalities of the speakers, each of whom has his/her particular way of recounting events.

The reader may note that portions of some testimonies are inconsistent with or directly contradicted by others. These anomalies have been left unedited with the understanding that different people often have different perspectives on the same series of events. Whether one narrator or another is to be regarded as 'unreliable' is a matter best left to the reader.

Jason Poe

*P**ow!*
The murals hit me hard. First came terror, then awe. It was only after I'd taken them in that I began to feel their immense power.

'The Locust Street Murals,' as we later called them, covered all four walls of that little room, and the strange menacing figures all seemed to be staring at me, meeting my eyes with theirs, following me as I turned from one to the next. Clearly, they told some kind of story. I had no idea what the story was, but from the first I knew I had to uncover it. I was equally determined to discover who had told this story, the name of the artist who'd painted these figures.

I'd been photographing the interiors of abandoned houses for a couple of years, sneaking in at night, looking around, finding something interesting and poignant, then setting up my camera and using my miner's headlamp to paint it with light. These long slow exposures were parts of a project I called *Leavings: The Things They Left Behind*, which I later hoped to assemble for exhibition, and, if the images were strong enough, publish together as a book.

There were so many abandoned houses in the city that the project took on a boundless quality. My close friend, Hannah, after looking at a huge number of my images, kindly suggested that perhaps it was time for me to stop. 'You may have a problem with repetition,' she told me. 'You need to decide when you've made your point.'

She was right: I was repeating myself. But I wasn't ready to call a halt. There was something missing, I told her, something I was after, and I didn't want to stop until I found it. I shrugged when she asked me what this something was. 'I wish I knew,' I said.

Whenever I entered a house, I had a pretty good idea what I was looking for: the detritus folks abandon when they hurriedly leave a place – upended furniture, unwashed dishes, gunked-up cooking equipment, torn bedding, unlaundered clothes, the scattered food containers out of which they ate their final at-home meal. I often found broken toys, discarded school books, crumpled newspapers open to the *Help Wanted* pages. But I was after the unusual object that spoke of the anguish of people who had left in a rush because their mortgage was underwater or they couldn't make rent: a final eviction notice, heap of unpaid bills, dented old tuba wrapped in soiled high-school band uniform, perhaps a treasured set of drums that unhappily hadn't made it into the family car.

Best of all, I'd discover oddities, the images of which I treasured most because they seemed so telling – a painting on black velvet of a movie star hanging crooked on a wall, a ragged stuffed donkey tucked neatly by a child into a crib. In one house I came upon a rusted gynecological examination table with stirrups, suggesting the place had been an unlicensed abortion clinic. In another I slipped on the scattered beads of a rosary, perhaps ripped apart in despair. And, too often, I found messages of anger and contempt directed at mortgage lenders and landlords: smashed toilets, paint flung at walls, pet excrement and opened cans of food deliberately set out to attract vermin and flies.

Always I'd ask myself: *What went wrong in this house? Who used to live here? What made them leave?* It was a melancholy quest I was on.

I harbored the notion (perhaps naïve) that such abandoned objects told stories of the people who had left, their anger, despair, feelings of having been beaten down by life. And when I photographed them, I didn't try to aestheticize the way some photographers do when they shoot pictures of decayed buildings, reveling in mold and peeling paint. I did not, I told my students and colleagues, view myself as that kind of artist. I'm a documentarian, I told them, using still lives to tell stories of broken hardscrabble lives, and, by extension, the breakdown of our rust-belt town, Calista.

As always, we'd chosen the house carefully. Tally, my former student at Calista Art Institute, had scouted it out.

'There's this boarded-up gothic place standing apart on Locust,' he told me as we lunched together in the cafeteria at CAI. He passed me his cell phone. I liked what I saw. There was a small square gazebo perched on top, with a little railing around it, like a widow's walk on a coastal house, except there was no coast in sight.

'Looks untouched,' Tally told me. 'Most of the places around have been torn down. I thought you'd like the turret.'

'I do,' I told him. 'I also like that it's on Locust. Is there a way in?'

'Yeah, there's a way,' he said.

We went to see it on a warm June afternoon. I knew the area, an eclectic neighborhood of houses in different styles, most set far back from the street. Many of the abandoned ones had been bulldozed in accordance with the city's *Tear Down the Blight* program. There'd been talk of giving the land beneath these teardowns to local residents for use as community gardens. I'd yet to see one. I'd only found broken foundations, piles of rubble and empty bramble-choked fields.

Locust Street fascinated me. The old Kenyon-Garfield Observatory stood on a rise at one end surmounted by the slotted dome that had once housed its fine Schmidt telescope. It was an anomaly in the neighborhood, a reminder of better days. The telescope had been relocated years before. The observatory building, long abandoned by Calista State University, had so far escaped local vandals due to a high-security fence and live-in watchman.

There were the two famous crime scenes near the other end of Locust that gave the street its notoriety: a house in which a middle-aged couple had imprisoned a young Latina for nearly a decade, and a murder venue just a block away to which a skinhead serial killer had lured black prostitutes for slaughter.

The imprisoned woman had been abducted on her way to school, then chained up in the attic to be used as a sex slave. As for the serial killer, when he was finally caught, the cops started digging around his place. They found four bodies buried in the crawlspace and seven more in shallow graves in the backyard. After that, TV anchors and reporters at local stations referred to Locust as 'Street of Horror.'

Tally was right. The gothic place did seem different from its neighbors, and the turret on top gave it the look of a classic haunted house. There were even decorative spikes protruding from the roof of the gazebo like a structure in a macabre cartoon by Charles Addams.

We slowed down as we passed, circled the block, then passed it slowly again.

'Best not to hang around and show interest,' Tally said as he picked up speed.

He had, he told me, checked it out three nights in a row.

'No one's lived there in years. Water, electric and gas all turned off. It's not considered abandoned 'cause the taxes are paid up. There're loose boards on a cellar window round back. Wouldn't be hard to jimmy,' he said.

'How do you know about the taxes?'

He glanced at me. 'Hall of Records. You know I always check, Jase. Listed to a corporation with an address on Doverland. I checked it out. Turned out to be a CPA's office in a shopping strip.'

'So somebody's paying taxes, but there're no utilities. What makes you so sure it hasn't been touched?'

Tally shrugged. 'Just a feeling. Maybe someone's been in there once or twice, but there're no signs it's been used as a crack house or occupied by homeless.' He glanced at me. 'Something about it, isn't there?' He stopped the car in front of the observatory. 'An aura. Like *Stay outta here! We mean it!* And for some reason the locals are respecting that.'

'I think you're being a little mystical,' I told him.

He shook his head. 'Maybe something spooky happened there once and people don't wanna mess around in it. Anyway, there's no one living near. A patrol car passes around midnight. Otherwise, it's real quiet. I spent a couple of hours in the bushes behind. Parked here then walked back. Didn't see a soul.' He paused, gestured toward the observatory dome. 'No moon tomorrow night. What'd you think?'

I wasn't sure. Going in through a cellar window could be risky if that was also the only way out. What if Tally was wrong and I encountered someone inside – crack user, copper thief, maniac with a vicious dog? Tally waiting outside would have my back; we'd be in contact texting back and forth . . . but still . . .

'Could attract attention if my lighting shows through the boards.'

'Boarding looks tight,' he said.

I thought about it. 'Let's try tomorrow.'

He grinned. 'Yeah, I kinda thought you'd go for it.'

We'd been working together on *Leavings* since I conceived the project, an odd pair of urban explorers, as we liked to describe ourselves: me, the white late-forties former conflict photographer, now instructor in photography at CAI, and Tally, my talented twenty-something former student, eking out a living as a wedding photographer in the African American community. We'd worked out a partnership: I'd take the pictures; Tally would handle scouting, protection and transport. His battered Honda ran well and didn't stand out in poor neighborhoods. We'd split anything we made from print sales or a book, but money wouldn't be the point. We both loved the combination of photography and risk, plus Tally had special feelings for his home town. 'It's about the busted American Dream here, isn't it?' he asked when I first proposed the project. Yeah, that's what it'll be about, I told him, adding that it was great that he got it right away. 'I know why you want to do this, Jase. You need the rush,' Tally said. I was glad he got that too.

I wasn't inside a couple of minutes when I sensed this house was different. Soon as I inspected the main floor I understood this wasn't a typical residence. The dining table was long enough to accommodate more than a dozen people, and I found a standing gong in the kitchen. Could be a dinner bell, I thought, suggesting a lot of people had once lived there.

I liked houses where it turned out there'd been a lot more going on inside than you could guess from the exterior. Perhaps this one had been an unlicensed boarding house, or group home for the mentally handicapped.

The place was moderately ratty. There were the usual signs of disuse and decay – cobwebs, rodent droppings – but no sign of black mold. One oddity: the words *A Caring Place* meticulously stenciled on the living-room wall, with a huge 666, the satanic number, crudely spray-painted on top as if to negate the good intentions beneath.

Maybe this was some kind of cult house or splinter church that went bad.

I banded my miner's lamp to my forehead, texted Tally, then cautiously played the beam on the windows. Tally texted back that no light was seeping out. Relieved, I set down my tripod, battery unit and camera pack, and continued to explore.

The stairs were in OK shape. A couple of risers were missing, and one step started to give when I put my foot on it. I warned myself to be careful, then continued the climb. I counted three bedrooms and a bath on the second floor and one more on the

third, with cots and double-decker bunks in each. Also on the third
was a master suite with adjoining study and private bath. Bedding
and clothes were strewn about. There were towels scattered on the
bathroom floors, old toothbrushes and toothpaste tubes in the sinks.
All those beds – definitely a lot of people used to live here . . .
I remember thinking that this was the kind of house I liked –
stuff scattered about and a mysterious backstory suggested by that
666 sprayed on the wall below.

In the third-floor hallway I ran into a hanging rope. Figuring it
for an attic ladder drawstring, I checked out the ceiling. My head
lamp picked up the outlines of a trapdoor, an entrance hatch to
the gazebo structure on the roof. When I pulled on the rope, the
trap door dropped open. I pulled on the bottom rung of the attached
ladder. It telescoped down to the floor.
    I texted Tally that I was going up to the gazebo.
    Circle the house and check again for light leaks, I texted.
Remember there're windows on all four sides.
    Roger that! he texted back.
    The ladder held steady. A musty smell enveloped me as I
approached the top. My breathing stirred up dust as I stuck my
head through the hatch. I remember thinking: *No one's been up
here in years . . .*
    That's when I caught sight of the murals.
    No light, Tally texted, but I didn't respond, just crawled in, then
stood still in the center of the ten-foot-square structure and gazed
incredulously at the walls.
    On numerous expeditions into abandoned houses I'd never come
across anything like this: all four walls covered with artwork, on
each a row of six painted life-size, head-to-foot people staring out
at me . . . or maybe at each other. These people, men and women,
did not appear friendly. There was intensity about them, ferocity
in their postures and the sets of their eyes. Gazing at them, I felt
them staring back. I knew at once I was looking at something
extraordinary.
    I texted Tally: *Pay dirt! Get settled. I'll be up here a while.*

It didn't matter that the murals didn't fit with my theme of 'The
Things They Left Behind.' I knew I had to document them.
The turret room was small, which made it difficult to take good

photographs. I'd have to go wide-angle to completely capture each wall. Since there're distortion issues with wide-angle lenses, I decided to shoot each wall from as far back as I could, then use a normal lens to document details. Later, using software, I could combine the images on my computer.

Full coverage would take time. My head lamp didn't throw off much light, but it helped that the walls were pale and the images were painted in shades of grays and blacks. Assured by Tally that no light was leaking out, I went downstairs to fetch my equipment. Back in the gazebo, I set up my master lights and set to work on the first wall.

The air in that attic was close. As I made exposure after exposure, standing very still so as not to shake my tripod and blur the images, I noticed that some of the murals were more finished than others. Looking closely, I saw that the figures on one wall and on a portion of another were drawn in a combination of charcoal and black crayon, while the rest were painted with black acrylic. This told me that whoever had drawn them had left behind a work-in-progress – as did a box of charcoal stubs and crayons, several cans of black paint and a vase of brushes I found stashed against one of the walls.

I didn't notice the bedrolls scrunched in a corner until I finished documenting two of the walls. Had the artist been so obsessed that he'd slept up here inside his work? Had he been awakened by someone in the middle of the night, forced to make a hurried departure? Who *was* he? What had he been trying to say? And how could he have left such a powerful work unfinished?

At first I thought that the figures on each wall were staring across the room at the figures on the wall opposite. But standing in the center of the gazebo while shooting sections, it occurred to me that just as I was staring through my lens at the people painted on the walls, they in turn were staring back at me. This, I realized, could account for the powerful effect of the murals: that it had been the intention of the artist, whoever he was, to draw the people on the walls as watchers, turning viewers who entered the attic room into objects of *their* inspection.

The eyes! There was no escaping them. They were sharp, hard, and all focused on whomever stood before them. Whenever I moved, the eyes uncannily seemed to follow me.

They were so strange, those people, frozen in space, their postures oddly angular, gestures exaggerated, bodies surmounted by slightly oversized heads. They were posed weirdly too: some in the foreground; others, darker, hovering just behind. And then I saw that in many cases the figures were doubled – the ones perched behind drawn as shadow doubles of the ones in front. The expressions on the faces of the front figures were stern but otherwise without affect, while the expressions on their shadowed doubles smirked, some showing unguarded cruelty, ferocity and deceit.

This, I gathered, had been the artist's intention: to show the two-faced character of his subjects, the false blank faces they showed the world and their true faces, Janus faces they kept concealed.

And then there was the little girl with the puppy crouching in the far right just behind one of the women's legs.

Who was she? And what was she doing there? Had she been asleep, heard something, come downstairs to see what was going on, and then snuck with her dog into a corner of the room, from which she peered out fascinated and unnoticed, a witness to the scene?

Sensing the power of these markings, I realized something strongly felt was being expressed, perhaps some sort of malevolent violation. I also knew this wasn't the time to try to decode the murals.

Concentrate, document, analyze them when I get home.

Tally texted: *Cops just passed a second time. Time to get out!*
Almost done. Gimme ten minutes, I texted back.

Half an hour later I knew it was time to go. The room had grown hot, I was sweating, my lungs ached, the musty air I'd been breathing was bad and my eyes were swelling with fatigue. I was starting to feel light-headed too.

Checking the walls to make certain I'd photographed every inch of them, I noticed for the first time something that should have been obvious from the start: the windows of the turret room weren't just boarded up on the outside; they'd been boarded on the interior as well. This told me the walls had been prepped, a smooth surface created on which to paint. It was only after I was back down in the third-floor hallway, pulling the rope that closed the attic trap-door, that it occurred to me that this might make it possible to detach the murals from the walls if someone wanted to remove them from the house.

*   *   *

'Man, you were up there four hours!' Tally whispered as I wriggled through the cellar window.

Once outside, I took deep breaths. I was glad to be out in open air.

'Worth it. You'll see,' I told him, as we replaced the boards that covered the window.

We walked in silence back to Tally's car. It was two a.m. An owl hooted in the distance. My nostrils caught a feint aroma of smoke. The air buzzed with the sounds of insects. We didn't see a single soul or passing vehicle.

Tally drove toward the city. When we reached a deserted shopping strip, I asked him to pull into the parking lot. There I pulled out my camera, accessed my last card of photos, passed it to Tally and watched him as he examined them.

'What *is* this?'

'You tell me.'

'Painted on the walls?' I nodded. 'They look big.'

'Life-size.'

'Holy shit!' He turned to me. 'Who *are* these people?'

'I've no idea.'

'There's no background? They're just standing there like they're in limbo or something.'

'No need for a background. They're right there in the room.'

'Spectacular!'

'Yeah!'

Again he turned to me. 'You wanna find out who made this art?'

'More than anything,' I told him.

Downtown Calista loomed as we approached on the interstate. It's generally considered to be an ugly city, but sometimes, approaching from the east, I'm moved by the buildings clustered against the sky. At this hour it was silent except for the distant sound of sirens.

'Fire engines,' Tally murmured. His ear could tell the difference between police and fire.

The city was dark except for streetlights, an occasional car, and Calista's signature twin office buildings, Tower of the Great Lakes and Tower of the Great Plains, lit inside for the night cleaning crews.

Tally drove along Calista River to the Capehart Building, a hundred-year-old six-story redbrick structure in the old warehouse district converted into live/work lofts. Several CAI teachers lived there. To buy into the Capehart you had to prove you were an artist, a rule that infuriated rich folks who longed to live in urban lofts with downtown views. They retaliated by calling it 'the artsy-fartsy complex,' and those of us qualified to live there 'pretentious assholes who couldn't make it in New York.' Fine with us! We laughed off their contempt. Calista might not be the Athens of America, but if you worked in the arts, you could live there reasonably well for not much money.

'Get some sleep,' I told Tally. 'We'll talk tomorrow. We gotta find out everything we can about that house.'

Tally nodded. 'Those people on the walls, Jase – they're not real, they're nightmare people, right?'

'Sometimes nightmare people can be more real than real people,' I told him as I stepped out of the car.

I know quite a bit about nightmares, have had my share, always based on a horrible experience in Aleppo. I lived in that hellhole for two months, documenting its bombardment and destruction, the agony of its inhabitants. I became close to a particular family, the Daouds – Ayman, Rasha and their four kids.

Ayman was a doctor who worked in a secret basement hospital, treating people wounded in the bombardment. I spent a lot of time with him and the injured he was tending to. They would look at me and then at my lens, and it was at these moments of eye/lens contact that I'd trip the shutter. The result was my exhibition and later my book, *The Eyes of Aleppo*, in which every image is of a person whose eyes express his/her perplexity, courage or suffering, and sometimes all three, as they meet the eyes of the beholder.

The Daouds were terrific people, educated and surprisingly optimistic considering the terrible conditions in which they lived. While Ayman treated the wounded, Rasha home-schooled the kids. All four were graceful and full of life, laughing as they played in the rubble on those rare occasions they were allowed outside.

One day, just before the end of my stay, I gathered them in a courtyard for a family group photograph. I arranged them, went back to my tripod, instructed them all to look directly at my lens, then started clicking off images. At first the kids forced themselves to peer at me with gravity, then they'd break into giggles. I got so involved trying to catch the family in different moods that I didn't hear the screech of the barrel bomb until just a couple of seconds before it hit. Soon as I heard it, I dove for the ground and covered up. The Daoud family took a direct hit. When I finally looked up, I saw their broken bodies, limbs scattered about. All six were dead. The roar of the explosion was so loud I went deaf. I went into shock and then, on auto-pilot, stumbled around trying to photograph what was left of them.

I didn't know it at the time, but the explosion had broken my camera. Perhaps it was a blessing that none of my images, of the family portrait session and its macabre aftermath, were recorded.

The next day I left Aleppo resolving never to go to war again. My 'I'll go anywhere there's a fight' reputation, which I'd so carefully nurtured, was blown up by that barrel bomb. I'd gone to Aleppo to be a witness. That was how I always saw my role. I left the city broken, burned out on empathy, finished with conflict photography.

Those unrecorded images of the Daoud family were etched into my brain. They still come to me sometimes while I sleep. It's always the sound of the kids' giggles that wakes me. Then I lie in bed, coated with sweat, gasping at images I can't shake off. The doctors called it PTSD, gave me pills, sent me to psychiatrists. I even went on my own to a hypnotist for help. It's been ten years since I last worked a war. The flashbacks come less often now. But still they come, nightmares, more intense and more real, sometimes, than the reality of my daily life.

I'd been what they call 'a war lover' – a hard-drinking guy in a safari jacket and a bunch of cameras specializing in pictures of carnage and conflict. I'd worked wars in Iraq, Afghanistan and Libya; street riots in Cairo and Kiev; endless chaos in Mogadishu. I was the fearless London-based freelancer, packed and ready to go at a moment's notice, the guy they called whenever a fight broke out. My JPOE byline on a photo was a seal of authenticity. I took a statement of the great Robert Capa and had it printed on the backs of my business cards: 'If your pictures aren't good enough, it's because you aren't close enough. You must be part of the event.'

Aleppo was the turning point. I'd gotten too close too many times, and suddenly couldn't do it anymore. My hands shook. I could no longer hold my camera steady. Maybe it was burnout, or, more likely, loss of nerve. Whatever the reason, I knew it was time to close the heroic photojournalist act with which I'd made my name. My agency offered me a photo-editing job. I tried it, didn't like it. A friend mentioned an opening in the photography department at Calista Art Institute. I applied, got the job, have been at it now for ten years. These nights the nightmares come less often, and during the day I get to play the grizzled ex-war shutterbug star, teaching kids the photojournalism trade. It's a good life, and I have my personal projects, the latest being *Leavings*.

Home from our Locust Street run, I slept a couple of hours, woke at five, sat down at my laptop, downloaded my photos, then started going through them. They were clean. The artwork on the walls showed clear. Reviewing the images, I asked myself: Were these murals really as powerful as I'd first thought, or had coming upon them unexpectedly clouded my judgment? Were they really, as I'd thought, some species of masterpiece, or merely a primitive effort by an unschooled artist? Were the people in them made-up 'nightmare people,' as Tally said, or, as I now viewed them, a cathartic vision of actual people the artist may have known or met in some kind of traumatic encounter, which he had then worked to exorcize by drawing them vividly in shades of black on the interior gazebo walls?

I waited until seven thirty to phone Hannah. We'd become lovers shortly after I moved to Calista, were now colleagues and best friends, occasionally 'friends with benefits' too. That's how Hannah sometimes chooses to describe our current relations, though depending on her mood she sometimes calls us, with ironic vulgarity, 'hook-up mates.' She knows I hate that expression, which, I suppose, is why she uses it, as in: 'Hey, Jase! I'm lying up here horny as hell. Mind if I come down for a mercy fuck?'

But aside from these diversions, we remain close. She teaches weaving and textile art at CAI, and is, as I've assured her numerous times, among the smartest of my friends. I know her habits, that she likes to get up early, go out for a run along Riverwalk above the Calista River, then return home for a light breakfast before heading over to the Institute.

'Getting you at a bad time?' I asked.

'Been up since six,' she said. 'What's going on?'

'I'd like to come up and show you something, if you got time.'
'Sure. Come up. We'll have coffee. I don't have class until eleven.'
Carrying my laptop, I took the elevator to the penthouse floor. Hers was the only loft up there, surrounded by terraces on three sides. It was the most luxurious residence at the Capehart, not part of the original building but added by the developer. I once overheard people in the cafeteria at CAI wondering aloud how an art teacher could afford such a place. Hannah didn't reveal much to colleagues about her background, but I knew, because she'd told me, that her grandfather, a local industrialist, had left her and her brother a pile of money. She was a Calista native who, after years of working in textile design in New York, returned home to receive her inheritance, then decided to stay on to teach.

At fifty-two, she was eight years older than me, a difference that never bothered either of us. I'd been attracted to her from the first time we met at a start-of-school faculty meeting at CAI. Our three-year affair, I liked to tell her, had made it possible for me to adapt to a city I hadn't started out liking very much . . . not to mention the fact, as I also liked to tell her, that she was the best lover I'd ever had.

'Better than all those dyed-blond TV news girls you hooked up with in exotic hotel bars?'

'Yeah, because they were always in a hurry, and you're a woman who likes to take her time.'

She liked hearing that, but then she asked, 'Why aren't we still together?'

'I think we are,' I answered, 'in our own way.'

'You mean like fuck buddies, Jase?'

I scowled. 'I prefer "romantic friends."'

'Oh, I know you prefer genteel language,' she said, 'but I like the expression on your face when I go vulgar. You always look *so shocked*!'

She enjoyed that kind of banter, and so did I. We felt it was the best part of our friendship.

She's looking really good, I thought, as she embraced me that morning at her penthouse door. Her hair was still wet from her shower. She pulled back and gazed at me.

'Wow, you look like crap, Jase. Been up all night? What's so important you've got to show it to me now?'

Hannah Sachs

loved Jason, always will . . . but I won't claim I loved his *Leavings* project. I liked it at first. He had a point of view and he came up with some great images. But a lot of serious photographers had worked that ruined-buildings-in-decaying-rust-belt-towns trope. I'd seen beautifully produced oversized books devoted to abandoned hospitals, schools and movie theaters in cities like Detroit. And even though Jason's obsessive pursuit of stuff left behind in abandoned houses was unique, I didn't see it leading anywhere. I also found it overly melancholic. He wasn't looking for beauty in the ruins and mold like the other 'lust-for-rust' guys. He seemed intent on straight documentation. I guess I thought he was trying to say something that people already knew.

I think the stuff he found in those houses meant something special to him, something he couldn't explain. He had a tenderness toward people who lacked privilege and struggled to get by. Who wouldn't love a guy like that?

He told me many times that his conflict photographer days had burned him out on photographing people under stress. He'd decided, he told me, to devote himself to still-life work – not, he emphasized, beautifully lit arrangements of objects with different and intriguing shapes, but, as he put it, 'stills that tell a story.' But there was plenty of risk, physical as well as legal, breaking into abandoned houses. That's why he partnered up with Tally; he needed someone to watch his back. So in a sense, I thought, his exploration into the artifacts of ruined lives was akin to his former career – pursuit of danger, adventure and the high he got from not knowing what might happen next.

He knew I felt this way. We frequently exchanged critiques, while always respecting each other's intentions. And even when our comments were less than fully enthusiastic, we always listened carefully to what the other had to say.

My personal opinion: there was a storehouse of hurt in Jason, a sadness in his background that made left-behind stuff meaningful to him. I don't know where that came from. Maybe it was his feeling that when his mom abandoned the family, *he* had been the 'stuff' that had been left. When I asked him one time if this was true, he shrugged, but didn't deny it. Still, no question he believed in his project, which made me think that his conviction would make it work. So even if I didn't adore what he was doing, I never tried to discourage him.

When he called early that Friday morning, asking to come up and show me some images, I figured they'd be from his *Leavings* series, and that maybe he felt he'd made a breakthrough. But when I opened my door and saw the glow in his eyes, I was pretty sure this visit was about something else. And then when he showed me the images and told me how he'd discovered them, I understood his excitement . . . for I felt it too.

I think 'enraptured' would be a better word. Or ravished. Or in thrall. And his tale, the way he told it, added extra heat to his discovery.

'It was a eureka moment,' he said. 'Like this is what I've been waiting to find since Tally and I started on the project. Then to just stumble on it in that nothing house! I knew as soon as I poked my head through the hole in the floor that this was something big!' He paused. 'But of course it wasn't a "nothing house." It was a strange house, not like any other – on a strange street, too. The whole place gave off a vibe.' He gazed at me. 'What'd you think?'

I had some thoughts but wasn't ready to express them. He was excited enough, keyed up like an artist in a manic fit of creativity, and I could see that he was struggling to stay calm. Anyway, I tend to distrust my first reactions. He'd barely slept, and now he'd come to me for validation. I wanted to be sure my own excitement derived from the power of the murals, and not because I'd been swept up in his feverish account of finding them.

'The size of them! The way they dominate that little room. I know my images can't convey that.'

'Hey, take a breath,' I told him. 'Take your coffee out on the terrace while I study them. I'll join you in a while and then we'll talk.'

'Sure, Hannah. Cast a cold eye.' He smiled. 'You're good at that.'

OK, I thought, after he'd left me alone, *this isn't about Jason's photography. It's about a set of murals he discovered and documented. So forget these are pictures of pictures. Look at these murals as a work of art.*

As I ran the images through his laptop, peering closely, trying to piece them together in my head, I had to admit that the cumulative effect was compelling. And, I thought, it would be even more so if I'd come upon them the way he'd described. There was, I thought, an 'outsider art' aspect to them, a mix of sophistication and naïveté. Perhaps they were by an artist who was talented yet not fully skilled. The drawing struck me as a bit cartoonish. The expressions on the characters' faces weren't subtle. There was no doubt they were leering. The double-faced figures, which Jason said he found so evocative, struck me as attempts at psychological portraiture. But I found the overall concept powerful: full-length, life-size frontal images of people on four walls facing one another, or perhaps observing something in between. And on the far right of one wall, a little girl on hands and knees with a puppy, peering with eyes filled with wonderment from behind an adult woman's legs – that was extraordinary, I thought, as if she were a voyeur who had snuck into the scene and was gazing out at something forbidden.

I was also impressed by the scope of the work, the commitment by the artist to a major project. These murals must have meant a great deal to him. They spoke of a huge investment of emotion. What else would compel someone to climb into an attic, seal up the windows, then create something on such a scale? In this sense it reminded me of one of those weirdly powerful outsider artworks that rare individuals have created out of an inexplicable inner need, works like the Watts Towers in LA, or the obsessive drawings of Henry Barger, works that perhaps started out small but then grew very large, illustrating stories they were seeking to tell themselves which they likely couldn't tell any other way.

Looking back, I think it was the figures' eyes that got to Jason. He had this thing for eyes. His book on Aleppo was called *The Eyes of Aleppo*. In every photo there was someone looking straight at his lens, making direct eye contact with the viewer. In a way, I think the murals are also about the figures' eyes. Some people think it's the mouths, the somewhat cruel way they're turned. But I think to Jason it was those people's eyes. What were they telling him? When I asked him about that, he shrugged. But I felt that he had seen eyes like those before, sometime in his life. Or were they his own eyes, and he'd seen them in a mirror?

Jason was looking for something; he didn't know what. He told me this when I asked him why he kept going on his *Leavings* project long after he had more than enough images.

'I keep thinking,' he said.

'Thinking what?' I asked.

'There's more.'

'More what?'

'More to be seen, to be found.'

Well, now it seemed he'd found that 'more.' Stumbled upon it, as he put it. And now he was hooked!

I must have spent an hour scrolling through the images before I went on to my terrace to talk to him. I found him sound asleep on one of my chaises longues. Smoke hung in the air. There'd recently been a lot of fires in the city. The sun had risen and was already beating down. Reluctant to wake him, I rolled a sun umbrella to the chaise and arranged it so it shadowed his face. Then I went back inside, knowing sooner or later he'd wake up and come back in to talk.

He appeared half an hour later, rubbing his eyes.

'Sorry I fell off,' he said. 'Barely slept last night. I'm thirsty as hell.'

I poured him a glass of water. He thanked me for setting up the umbrella.

'It's wicked hot out there. I didn't want my best friend to get burned.' I looked at him. 'We have a lot to talk about.'

He listened closely as I told him what I thought about the murals.

'They're not like anything else I've seen. That alone makes them interesting. I think they might be about feelings . . . rejection and humiliation. The frontality of them – I find that extraordinary. And I love the little girl and the dog. Also the consistency of the artist's vision. I think whoever painted these knew exactly what he wanted to do from the start. Fill up the four walls. Arrange the same number of figures on each. Show them all reacting to each other or to whatever was happening in the middle of the room.'

'What do you suppose that was?'

'From reading their faces, something dark. That's why these murals are so powerful. We can't see what they're seeing, but we can imagine it based on their collective gaze, their malice and scorn. And the little girl – she's different, still uncorrupted. That tells us something too.' I paused. 'We keep saying "he" wanted this, "he" painted that. What if the artist wasn't a "he"? Maybe it was that girl. Maybe this whole thing is about a memory of something she saw—'

'That she wasn't supposed to see. Like she snuck in there, nobody noticed her, and then she saw . . . whatever.'

'Yeah, that's what I'm thinking too.'

He told me he wanted to make a model of the room – piece his images together, blow them up, laminate them on to cardboard, then set them up facing one another exactly as arranged on the walls. He thought that would give him a better idea of the work and ignite new insights.

'I asked Tally to find out whatever he can about the house – who owns it, why they're still paying taxes on it, why there're all those bunk beds upstairs, what the hell was going on in there. I also want to go back and take another look.' He paused. 'Would you come with me?'

I thought about it. That would be a way for him to test his first impression and for me to experience the work firsthand. But I was hesitant. I didn't know if I could handle sneaking in, crawling in through a rear window, taking the chance of being caught.

'What about first getting an outside opinion? I have a friend, Anna, who wrote her doctoral thesis on *art brut*. She works in fundraising at CMA, also curates their outsider art collection. She found a donor who's into it, persuaded her to fund some acquisitions. Turns out the public loves that stuff. She's trying to get the museum to establish a department of outsider art.'

Jason was skeptical, said he was a long way from wanting to reveal what he'd found. Also, he didn't want to admit to breaking into a property that hadn't been legally abandoned.

'We'll just show her your photos and ask her to evaluate them. We'll set ground rules – no questions about where you found them. I've known her a long time. She really knows the field, always attends the annual Outsider Art Fair in New York. I think if we showed her these photos, she'd tell us honestly what she thinks.'

It took Jason the weekend to stitch together four master images, print them out on four-foot-wide sheets, laminate them and construct his model. Saturday and Sunday we were in and out of each other's lofts numerous times. Once he had the model built and set up on a table, we designated the walls A, B, C and D. Then we began to see things in them we hadn't fully noticed before.

The little girl crouching in the corner of Wall A was depicted further back than we first thought, not close to the legs of the woman beside her, but in what looked like a doorway lost in the gloom behind.

Although we'd thought the four sets of figures were standing in limbo, we were now able to make out a kind of structure behind them on Wall C. Perhaps a chimney or maybe a tall window; there was something structural back there left undefined.

We also observed that a nearly identical pair of characters, a double-faced man and woman in the center of Wall A, appeared again on Wall C.

'I'm starting to see these people as chess pieces,' Jason said. 'That pair in the middle, King and Queen, opposing another King and Queen across the way.'

But he was quick to agree that the chess analogy didn't hold. So why did the artist repeat this pair? What role had they played in the drama . . . if, in fact, a drama was what this work was about?

'I think this thing is based on a memory, but stylized and distorted like in a dream.'

'Yes,' I agreed. 'A haunting vision by a haunted artist. There's a story in there.'

'A mystery story,' Jason said.

Tally Vaughan

Jason wanted me to research the house. Since I'd already checked out the address at the Hall of Records, I decided to go back to Locust Street and see what I could find out from the locals.

I parked in my usual spot, just outside the gates to the Kenyon-Garfield Observatory, then took a long slow walk through the neighborhood. Although it was two o'clock on a pleasant autumn Saturday afternoon, I didn't encounter any pedestrians, or even kids riding bikes or playing pick-up games in the fields.

There'd been quite a few tear-downs. Most of the houses still standing looked to be in poor shape. At least half were abandoned.

Although others showed signs of being occupied, there was an eerie silence – no one puttering around in a garden or cleaning up a yard, no sounds of TVs issuing through open windows, or wash hanging on outdoor lines. Far as I could see, Locust Street was dead.

Returning to my car, I spotted an old guy raking leaves in front of the observatory. I called out to him. He turned, studied me for a moment, then started down the slope toward where I was standing outside the gate.

'Yo!'

'Yo, yourself,' he said. He looked to be in his sixties, African American, friendly face. 'Can I help you?'

'Not sure,' I said. 'I'm kinda curious about the neighborhood.'

He nodded. 'Folks *are* curious about it. Every so often someone comes by, asking me to point them to the murder house.'

'Couple blocks down the street, right?'

'Number 2462 before they tore it down. They razed it after the trial. That was about ten years ago.'

'Why'd they raze it?'

'They thought they'd find more bodies. They didn't. Also, they didn't want folks turning it into some kind of shrine. More folks lived here back then. They didn't like Locust being called "Street of Horror" and all those rubbernecks coming around. So the city tore it down. Some are disappointed when I tell them that. Others are bitter they came all this way for nothing.'

Hmmm. 'What about the house where that couple kept the girl?'

'We called that one the bondage house. Tore it down, too. The prisoner-girl – she got ownership, part of her reparations package. She wanted it obliterated from the face of the earth. She was there the day they bulldozed it. We all watched, everyone in the neighborhood. She looked happy when the walls collapsed, or at least pretended she was. My opinion, I don't think it was all that satisfying to her, considering all she'd gone through in there.'

He was well spoken, educated, used words like 'reparations,' 'obliterated,' and was clearly well versed in local goings-on. He told me he'd been caretaker and watchman at the observatory for fifteen years, ever since the university took out the big telescope and closed the place down. He told me he lived there with his wife the first couple of years, but then she left because she couldn't take the loneliness. He liked the job, liked leading a solitary life, and so decided to stay on.

'There're all sorts of interesting things going on around here if you're patient and stare hard enough. Like the murder house. I had a feeling something bad was going on in there. The guy was a loner, quiet, polite, but you could see the weirdness in his eyes. 'Course, if I'd known what he was doing, I'd have spoken up.' He shook his head. 'Same with the bondage house. The couple lived there – they had this furtive way about them. I noticed they never went out together. It was like one always stayed home to guard. No way of knowing they had a girl locked up in there. They say she was chained in the cellar all those years without even a glimpse of daylight.'

He looked straight into my eyes then. 'Aren't you going to ask about that one?' He gestured with his head toward the gothic house with the turret. 'I think that's the one you're interested in.'

I felt a chill when he said that, but did my best not to show it. 'Yeah, I was going to ask you about it too.'

He smiled, a little grin to himself. He must have noticed me surveilling it.

'I call that one the cult house,' he said. 'I saw you and the white fella go in there Thursday night.'

He didn't speak accusingly, simply stated what he'd observed. From the way he spoke, I knew there was no point denying it.

'Seems like you know everything going on around here,' I said.

'Well, see, that's the watchman's job. Remember, this here's an observatory. Up here on the rise is a good place to *observe*.'

'It was pitch-dark Thursday night. Barely a sliver of moon.'

'When I took this job, they issued me a pair of night-vision goggles. They were kinda cheesy, so I saved up my money and bought a really good military surplus pair. With the infrared, I can see all sorts of stuff. I saw you two clear as day. What with these fires breaking out, I stay on my toes. Last night I heard sirens. When I hear them, I get up, go outside and look around for a glow.'

'Then you know I didn't go in.'

He nodded. 'The white fella did. He was in there a long time. Didn't come out with anything more than he took in with him, so I knew you weren't robbers. Not that there's anything worth taking in there. If there were, it'd have been taken long ago.' He met my eyes. 'I'm curious what you were doing.'

'I'm curious why you call it the cult house.'

He opened the gate. 'I'm Oscar.' He offered his hand.

'I'm Tally.' We shook.

'Come on up the hill. We'll talk.'

I felt relaxed sitting with him on the terrace in front of the main entrance to the observatory. He had a couple of Adirondack chairs set up there and a little table in between. He went inside, came back with a couple of beers. We each took a quaff, then sat back.

'You go first,' he said.

I told him about our *Leavings* project, the concept behind it and how we'd been going about the work.

'Risky going in cold like that,' he said.

'Sure, because you never know what you'll run into.' I told him about a couple of close calls. He was particularly interested in the time we stumbled into a crack house where a guy pulled out a gun, thinking we were undercover cops. I told him how we talked our way out of that, and how afterwards I spent a lot more time scouting houses before deciding they were worth going into.

I pulled out my phone, showed him some of Jason's photos. He peered at them, nodded, said he understood what we were trying to do.

'This 'hood's seen better days,' he said. 'It's shriveled down last few years. More crime since folks abandoned places and moved out. I gotta keep my eyes open. The observatory's big and there's still plenty of stuff worth stealing inside.'

'Tell me about the cult house, Oscar. Why do you call it that?'

'There was a group living in there, some kind of cult. What I hear, a couple of rich teenage girls joined up and their parents weren't happy about it. So they got the cops to raid the place. When they did, all hell broke loose. There was a fight and one of the cops got scratched up. They took the girls away, arrested the leaders, closed the place down, and it's been shut tight ever since. This is all hearsay, understand, 'cause I wasn't living here back then.'

'How long ago?'

'The raid – maybe twenty-five years.'

'And it's been boarded up ever since?'

'Far as I know.'

'My partner, Jason, says things inside look untouched – that the kitchen appliances are still there and no one's gone in and ripped out the copper.'

'I think folks are still spooked by the place. Also, there's this woman comes by every so often. People think maybe she owns it and they don't want to mess with an owned house.'

'"Comes by"?'

'I never saw her go inside. She drives up, parks out front, then just sits there in her car, staring at it. Sometimes she gets out and walks around back. If she sees something broken or loose, like that board you pried off, she'll make a note, then a couple days later a handyman'll show up and fix it.'

'How long does she stay?'

'An hour sometimes, other times less.'

'How often?'

'Every month or so. It's not like she's regular about it. More like she's checking time to time that it's still there and no one's messed with it.'

'Can you describe her?'

He shrugged. 'Nice-looking. Middle-aged. Drives one of those Japanese cars – Toyota, Honda or whatever.'

'You think she's the owner?'

He shrugged again. 'Maybe, or maybe she works for a property management firm. If she's the owner, I doubt she could sell it now, even if she wanted to. Places around here aren't worth nothing. Locust's got a bad rep. And I doubt anyone'd rent it. Too big to heat in winter or air-condition in summer. No one wants to live around here anymore.'

'What about this place?'

'The observatory? They don't know what to do with it. Few years ago a fella came around, said he was interested in buying it, turning it into condos, which didn't make sense to me, 'cause who'd want to live around here anyway? Whatever his deal was, he couldn't come to terms with the university. See, when they built this place a hundred years ago, it was dark here at night, and this hill was a good spot to observe the stars. But then Calista grew around it, and that made for too much city light at night. So they took the big telescope out and shipped it to an observatory in Arizona, and now this place sits here rotting away, just like the cult house down the hill.'

As I drove off, I thought about some of the things he'd said. I had a hunch he knew who the woman was. His vague description of her didn't fit with his self-assigned role as keen observer of local goings-on. Also, it would make sense for an absentee owner to hire the resident caretaker next door to keep an eye on the place and make exterior repairs as needed. But if that were true, why hadn't Oscar owned up to it? On the other hand, why should he? He didn't know me and had no reason to confide. He'd seemed chatty, but I had a feeling he'd told me only as much as he wanted to reveal.

I phoned Jason. He was excited by what I'd found out: that the house had a history, that serious stuff had gone down in there, that there'd been a cult and two girls from wealthy families had joined it, and that now, twenty-five years later, a middle-aged woman came around every so often to stare at the house from her car. But he got upset when I told him Oscar had night-vision equipment and had seen us go in.

'Shit! Do you think he'll report us?'

'I don't. He knows we didn't vandalize or steal, so he doesn't care.'

'Still . . .'

'It's unnerving.'

'That woman – could she have been staring at the tower room?'

I told him Oscar didn't say, but that I suspected he knew who the woman was.

'Then he'll tell her we were in there,' Jason said.

'He might.'

'Hard to believe whoever owns the place doesn't know about the murals.'

That was Jason's big concern – not that we'd be reported for breaking and entering, but the likely possibility that his coming upon the murals was not actually his discovery, that other people knew about them and had seen them. It seemed possible, though improbable, that no one had been in the tower room since the raid and the house was sealed off. But even if that were true, someone had painted the murals, someone had provided the artist with materials and someone had installed plywood boards as a painting surface on all four walls of the room. Twenty-five years was a long time ago, but not so long as to preclude the likelihood that there were still living witnesses.

Jason Poe

When Tally told me we'd been seen, I knew there was no way I could sneak back in with Hannah. Which, she said, was fine with her, as she wasn't all that keen on crawling in through a basement window.

As we talked over our next step, we agreed there were two things we wanted to know. What was the story *behind* the murals – the identity and intention of the artist? And what was the story told *by* the murals – was it a fantasy or a real experience?

After Tally pointed out that it would take forever to search through hundreds of back issues of local papers, Hannah reminded me that newspapers keep morgue files, folders of clippings from past issues arranged by subject matter, as reference material for reporters.

Soon as she said that, I knew whom to call: Joan Nguyen, a young reporter for the *Calista Times-Dispatch* who'd interviewed me a couple of years before in connection with an exhibition of my war photographs. Joan struck me as smart, was interested in my work – and perhaps, I thought at the time, also interested in me. We met for drinks a couple of times, but neither of us followed up. She was attractive and fun to be with, but, I felt, too young for me. I liked her but couldn't see myself, the rueful, older guy with the lived-in face, dating the bouncy, fresh-faced gal with the idolatrous gleam in her gorgeous Asian eyes.

Still, we kept in touch. She'd call me every so often to ask me a question about photography, and sometimes just to check in. She was also supportive of my *Leavings* project, approving of the images I showed her.

'I don't want to lose track of you,' she told me one time. 'I meet a lot of people through work – sometimes it gets pretty intense, but after the article comes out we never see each other again.'

'No reason to lose track,' I assured her, though I wasn't at all clear how we could make that work. Now, I knew, it was my turn to call her, not to cash in on what I'd imagined might be her lingering affection, but to entice her to help me by offering her an exclusive.

We met in the Casablanca Room at the Alhambra, a funky Moorish-style hotel on the edge of the warehouse district. The place had literary pretensions. It offered special rates to visiting writers on tour, and created the Casablanca Room as a congenial space for members of the working press. With its alcoves and Moorish arches, enlarged movie stills of Bogart and Bergman, Middle Eastern mezes, and an antique juke box stocked with songs sung by Piaf and Juliette Greco, the room had a retro, noirish charm.

'I do like this joint,' Joan said, as she edged into the alcove where I was waiting. 'I especially like meeting you here to discuss something *confidential*.' She gazed at me from across the little table. 'I adore secrets,' she whispered.

She looked great. Her skin was pale, her black bangs hung down to her eyebrows, and there were silver studs in her ear lobes. She wore jeans and a *Calista Strong* T-shirt that clung to her slim torso. As always, I felt drawn to her dark, liquid, querying eyes.

We spent a few minutes catching up. She told me she was the junior member of an investigative team working on a story about cop corruption on the West Side.

I asked her if she liked investigative work.

'Love it!' she said. 'It's fun to write features, but that's real journalism.' She lowered her voice. 'There's a major story to be done about the spate of fires. Are they being set by an arsonist, or maybe by more than one? Hard to see a pattern – a synagogue in Little Warsaw, an abandoned house in Gunktown, a homeless guy doused, then set on fire behind the zoo. Some set with accelerants, others by souped-up Molotov cocktails. I told Josh, my editor, I have feelers out and that if I come up with something, I want to be lead reporter. He said, "Sure, Joan, you bring it in, it's yours."' She gazed at me. 'I like it that working that kind of story can be dangerous. I know you understand that.'

Listening to her, I began to view her differently, no longer as a laid-back cultural news journalist, but more akin to the ambitious young women reporters I used to meet and hook up with in hotel bars in Baghdad and Kabul.

'My dangerous days are long behind me,' I reminded her.

'Really? You told me you've had some close calls.'

'Nothing serious. Tally covers my back.'

'Is he armed?'

'I'm not going to answer that.'

'Well . . . OK . . .' She smiled.

'No, he's not armed. We made a decision early on we wouldn't go into a place if we thought we'd need a gun.'

We talked a while more, ordered a second round, munched on slivers of pita dipped in hummus, until finally she expressed some exasperation, which was what I was waiting for her to do.

'So, Jase, why are we meeting? What's going on?'

I told her I'd stumbled on something inside a house, something I believed was extraordinary. I told her the house had a history, that years ago a cult was living there, there was a raid, arrests and a cop was injured.

'I'm hoping your paper has a file on it. If so, I'm hoping you'll copy it for me.'

'*Times-Dispatch* files aren't for public use.'

'I know.'

'You want me to break the rules?' I nodded. 'What's in it for me?'

'If the story plays out, you get an exclusive.'

'What's the story?'

'Can't tell you that now.'

'Come on, Jase. Do I have to pull it out of you?'

'So far the only other people who know are Tally and Hannah. If I tell you, that'll make four. I don't want this to get out.'

She smiled, brought her fingers to her lips, mimed turning a key.

I nodded, told her about the murals, showed her the photos I'd transferred to my phone. She studied them a while, then handed the phone back.

'You really think there's a story?'

'Maybe a big one. Don't know yet.'

'These murals really grabbed you, huh?'

'Phone images can't convey how strong they are. When I first saw them, I felt like maybe that French farmer did when he stumbled into the cave at Lascaux. He shines his flashlight around and suddenly sees those incredible prehistoric wall paintings made by people thirty thousand years before.'

'Surely you can't compare—'

'I'm not saying what I found is anywhere near that important.
Just trying to convey how it felt. DERP work—'

'What's that?'

'Derelict and Ruined Places – like storm-drain entrances,
boarded-up buildings, padlocked gates. Caves, catacombs, World
War One and Two bunkers. When you go into places like that,
you never know what you're going to find. Usually nothing. Then
it happens! As it did to me the other night. So how could I not
be excited?'

She peered at me, large eyes wide. 'OK, Jase – I'll get you
what we have on the house, cult, raid and anything else I can find.
And if you need more help, I'll do some follow-up. But I have to
be the only reporter in on this. If there's a story, I gotta be the
one who writes it. Deal?'

'Yeah, deal,' I assured her.

The following day I found an oversize envelope in my box at CAI.
No return address, just a cartoon smile. Joan had come through
for me fast.

CALISTA TIMES-DISPATCH, Police Blotter,
August 17, 1993

Police raided a house at 1160 Locust Street last night based
on a tip from a confidential informant. There was a scuffle
during the raid and one officer was injured. 'They put up a
fight. They didn't want us to come in, even though we had
a warrant,' said CPD Captain Walter Loetz.

The three-story house is owned by Theodore and Elizabeth
Schechtner, social workers who, according to police, lead a
cult under the guise of running a halfway house for teen
runaways.

'There were signs of satanism in the house, the number 666
and other satanic symbols drawn on the walls, an upside-down
crucifix and assorted paraphernalia,' Loetz said. 'The informant
told us the Schechtners were holding several female teens
against their will.'

The Schechtners were arrested during the fracas, and are
being held in City Jail awaiting arraignment. The teenage
residents have been turned over to Child Protective Services.

CALISTA TIMES-DISPATCH, Police Blotter,
August 18, 1993

Clinical psychologists Theodore and Elizabeth Schechtner were arraigned in Criminal Court this morning for refusing entry to police with a valid search warrant, resisting arrest, injuring an officer, running an unlicensed halfway house for minors, inducting minors into a satanic cult, holding minors in the house against their will, providing minors with illegal drugs, and other charges.

The Schechtners' attorney, Spencer Addams, protested the description of his clients as cult leaders. 'There is no cult and there was nothing satanic going on in the house,' he said. 'The Schechtners are an idealistic couple with advanced academic degrees who are licensed to practice psychotherapy. Moreover their house, called A Caring Place, is a licensed refuge for runaway kids. They specialize in the treatment of troubled adolescents. No person has ever been held in the house against his or her will.'

Captain Loetz then testified that he had found two teenage girls hiding in an attic room, the walls of which were covered with 'satanic style' paintings. When he tried to enter the attic, the girls became hysterical and refused to let him in. Police had to restrain them in order to effect a rescue.

'The girls scratched and bit me,' Loetz said. 'They seemed delusional, shrieking and hollering. I believe they were high on drugs, probably LSD.' The detective showed what he said were scratches and bite marks on his hands and arms.

Judge Stephanie Bates set bail for the Schechtners at $100,000 each.

CALISTA TIMES-DISPATCH, August 24, 1993

CULT HOUSE ATTORNEY SAYS
'THERE NEVER WAS A CULT'
by Steve Dorfman

Spencer Addams, attorney for Drs Theodore and Elizabeth Schechtner, arrested and charged with running an unlicensed halfway house on Locust Street, insists his clients are reputable licensed psychotherapists and are wrongly accused of leading a satanic cult.

In an interview in his Bush Building office, Addams stated: 'The police claim they found 666 inscribed on a wall and an upside-down crucifix erected in the main room, and that this is proof of satanism. In fact, certain persons who entered the house with the police spray-painted the symbol and erected the crucifix in that position. The police also claim they found wall murals filled with "satanic content" in the attic. I've seen the murals. They are not satanic, rather the result of an art therapy project.'

When asked to identify the 'persons' who brought in the crucifix, Addams stated that they were 'so-called cult deprogrammers' hired by the prominent Cobb family to rescue their daughter and her friend from the house, deprogram them and then return them to their respective homes.

'There's more to this case than meets the eye,' Addams said. 'The Cobb girl and her friend ran away from home and voluntarily took refuge at A Caring Place. The Schechtners are not satanists. They are secular professionals greatly respected in Calista for their skill and compassion working with troubled adolescents. The police raid was a ruse, engineered by the Cobb family to force the return of their daughter. The police collaborated with the deprogrammers to provide them with entry to the house, and then helped them by forcibly removing the girls. Neither girl was turned over to Protective Services. Both were taken away by the deprogrammers and have not been seen since. In fact, both girls were in the process of petitioning for emancipation from parental control when the raid occurred. The Schechtners were assisting them with this, and the raid was undertaken to disrupt the emancipation process.'

Addams claims that the warrant for entry to the house was defective as it was signed by Judge Neville Brown, who, before taking the bench, was a Cobb Industries house attorney.

'I'm not saying there was collusion between Judge Brown and the Cobbs. But this doesn't pass the smell test. Meanwhile, my clients are being held in jail because they can't raise the exorbitant bail set by Judge Bates.'

Addams declined to identify the deprogrammers, saying only that they were employees of an out-of-state firm that specializes in deprogramming children. Addams says he is filing a habeas corpus writ on behalf of his clients to force a hearing on these claims.

The Cobb family, owners of Cobb Industries, is well known in Calista for its philanthropy. A spokesperson at the company, reached by phone, said she was not authorized to speak for the family. She refused comment on Addams's claims. 'We believe this matter is best settled in court,' she said.

Judge Brown's clerk, reached by phone, called Addams's claims concerning His Honor 'reckless and absurd.'

'This is an attorney known for making unsubstantiated claims,' the clerk said. 'We expect he will be sanctioned by Judge Bates for his outburst.'

[Editor's Note: The minors referred to in the story have not been named in accordance with *Times-Dispatch* policy.]

CALISTA TIMES-DISPATCH, September 1, 1993

AROUND TOWN . . .
by Waldo Channing

People are talking about . . . a major brouhaha involving Horace and Elena Cobb and their wayward teenage daughter, Courtney. The way *we* hear it (and our sources are very reliable), young Cobb and her best friend, Penny Dawson, disappeared six weeks ago from an after-school art class at Danzig Heights Community Center. The Cobb and Dawson families, believing their daughters were abducted, called Calista Police. In the absence of ransom demands, the police concluded that the girls were runaways.

Horace and Elena went on local TV begging their daughter to return home. They also offered $50,000 to anyone with information that would lead to her return.

According to my sources, there has been much consternation of late within the Cobb family. Young Courtney, I am told, was at 'sword points' with both parents and had threatened to run away several times. She also, I am told, attempted suicide last year, and was fortunately discovered in time by a servant who immediately called in medics. The girl recovered and was placed in psychotherapy with Dr Reginald Holden, a specialist in the treatment of troubled adolescents.

This is where the plot thickens! Courtney told her parents that Dr Holden had fondled her in a lascivious manner. Now two other psychologists, Drs Elizabeth and Theodore Schechtner, are accused of having harbored the girls in a halfway house which they call A Caring Place, and which they own and run on Locust Street within spitting distance of the old Kenyon-Garfield Observatory.

Big Question: Why did the Schechtners not contact the parents of the girls to tell them their daughters were safe? I am told that their failure to do so could be construed as criminal.

But there is more . . . much more . . . including claims that the Schechtners were the leaders of a satanist cult, and that they used their clinical practices to recruit young patients and seduce them into joining it.

The Schechtners vigorously deny this, and their attorney, Spencer Addams (he of the infamous Dacoite Case), claims the girls were in the process of petitioning to be liberated minors with the help of the Schechtners, on the basis that the Cobb and Dawson households were unsafe environments.

There are rumors of physical abuse by parents . . . something this columnist finds nearly impossible to believe. I don't know the Dawsons, but Horace and Elena Cobb are friends of many years' standing, and are part of a group this column refers to as 'The Happy Few' in stories about local society goings-on.

Adding to the melodrama is the fact that the two girls fought the raiders tooth and nail before being handcuffed and dragged from the premises. They are both, we are told, in an out-of-state deprogramming facility undergoing appropriate therapy.

There are other rumors which we have not been able to verify, which are too scandalous to report here. Let it simply be said that as far as this column is concerned, the Drs Schechtner would appear to be unscrupulous psychologists and the Cobb and Dawson families have been gravely wronged.

Stay tuned . . .

Wow! This was dynamite. Things were starting to fit together. And there were more clippings in Joan's envelope: stories about pre-trial hearings, reports of videotaped interviews by psychologists of teens rescued from the house regarding satanic practices – being made to strip naked, make confessions and perform perverse sexual acts with each other and the Schechtners in a 'weirdly painted attic room.'

These claims were vigorously disputed during cross-examination by attorney Spencer Addams. He tried to show that these videotaped statements were coerced, made under duress, or were the result of brainwashing by the interviewing psychologists. He tried to rattle the psychologists by demanding to know how much they had been paid to bend the teenagers' stories. After objections by the prosecutor, Judge Bates admonished Addams for bullying these witnesses. Addams went on to assert that the Schechtners were licensed, their house was licensed, and that there was no cult.

Of course, I was struck by these claims of 'perverse sexual acts' enacted in the 'weirdly painted attic room,' as this threw a new and unexpected light on the murals.

Yes, it did seem conceivable that the people depicted on the walls were created to stand as witnesses to acts taking place in the middle of that room. Indeed, there was a diabolic aspect to their cold, leering faces.

I wondered: Could this possibly be true? Could the murals have served such a purpose?

Possible, I thought, but not likely, although I wasn't sure why I felt that. Something about those painted people still struck me as an attempt to tell a story, not just to ornament the walls of a cult-oriented orgy room.

I learned from the clippings that suddenly, and without explanation, the case against both Drs Schechtner was dismissed and they were set free. There were rumors that a private settlement had been made, which the parties and the prosecutors refused to confirm or explain. After this, news of the scandal disappeared from the newspaper, except for a follow-up column, one year later, by the society columnist Waldo Channing:

CALISTA TIMES-DISPATCH, November 1, 1994

AROUND TOWN . . .
by Waldo Channing

People are talking about . . . the odd outcome of the Cobb family brouhaha, reported in detail in this column last year. Young Courtney Cobb, daughter of Horace and Elena, has not returned to the family home in Calista, even though more than a year has passed since she was spirited away by de-programmers from a 'cult house' on Locust Street to an unnamed 'out-of-state rehab facility.'

Teachers and friends of the girl at the Ashley-Burnett School, concerned about her well-being, received no responses to their inquiries from her family. Her parents and two older brothers refuse to answer questions regarding her mental and physical state, all offering the same by-rote answer: 'This is a private family matter and we intend to keep it that way.'

In view of the fact that Courtney's friend, Penny Dawson, has emerged from rehab, and is now a student at the San Francisco Art Institute, people are troubled by Courtney's continuing unexplained absence. Your columnist has made similar inquiries and received the same stock non-response. *Strange* . . .

Meantime, the formerly jailed married psychologists, Theodore and Elizabeth Schechtner, have departed Calista, because, according to their attorney, Spencer Addams, 'the outrageous charges brought against them have ruined their professional reputations.' Addams tells this column that the Schechtners have relocated out of state in order to move on with their lives. When asked about rumors of a private settle-ment, Addams waved the question off. 'The point,' he said, 'is that the community has lost two fine practitioners, and that what was taken from them, their good names and reputations, cannot be repaired by any amount of money.'

This was the last dated clipping in the envelope. Joan had given me a trove of material. Some things I had wondered about were explained, while others remained mysterious. But at least I had a context for the artwork. The question now was whether the murals were as powerful as I'd first thought, or whether I'd been seduced by the 'strange' (to use Waldo Channing's word) circumstances in which I'd discovered them.

Hannah would take up the aesthetic value issues with her friend, Anna von Arx. She wanted me to accompany her, but I decided it would be better if she made the presentation on her own. I prepared a small twelve-inch-per-wall model of the murals with hinges on each wall to enable her to fold up 'the room' and carry it flat to her meeting.

Hannah Sachs

I phoned Anna to set up a meeting. I told her I had something interesting to show her, about which I was eager to hear her opinion. As we talked, I noticed strain in her voice.

'Something the matter?' I asked.

'I'm really glad you called, Hannah. I'll tell you all about it at lunch.'

At her suggestion we met at Giovanni's, a red-checkered-tablecloth trattoria in the Little Italy district on Chandler Hill. I was surprised at this choice; I'd expected she'd want to meet closer to the museum. It was raining when I arrived, one of those summer storms that come out of nowhere – the sky turns dark, the rain beats down hard for a quarter-hour, then suddenly the sun re-emerges, pouring down dazzling light.

After we settled into a booth, I asked her why she'd chosen the place.

'It's quiet, the food's good and it's unlikely any of my co-workers will be lunching here.'

'So, tell me – what is going on?'

As she launched into her saga, tears filled her eyes. She told me she'd been having an affair with Anders Carlsen, director of the museum.

'It's been going on a year,' she said. 'Of course, we've kept it secret. Intimate relationships between staff aren't permitted and are regarded as especially egregious when there's such a disparity in status. Also, Anders is married and has young kids. Now he wants to leave his wife and move in with me, which means I'll have to quit my job.'

She took a breath. 'I love this job – not the fundraising part so much, but developing a department of outsider art. I've pushed through some amazing acquisitions. If I go along with Anders, that'll end. I'll be labeled a home-breaker . . . you know, "that little blond bitch who used to work in the museum." And if I break up with him, I'll have to leave anyway. It would be impossible to stay on and act like nothing happened. Meantime, some nasty person wrote an anonymous letter to the board chairman. When he asked Anders about it, Anders grinned and gave an ambiguous shrug as if to say "How could that possibly be true?" Now, if he moves in with me, he'll look like a liar. The new plan is for me to quit, then a few weeks later he'll leave his wife and take an apartment near mine. That way, if we're discreet, we can continue without a scandal. But I lose either way.'

'How do you feel about the guy?'

'I like him a lot.'

'And?'

'He claims he adores me.'

'He's putting you in a difficult position.'

'Awful!'

'So what're you going to do?'

'Don't know yet.' She wiped her eyes and forced a smile.

I felt badly for her. We'd been classmates at Ashley-Burnett. While I'd gone on to study textile art at Cranbrook, she'd gone to NYU, then to the Courtauld in London, where she'd earned her doctorate in art history. After my years working in New York, and hers at museums in Houston, Portland and Minneapolis, we'd both coincidentally landed back in our hometown.

We quickly reconnected and fell back into our high-school habit of sharing intimate details about our lives. She knew all about my relationship with Jason, and I knew all about her unhappy marriage and bitter divorce. But I hadn't known until that day about her affair with Anders Carlsen.

Her situation struck me as fairly miserable. I had only met Carlsen once, at a museum opening, and was not impressed by his self-important hauteur. The dish on him was that he was arrogant toward subordinates and obsequious toward museum board members and wealthy donors. So what was my lovely friend doing with this guy, and why had she allowed him to put her in such an awful bind?

'Now your turn,' she said. 'What's going on with you? The interesting thing you want to show me – it's in the portfolio, right?'

'After what you just told me, I don't know if this is a good time to bring it out.'

'Please, Hannah – show me what you've got. Anything to take my mind off this damn . . . I don't know . . . whatever.'

I told her Jason had come upon a room in an abandoned house with all four walls covered in murals, and that in the portfolio I had a small collapsible model of the room with photos of the murals mounted on the walls. I told her I'd like to hear what she thought of them, whether she saw them as works of outsider art or perhaps something else. Also, that I'd appreciate it if she didn't ask me questions about where Jason stumbled on them and to please not mention them to anyone else.

'So what you want from me is . . .'

'Whatever you care to say. Jason and I have our thoughts. I'm bringing this to you for an outside opinion.'

'You've gotten me excited,' she said, as I brought out the small model, set it up on the table so she could see how the murals filled the room, then opened it flat to give her an unobstructed view of the four walls.

She studied them for a while, asked the dimensions of the room and then how close the paintings came to the ceiling. She nodded when I explained that the ceiling was a four-way roof.

'I get it – like a gazebo or cupola,' she said. 'But no windows?'

'They're boarded up. The murals are painted on plywood.'

She erected the model again, studied it, then laid it flat and studied it some more.

'Pretty spectacular,' she said. 'I'd love to know who did these. Is this outsider art? Not literally. Clearly the artist had some training. But it does have an outsider quality in the way it takes you into the artist's world, a world totally unlike your own.'

She squinted at the model. 'This is certainly not a happy set of murals. It seems to have been generated by dark emotions. One rarely finds such an intense vision. Nothing improvised here. Whoever created this knew from the start what he wanted to do. He had a plan and carried it out. Powerfully, I'd say. I can just imagine standing in the center of this room, seeing this, turning and seeing the other walls. It would make for a compelling experience.'

She looked up at me. 'I know I'm not supposed to ask where Jason found this. But I do wonder whether he found it at night?'

'That's when he goes into places.'

'I ask because I see this as a night-time experience. I don't see any lights in the room. Are there?'

'Don't know. The power was shut off.'

'OK, I won't ask anything else. You want my evaluation – aesthetic, not monetary. I'd say this is an extraordinary work, and I say this without knowing the story behind it. That's the thing about really good outsider art: it's great to know the backstory – who the artist was and what he was thinking – but with the best works you don't really need to know. They stand up on their own.' She paused. 'This is an enigmatic work. It's filled with mystery. I can imagine people seeing it, then making up stories to explain it, and I think everyone's story would be different.'

'Like a Rorschach? Their stories would tell more about them than about the work?'

She nodded. 'These murals don't need interpretation. I think they work on their own terms. What I'm saying is they're strong enough to embrace a multitude of interpretations and that in the end it doesn't matter what the actual story is or was. The power comes from the feelings they evoke – fear, menace, awe. It's been a long time since I've seen such an emotional and, at the same time, disciplined piece.'

'Do you think it could be important?'

'Absolutely! Sure, there're some technical weaknesses. Also some naïveté. I'm certainly not saying these murals are mind-blowingly magnificent, though I might change my mind if I saw them in place. But like all important works, these represent a powerful unified vision. What more can you ask from a work of art?'

I was thrilled by her enthusiasm. It coincided with mine and Jason's. But I didn't agree that the backstory was irrelevant. To me, as to Jason, the story behind the murals was the key to understanding them.

As we left the restaurant, the rain started up again. We unfurled our umbrellas and promised to stay in closer touch. Then I hurried back to CAI to tell Jason what Anna had said.

'We weren't deluding ourselves – that's a relief,' he said. 'But you're right – we *have* to find out who created these and what they're about.' He told me he couldn't imagine war photos without captions to give them context. He recognized that the murals weren't documents, but he was certain they told a story.

He said he was going to ask Joan to do some more research on the Cobb parents, the Schechtners, Courtney Cobb and Penny Dawson, the lawyer, Spencer Addams, and the society columnist, Channing, who, Jase told me, sounded like a jerk.

'There were plenty of people living in that house. They can't all be dead. There's gotta be someone still around who knows stuff. Also why are these murals not known? Could they have been deliberately hidden away?'

Anna called me that night.

'I can't stop thinking about those murals,' she told me. 'They're haunting, you know – like a dream. Anyway, I feel haunted by them. Also . . .'

'*What?*' I asked.

'Something in them . . . I don't know, I could be wrong . . . but there's something in them that seemed . . . familiar somehow.'

Joan Nguyen

I really like Jason, though perhaps not in the way he thinks. He's an interesting guy, very talented, and flawed just like the rest of us. I admire him but certainly don't idealize him. That said, I was happy to pull that set of clippings for him. But when he came back to me for more, I told him I wanted to be let in on the story as it progressed, not just at the end. I told him if he'd go along with that, I'd be happy to put in some real effort.

'That means writing about you, Jase, because often the story of the quest is more interesting than the end result.'

I think that's what convinced him. Like most people, he'd be delighted to play a starring role. I'm not saying he was vainglorious, but he did have an ego. Why else would a guy go around the world covering wars, if not, at least in part, for the glory?

'OK,' he said. 'You're in.' Then he handed me a list of people about whom he wanted info.

I told him right off that Horace and Elena Cobb were deceased, that Cobb Industries, originally a steel company, was now under the leadership of their sons, Jack and Kevin Cobb, a very lucrative, privately held chemical and paint manufacturer, and perhaps the biggest industrial polluter in the state. I told him that the Cobb brothers were movers and shakers, major backers of the Calista Museum of Art and the Calista Symphony, and that they were also self-styled libertarians who made large financial contributions to national ultra-conservative causes and backed ultra-conservative candidates and office holders.

'I never heard they had a sister,' I told him.

As for Waldo Channing, he too was long gone, and yes, I had to agree, based on his columns, he'd been a bit of a horse's ass.

'He was pretty powerful here back in the day,' I told Jase, 'when society newspaper columnists reigned over American cities.'

I said I'd see what we had on the Schechtners and their lawyer, Spencer Addams, and look for anything on Courtney Cobb and Penny Dawson. I told him I'd check our morgue files as well as Facebook and other sources.

'We have ways of finding people even when they don't want to be found.'

It was fairly clear that Courtney and Penny were key to the story. They had met and become friends at after-school art classes and they'd been dragged kicking and screaming from the Locust Street house attic. One of them must have been the artist who painted the murals, possibly with the assistance of the other.

How to find them? To get a better understanding of the layout, I drove slowly by the house. I didn't want to attract the attention of the nosy observatory caretaker, so I didn't stop in front.

Indeed, the house did look creepy, like a location for a horror film. It seemed almost too obvious a place for a cult. Maybe there'd been a cult or maybe there hadn't. That, I decided, was worth looking into.

I started with Penny Dawson. Channing reported she'd enrolled at SFAI. As expected, the Institute refused to answer inquiries regarding alumni, but the nice woman did agree to pass on a message to Ms Dawson. My message was simple: 'Please contact me, Joan Nguyen, at the *Calista Times-Dispatch*. I'm working on a story, your name came up and I'd like to ask you about a couple things.'

Next I called the Danzig Heights Community Center to ask about art classes. Turned out they used to offer them to young people but discontinued doing so years before. The center was now serving the senior community. I asked if any of the art teachers from twenty-five years ago were still there. The manager said she'd ask around.

I had one excellent source at the Calista Police Department, Damon Malonas, a Greek-American police officer and talented Sunday painter I'd featured in an article. He liked me enough to tell me what he knew about the shakedown activity on the West Side. Because I'd brought him in, I was assigned to assist the two-man investigative team working the story.

The lead writers had their sources. Damon was mine. Every so often we'd meet at a Korean restaurant after his shift. If anyone found out he was spilling to me, he could be in serious danger. Damon had taken a chance, but as he put it the first time he broached his concerns, 'I feel a lot safer talking to you than taking my story to CPD Internal Affairs.'

I emailed him requesting a meeting. Bulgogi East, a grilled-meats restaurant on East Monroe, was a fairly busy place, but they had a quiet backroom with tables set against the walls. Damon felt safe there. It wasn't a cop hang-out. And the staff there seemed to like me, probably because I'm of Asian heritage.

He didn't have any new leads, but said he'd be willing to help me out by pulling the old file on the raid at A Caring House, and also find out how I could get hold of Captain Walter Loetz, likely long retired.

When I asked Damon if he knew anything about an arson investigation concerning the fires, he shook his head but promised to check with his brother-in-law.

'He's a fireman. If he knows something, I'll put you in touch.'

He got back to me the next day on Walter Loetz, retired and now living in an Akron suburb. Turned out this guy ended his career at a lot higher rank than captain. He retired as Deputy Chief of Operations.

I looked him up, found his phone number, thought about cold-calling him, then decided to check first with Jase.

'I think I ought to read the file first,' I told him. 'I'll get further with Loetz if I can show I'm familiar with his notes.'

* * *

Two days later, to my great surprise, I got a call back from Penny Dawson. The SFAI Alumni Office had passed on my message, but Penny sounded perturbed. What could I possibly want with her? She'd been living down in the Florida Keys the last fifteen years. It had been decades since she'd set foot in Calista.

'Are you sure I'm the right Penny Dawson?' she asked.

'You were a friend of Courtney Cobb?'

I could hear her intake her breath. 'Is Courtney OK?' she asked, voice subdued.

'Don't know. I'm trying to find her.'

'Are you calling about A Caring Place on Locust?' I told her that I was. 'Haven't seen or heard from her since the night the cops yanked us out of there. They hustled us into separate cars. I've no idea where they took her.'

I told her I was concerned about Courtney, and that other people were as well. I told her the Cobb family refused to say anything about her, even to say whether she was still alive. I told her a friend of mine saw some artwork in the house and was trying to find out who had done it.

'They're still there – the wall paintings?' She sounded almost breathless.

'Yes, they're still there. What can you tell me about them?'

Long pause. 'You're coming at me out of the blue.' She sounded even more distraught than before. 'Let me think about this and call you back.'

'Sure . . .' I didn't want to lose her. 'Tell me a good time to call you, Penny. Can you give me your number?'

'I'll get back to you,' she said and hung up.

There was no caller ID on my phone. She either kept hers off or turned it off before she called me. Now I'd have to wait until she chose to call back . . . if she ever did.

I have to admit I was stunned. I wasn't prepared for her call and didn't think I'd handled it well. I hesitated before telling Jason, afraid he'd think I'd screwed up. He was nice about it.

'Look, you found her. Now we know she lives in the Keys. I think she'll call you back. Really, how can she resist asking what this is all about?'

A week passed without my hearing from her. I couldn't find any Dawsons listed in the Keys. I was starting to despair I'd never hear from her again, but brightened up when Damon called to say he had the August 16, 1993 file on the raid, and was in the process of copying it for me as we spoke.

'Fairly scanty,' he said. 'About what you'd expect on a one-night operation. There's the warrant application and some handwritten notes initialed by Loetz.'

He paused. 'About the fires, seems my brother-in-law knows stuff, but he's hesitant to talk. I vouched for you, so he's willing to meet. His name's Tony Delgado, real straight-arrow type. He'll meet you tomorrow night at eight p.m. in the parking lot behind the Haggerty Mall. He'll bring the photocopies with him. Park in the far north corner and leave your side window open. He'll pull up next to you. Then you can talk car-to-car.'

'Great! I love intrigue.'

'He's a little jumpy, Joan. He's never dealt with a reporter. Do your best to calm him down. I think it'll be worth your time.'

The mall parking lot was practically empty when I arrived, not surprising since most of the stores had closed. There was a cluster of cars near the multiplex, but otherwise a vast wasteland of empty pavement. I followed instructions, drove to the far north corner and parked. I checked my watch. I was five minutes early.

Tony Delgado swooped in beside me at eight fifteen. He drove a vintage Chevy that looked immaculately restored. He rolled down his window. He had the lean, taut face of a cardinal in a Renaissance painting, contradicted by a cherubic smile.

'You're Joan?' I nodded. 'Sorry I'm late. We live on the West Side. Don't shop much around here. Anyway, got something for you.' He stuck his arm out of his window. I reached out, took hold of a manila envelope. 'From Damon. He sends best regards.'

'Thanks.'

'So you wanna know about the fires, huh?'

'Anything you can tell me.'

'They're keeping us busy. Which is good. Most of the guys like that. Lotsa overtime. But, see, maybe we shouldn't be liking it so much, if you know what I mean.'

'Not sure I do.'

'I can't tell you much. There're all sorts of rumors. They brought in a crack arson investigation team from the state capital. We don't know them. They're working independent. They got their own headquarters someplace – an undisclosed location. It's headed up by a guy name of Nick Gallagher, a legend in the field. No one's sure what they're up to, but like I said, there're all these rumors.'

'What kind of rumors?'

He grinned. He didn't strike me as being at all jumpy. 'That there could be firemen involved. Otherwise, why so secretive?'

'Why would firemen set fires?'

'Because they're nuts. Because they love fire. Because it's love of fire that drew them to the department. To set them, then put them out. Save people. Become heroes. That's part of it, but it's really the flames they love. Not the smoke, but the flames. Flames turn them on. Anyway, that's what people are whispering about, 'cause, see, firemen-arsonists are Gallagher's specialty.'

Oh man! I felt tremors shoot up my legs. *If what he's saying is right, this really could be a big story.*

'Anything else you can tell me?'

He shook his head. 'Nothing – at least, not now. Thing is, when there're a lot of fires, unscrupulous people will use them for cover. They think like "Hey, there's a mad arsonist setting fires, so why don't I set one in my business and collect the insurance?"'

'You think that's what's happening?'

'Maybe. Bunch of fires'll bring the pyros out. The imitators and amateurs set the dangerous ones. Yeah, sure, we like the overtime, but we know if this keeps up, sooner or later some of us are going to get hurt.'

He said he had to get going, pick up his kids.

'Nice meeting you, Joan. My advice, try and find Gallagher. He's the guy you wanna talk to.'

And with that he revved up his engine, and sped away, leaving me alone in that forlorn mall parking lot with dark thoughts about firemen-arsonists and Damon's manila envelope in my lap.

The police file may have seemed scanty to Damon, but I found it fascinating. Loetz noted that he'd been bitten and scratched by the girls (referred to by their initials, C.C. and P.D.), but decided not to charge them since they were underage and 'clearly disturbed.' He described Dr Theodore Schechtner as 'vicious' and fingered him as the cult leader. He described Dr Elizabeth Schechtner as 'clearly subservient to her husband.' His only mention of the murals was that he found the two girls in 'the attic orgy room decorated with erotic wall paintings.'

Erotic! Really? Where did that come from?

He also mentioned that during the raid C.C.'s father was in a car parked outside the house. Loetz wrote: 'I asked him to be there so he'd see there was no mistreatment of his daughter.'

He wrote that the two minors, C.C. and P.D., at the request of their parents, were each turned over to separate male/female pairs of experienced deprogrammers from Cult Intervention & Recovery Services, Inc. of Buffalo, New York, while the other minors were turned over to Calista Child Protective Services for placement in licensed foster homes.

Accompanying Loetz's notes was a copy of his sworn search warrant request:

WARRANT APPLICATION

Confidential female informant, C.D., familiar with the house at 1160 Locust Street, East Calista, recognized C.C., a minor child, from a newspaper story. Incentivized by the offering of the reward money by the C. family, she went to a phone booth and called the contact number in the story to report that C.C. was being forcibly held in a windowless attic room in the house. Mr C., father of the minor, C.C., subsequently called Police Commissioner Hawkes who assigned me to investigate. I posted an officer in an unmarked car across the street. This officer (report attached) observed possible use of force by the two adults in the residence and the presence of seven minor children. Further investigation revealed that the residence is apparently not licensed as a halfway house, and although the adult occupants are licensed psychologists, they are not licensed as foster parents. Although the officer did not see C.C., this is understandable, if, as informant claims, she is being forcibly held in a windowless attic room. A warrant to search is hereby requested on the basis of the above information.

Sworn under penalty of perjury, Walter D. Loetz, Capt CPD

WARRANT GRANTED: HON. NEVILLE D. BROWN, JUDGE, CALISTA CRIMINAL COURT, AUGUST 16, 1993

The story behind the raid was starting to come together: a female informant with the initials C.D., apparently living in the house, reported that Courtney Cobb was living there in order to collect the $50,000 reward offered by her parents. I now also had the name of the deprogramming company. I looked it up. It had filed for bankruptcy in 1998 and was defunct.

Loetz, it was clear, had done an efficient job skewing his warrant request to Judge Brown. He had also skewed his accompanying notes using the terms 'orgy room,' 'erotic wall paintings' and 'forcibly held' in order to justify his arrest of the Schechtners. In Calista, a police captain was a ranking officer normally assigned to a command position. That he had been assigned to the case, led the raid and personally pulled the two girls out of the attic suggested he was under pressure from Commissioner Hawkes to take speedy action. That Loetz had done so could account for his subsequent rise at CPD where, as Deputy Chief of Operations, he qualified for a very comfortable pension.

I called Loetz. At first he wasn't keen to talk.

'I've been stung a few too many times by so-called journalists,' he said.

So-called!

He sounded like a hard-ass. To soften him up, I told him a little about myself and that I was working on a story about rumors concerning a raid he'd conducted a quarter-century before. He finally relented, said I sounded 'nice,' and that I should come by the following morning.

He lived in a vine-covered brick house across from a golf course on a pleasant residential street in upscale Fairlawn Heights. There was a decent-sized expanse of grass, a two-year-old Volvo parked in the drive, and a doormat with the name *Loetz* woven into the brush. Loetz greeted me at the door. He looked to be in his mid-seventies, tanned cheeks, white arching eyebrows, a fringe of white hair on either side of a bald pate. He was wearing a navy-blue tracksuit. I noted a certain courtliness in his manner as he ushered me into what he called 'my den.'

It was a typical suburban man cave – oversize TV, shelf of old sports trophies, signed photos of himself with high city officials, a framed newspaper article about his career, a cluster of family photos, a bag of golf clubs in the corner. Through the window I saw a swing set in the backyard.

'For the grandkids,' he said. 'I've got six. Make quite a racket when they're all here at once.'

I asked about Mrs Loetz. He told me she had dementia and was living in a nursing facility two miles away.

'I visit her every day,' he said.

Yes, indeed, he recalled the Locust Street raid. 'I got scratched up pretty good,' he said. 'You don't forget a thing like that.'

'I understand there was an informant.'

He grinned. 'She was after the reward money. I heard they paid it to her, too. Why not? Her info was on the mark and those families got their daughters back.' He studied me. 'What's your interest in this, Joan? It was a cut-and-dried operation.'

'I'm interested in the artwork in the attic. Remember it?'

He nodded. 'It was weird, scary, like all those characters were staring out at you from the walls.'

'You used the word "erotic" in your report.'

'Don't remember that. The plan was to get those kids out of there, out of that couple's control. We accomplished that. No complaints, except from their defense attorney who tried to make me out to be a liar. But you see, it wasn't about that couple – what was their name?'

'Schechtner.'

'Yeah, see, it wasn't about them. It was about getting those two girls out safe and sound. Really just the Cobb girl. The Commissioner, Jim Hawkes, wanted that girl found. I found her and delivered her.'

'Did Mr Cobb and Commissioner Hawkes have a relationship?'

'I heard they were golf buddies. Commish wanted this taken care of and he knew I could take care of it. So tell me, Joan – what's the story with those paintings?'

'That's what I'm wondering. I've seen photos of them. They're certainly not erotic. From what I've been able to find out, Courtney Cobb painted them. Did she say anything when you took her downstairs?'

'She was hollering. She acted crazed, like she was high on meth. But soon as we got outside and she saw her dad, she shut down and went limp. This deprogrammer couple hustled her into their car and drove off. Then her old man came up to me, thanked me for rescuing her. I remember something he said – "I know you can't take money, Walt. You're honest as the day is long. But if there's ever any way I can help you, now or in the future, don't hesitate to call." He handed me his card and drove off.'

'Did you ever call him?'

Loetz shook his head. 'I loved CPD. Wasn't interested in a corporate security job. Still, was nice to know someone so important felt he owed me a favor.'

Loetz was slick, but I didn't believe he'd never cashed in Cobb's offer. The ultra-sincere way he gazed into my eyes told me he was lying. Maybe he didn't take money from Cobb but got paid off in some untraceable way, such as box seats at professional sports events or scholarships for his daughters at the fancy private girls' school, Ashley-Burnett.

There comes a moment in an interview when it's time to bear down. So far Loetz hadn't told me much. I had a hunch he was concealing something, and that if I was going to get to it, I'd have to provoke him.

'There's corruption in CPD. Guess that's always been a problem. We're hearing rumors of a police shakedown operation on the West Side. I'm working that story.'

'If that's why you're here, you're wasting your time. I've been out of the department ten years.'

'I'm here about the raid, Mr Loetz. It doesn't pass the smell test. The Schechtners were charged with serious stuff, then suddenly they were let off. Like you said, it was all about getting the Cobb girl out of there. But funny thing – she hasn't been seen since.'

Loetz stared at me. 'Not sure what you mean by that.'

'No one's seen or heard from Courtney Cobb since the night you pulled her out of that house. I'm sure her family knows where she is, but they refuse to talk about her. Don't you find that strange?'

He shrugged, but I could tell I was making him uneasy. 'Families . . . sometimes hard to figure them out.'

'How did you figure the Cobb family?'

'I figured them for desperate. They wanted their daughter back and she didn't want to go back.'

'Did you think those deprogrammers were legit?'

'No idea. The family hired them.'

'You took the other kids down to CPS. Why not the two in the attic?'

'That wasn't the deal.'

'Oh, so there *was* a deal. What kind of deal?'

'Deliver Courtney to her dad. Everyone else, the kids, the Schechtners . . .' He shrugged again.

'Collateral damage?'

'Wouldn't put it that way. The other kids were well placed.'

'The Schechtners were ruined. No one would touch them. You'd branded them as satanists.'

He didn't respond.

'Wanna know what I think, Mr Loetz? This whole operation was about pleasing the Commissioner who had a personal relationship with the very wealthy, very powerful Horace Cobb.'

'You can sum it up that way if you want. Like I told you on the phone, I've been stung by reporters lotsa times.'

'Let's talk about the way *you* summed it up, when you went to Judge Brown for a warrant and later wrote up your report. You described the attic as an "orgy room," the murals as "erotic wall paintings." You claimed two girls were being "forcibly held" when there was absolutely no proof of that. On the contrary, later there was sworn testimony that the girls were there voluntarily and were in the process of applying to become liberated minors. You also claimed that the house, A Caring Place, wasn't licensed, but then it turned out that it was. You swore out your warrant application under penalty of perjury, but seems like there may have been some exaggeration involved.'

'I worked with the information I had. Under pressure, mistakes get made. I swore out that application based on belief.' Suddenly, he turned angry. 'Hey! I don't get why you're here. *What the hell do you want?*'

'I want the truth, Mr Loetz. I think you knew what was going on, and you worked very hard to make it legal.'

'What do *you* think was going on?'

'A reverse kidnapping.'

He scoffed. 'No such thing!'

'Sure about that? A kid runs away from home. Her family wants her back. They get the police to snatch her, then send her off with some so-called cult deprogrammers who brought in props like an upside-down crucifix and sprayed six-six-six on the walls to make the place look like a satanic cult house. Ever since that night no one – not her friends, her teachers, the girl who was with her in the house – have seen or heard from her.'

'Like I said, Ms Nguyen, there's no such thing as a reverse kidnapping. A family can't kidnap its own child.' He stood. 'I think it's time for you to go.'

At the door, he gazed into my eyes. 'You have a sweet face,' he said. 'Too bad you came all this way for nothing.'

But of course I hadn't come for nothing. I'd learned a lot and recorded the interview. That night I went over to the Capehart and played it for Jason and Hannah.

Jason Poe

I was impressed by how much information Joan got out of Loetz. Even though she did most of the talking, he never denied her interpretation of the raid.

It had been two weeks since Penny Dawson had hung up on Joan. I'd hoped Penny would call back and was disappointed that she hadn't. If anyone knew the backstory on the murals, she would be the one.

Joan offered to do a deep search for her. There were about 75,000 people living in the Florida Keys. If Penny hadn't fibbed about that, Joan thought it would be possible to find her. But even if we did, then what? We couldn't stalk her or harass her. That would only turn her off.

'First let's see if we can find her,' Joan said, 'then we'll figure out how to make an approach.'

I had lunch with Tally, told him I was ready to stop taking photos for *Leavings*.

He grinned. 'Finally!'

We had all the images, around twelve hundred, on our respective computers. I asked him to go through them and make a first cut, picking the ones he thought were the best. I'd do the same and then we'd compare. We agreed to limit our first cut to a hundred.

'So now we're going to work on the murals?'

I told him that's what I wanted us to do and that I was thinking about approaching the CPA firm where the tax bills for the house were sent. Maybe they'd give me the owner's name if I suggested I was interested in purchasing the place.

'It's not worth anything, according to Oscar,' Tally said. 'No one wants to buy around there. You'd have to think up a decent reason, like gutting it and then turning it into a photo studio. What'll you say if the CPA asks you to make an offer?'

'Tell him I'll need to make a top-to-bottom inspection first.'

'You really want to go back in there.'

'Oh, yeah! I want you to see those murals and I want to see them again.'

'Since whoever owns it hasn't abandoned it and Mystery Lady comes by every so often to check it out, I have a hunch the CPA firm will blow you off.'

Mystery Lady – I liked that. And I thought Tally was probably right. If she was the owner, showing interest in the property might be a good way to flush her out.

I decided to approach the CPA firm cold. I drove over to the address on Doverland Avenue, a short, nondescript, worn-down, two-story shopping strip – drugstore, pet grooming salon, seedy-looking barbershop on the ground level, with a couple of dentist offices and the offices of Meyers and Lee Certified Public Accountants upstairs.

There was a crabby-looking middle-aged lady at a desk in the front office. She gave me a stony-faced 'May I help you?'

I told her I was interested in a property, which, according to city tax records, was billed to her accounting firm.

'What's the address?'

'It's 1160 Locust.'

She nodded, told me to take a seat, then went to a back office, knocked on the door, entered and closed it behind her.

She returned a couple of minutes later.

'Mr Meyers asks why you're interested.'

I handed her my card. 'I'll tell him that myself.'

She looked at my card, gave me a dirty look, went back to the rear office, knocked and went in. This time when she came out, she gestured for me to enter.

An overweight guy in his fifties with a shaved head stood up from behind a desk.

'Jeff Meyers,' he said.

We shook hands. He motioned me to a seat, then studied my card.

'You teach at the Art Institute, Mr Poe. Photography Department, it says here.'

'Correct.'

'What's your interest in the Locust Street property?'

'I'm looking for a studio in an inexpensive neighborhood. The house intrigues me and it looks like it's been kept up.'

'To buy or lease?' he asked.

'Can't say yet. Need to get inside and check it out.'

'Well, whatever you have in mind, it's not going to happen. That property isn't for sale or for rent.'

'If that's the case, why ask why I'm interested and if I want to buy or lease?'

'Curious, I guess.'

'Will you at least pass on my interest to the owner?'

'Sure.' He stood up. 'I'm sorry you came all the way over here. It's usually best to call first, save yourself the time.'

The lady in the front smirked as I came back out.

'Edgar?' she asked.

'Excuse me?'

'Edgar Allan Poe – you related?'

I ignored her.

'Well, *excuse me!*' she said.

I didn't like Meyers much and I definitely didn't like his receptionist. Meyers's queries were intrusive and his front-office gal was rude. Why all this secrecy regarding 1160 Locust? Why were the taxes billed to a third-rate accounting firm? Why act so cagey about who owned the property? And who was the Mystery Lady who came by every so often to stare at the house?

Could all of this have something to do with the murals?

Rob Kraus, dean at CAI, was a busy guy. Besides running the school, hiring faculty and having to deal all day with difficult art students and temperamental teachers, he also taught a course, 'The Business of Art,' which every CAI student was required to take.

As Rob put it when he addressed us at the start of every year, 'Unlike most private art schools that only care about collecting tuition, I don't want to send our kids out into the world with any illusions. I want them to know how tough it is to make a career as an artist, how harsh the world is out there. I want them to understand that being an artist isn't just about the work you do in the studio. It's also about how you interact in a ruthlessly competitive society. Thus my course "The Business of Art," in which I instruct our aspiring artists on what they need to know to survive.'

To which I say, *Bravo!*

I liked Rob. He took his teaching seriously. He also knew a good deal about the legal aspects of fine art practice, which was why Hannah and I cornered him in the CAI cafeteria.

After some chatter about our curriculum and an exchange of gossip regarding extramarital goings-on at the museum, I broached a subject that had been bothering me regarding ownership of the Locust Street Murals.

'Here's a hypothetical, Rob. Say, forty years ago I give a dinner party in my New York City loft, and Willem de Kooning is one of the guests. He gets tipsy and asks if he can paint something on one of my walls . . . say, the bathroom to spruce it up. I tell him to go ahead, so he goes into the bathroom and he paints one of his terrific "angry woman" nudes on the tile wall. Assuming I own the loft, who owns the painting?'

'That's easy,' Rob said. 'He owns the rights to his image, but you own the actual work.'

'Even though I didn't pay him or commission it?'

'Doesn't matter. Also doesn't matter if he asked your permission to paint it. You own the wall so you own what's on the wall. This comes up all the time with graffiti artists or someone like Banksy who goes around the world stenciling and painting stuff on building walls. Their artwork belongs to the buildings' owners, who have a perfect right to paint it over if they want, or, in the case of Banksy, cut off that particular chunk of wall and then put it up for auction at Sotheby's.'

'Thanks, Rob, you've answered my question.'

'Don't mention it, Jase. Next time try me on something a little more taxing.'

After lunch I walked Hannah back to her studio. En route, I mentioned that since Rob seemed to know about Anders Carlsen's affair with Anna, it was safe to assume plenty of other people knew as well.

'Except for Carlsen's wife. I think Anna would die if she knew people were gabbing about it.'

When we reached her studio, she showed me two pieces she was working on. As I stood admiring them, she explained she was employing a new technique. She'd woven same-size pieces of blank cloth, taken them off her looms, painted similar abstract forms on them using different colored dyes, unraveled the pieces and was now in the process of reweaving them, combining the warp from the first piece with the weft from the second, and vice versa. The result of this laborious process would be a pair of twin-like weavings, each the ghost mirror image of the other.

I found this mind-blowing. 'Utterly brilliant!' I told her.

A couple days after my unpleasant visit to the offices of Meyers and Lee, I found a message on my voicemail: 'Hello, Mr Poe. My name's Cynthia Broderick. We haven't met. I'm calling because I understand you're interested in my Locust Street property. Call me back if you'd care to discuss.'

She had one of those upper-class accents – the kind Scott Fitzgerald described as 'full of money.'

I immediately returned her call. I have a vivid memory of our conversation, a turning point in our quest to discover the origin of the murals.

'Hello, Ms Broderick, this is Jason Poe.'

'Thanks for getting back to me.'

'What can I do for you?'

'I think it's more what I can do for you.'

'You own the house at 1160 Locust?'

'I do.'

'I take it you got my name from Jeff Meyers.'

'Seems you made quite an impression on him.'

'Oh?'

'He found you rather . . . hmm . . . presumptuous.'

'Did he?'

'His old bag of a secretary, Alice Confessore, didn't like you at all.'

'What didn't she like about me?'

'Your arrogance, she said.'

'I found her obnoxious.'

'I'm not surprised, Mr Poe.'

'Please call me Jason.'

'Please call me Cindy.' She paused. 'Those two, Meyers and Confessore – they're nasty. I rather like that in CPAs.'

'Well, to each his own . . .'

'I know who you are, Jason. I know your work. You were quite well known some years back – the fearless war photographer, the guy who liked to go in close. I remember seeing a photo of you in a safari jacket, cameras crisscrossing your torso like ammo belts. "Quite the intrepid photojournalist," I remember thinking at the time.'

'Guess I'll never live that one down.'

'Here's the thing, Jason – if I hadn't heard of you, I wouldn't have bothered to call. As Meyers told you, my Locust Street property isn't for sale. If you're wondering why, I guess you could say I'm holding on to it for sentimental reasons. But because I had heard of you, I did some internet research. What do you suppose I found? That in addition to your teaching duties at Calista Art Institute, you've been hard at work photographing stuff people leave behind when they abandon houses. This project, I understand, involves forays in the dead of night – intrusions not likely to be welcomed by property owners.' She paused. 'That sum it up?'

'My compliments on your research.'

'I think we should meet and discuss your interest in my property. Are you free this weekend?'

'I am.'

'Please come by my gallery tomorrow.'

She owns a gallery!

She gave me the address. 'I close at six. Six thirty would be good. Ring the bell and I'll let you in.'

Hannah Sachs

was working late in my studio at CAI when Jason called. He was down in his office on the second floor. Could he come up right away? *Of course!*

I'm no Nancy Drew, but as he recounted his conversation with Cindy Broderick, it didn't take me half a minute to deduce she was the Mystery Lady Tally had told us about.

I knew Cindy. The Calista art world's small. Everyone knows everyone else. A few years back I'd showed her my portfolio. She was respectful, but told me she didn't handle textile art. That was OK. The market for what I do is small. When I told this to Jason and he asked what her gallery was like, I was surprised he'd never set foot in it.

'You should have,' I told him. 'It's the best contemporary gallery in town. She specializes in pricey big names like Eric Fischl and Jennifer Bartlett.'

'Photography?'

'Some. I've seen a few good pieces there – a Mapplethorpe lily and a large multi-image collage by the Starns.'

Jason shrugged, said he was surprised people in Calista would be interested in stuff like that.

'You still think everyone here's a hick. Actually, there're several hundred committed collectors in town, of which maybe twenty are very serious.'

'So she deals in high-end art, yet holds on to a rotting old house on crummy Locust Street. What does that tell you?'

'I'm not sure.'

'She damn well knows what's in her attic. That's why she's holding on to it. Will you come with me tomorrow?'

'Of course! I've been waiting for you to ask.'

I told him what I knew about Cindy, which wasn't all that much. Yes, she had a plummy accent, but she wasn't from a moneyed background. She was local, smart, very good-looking, and had somehow wangled herself a scholarship to Mount Holyoke College. There she'd majored in Art History and French Lit. Presumably that's also where she acquired her social skills and way of speaking. After college she came back to Calista, got a job as an assistant at the Easton Gallery, met, dated and married a wealthy Social Register type named Carter Broderick, divorced him after a few years, and used her settlement money to buy out Lane Easton and take over his gallery when he retired.

'She's done well with it. She knows how to sell art. She waits for clients to come to her, then grooms them. She talks the usual gallery spiel about buying only what you love, and how it's always better to buy one really good piece than half a dozen minor works that'll just clog up your walls. There're women around town who don't care for her. They see her as an upstart and are probably jealous of her looks. But most people, men especially, are quite taken with her. She's honest, and she's willing to take back a piece if a client changes his mind. She also makes a practice of loaning pieces out, letting her clients live with them a while, but never pushing them to make a decision.'

'So, the gallerist of one's dreams,' Jase said. 'She was a little snooty about an old portrait someone took of me.'

'The one where you're draped with camera straps from your Hemingway days?'

'Yeah.'

'Sounds like she knew you and Tally were in her house.'

'Oscar, that old guy at the observatory – Tally thinks he keeps an eye on the place for her.'

The Easton Gallery was on Waverly Square, the best retail location in the East Side suburbs. The square, at the intersection of Waverly and Middlebrook, was near my alma mater, the private girls' school, Ashley-Burnett. The gallery was situated in a cluster of upscale shops including Gucci and Hermès boutiques; Cooks & Crooks, a bookstore specializing in cookbooks and mysteries; Tranche, a pâté and cheese shop; the Left Bank, a Parisian-style café; the Wizard of Odds, an antique store; and 'O', a sushi bar/Asian fusion restaurant.

Jason, as instructed, rang the bell. Through the window I could see Cindy moving toward us. She cocked her finger at me in recognition, unlocked the door, beckoned us in, then relocked it behind us.

'Hannah, Jason – of course! You know each other from CAI. Happy to see you guys. Let's go to my office.' She escorted us through three gallery rooms to the back.

'Next week we're opening a Dana Schutz exhibition. I'll send you invitations.'

She was gracious and well groomed – designer jeans, off-white blouse, turquoise and silver necklace, light eye make-up, glossed lips, light brown hair held into a ponytail by a chocolate-colored velvet scrunchie. And her voice, that moneyed, plummy tone noted by Jason, completed the picture of the archetypal gallerist – elegant, understated, mistress of the soft sell.

Her office was appointed with a sawhorse-style desk with inch-thick glass top, three-seat Corbusier couch and pair of Corbu grande comfort armchairs, all with matching chrome frames and fitted black leather cushions. There was a set of signed framed Rauschenberg prints on the walls, and a built-in wet bar with miniature fridge.

When Cindy asked what we'd like to drink, I asked for a glass of white wine. Jason opted for water.

'Oh, you sober *artistes*!' she said. 'Hope you don't mind if I have a real drink.'

She poured herself a Scotch and soda, then sat down in the power position in the center of the couch while we occupied the armchairs.

'I know you're here to discuss my house. But first' – she turned to me – 'tell me what you're up to, Hannah?'

She seemed genuinely interested, so I started to explain my deconstruction–reconstruction weaving technique.

'Fascinating! I'd love to see your new pieces. Would you be up for a studio visit?'

'Sure,' I said. 'But you told me you didn't handle textile art.'

'The gallery's doing well. I'm looking to expand our roster. Can't think of a better way than to work with select local artists.' She turned to Jason. 'Any thoughts about a *Leavings* exhibition?'

Oh, she was seductive, dangling the possibility of exhibiting our work and establishing a patronage relationship. She knew about artists, how much we need exposure, how enticed we'd be by even the hint of such an offer. I wondered: Was she softening us up for something, or was this just her way of establishing dominance?

'We've stopped taking pictures for *Leavings*,' Jason told her. 'We're in an editing phase. Like they say, "gotta kill your darlings."'

'*We?*'

'I'm working with a former student. He handles security and logistics, and he's got a terrific eye.'

'That's the African American kid?'

'I guess you know.'

Cindy smiled. 'I know you were inside my house. For quite a few hours, I understand.'

She didn't say it harshly or with reproach. She simply stated it as an incontrovertible fact.

'That's true,' Jason said. 'Sorry we didn't ask permission.'

'But you didn't know whom to ask, did you?' She posed the question coolly.

'We could have found out.'

She smiled. 'Don't worry about it. I won't go after you for trespassing. Wouldn't dream of it. But I *am* curious. What made you choose my house?'

'It stands out. There's something special about it.'

'Yes, there is, which I why I like it.'

'We assume you're the lady who stops by every so often and looks it over from her car.'

'Seems Oscar told your boy more than he should.'

I could see Jason tense up at the word 'boy.'

'We've been calling you "the Mystery Lady,"' I told her.

'Really! "Mystery Lady" – nice! Yes, I am that person. But maybe not so mysterious as you think.'

'It does seem mysterious,' Jason said. 'As if there's something—'

'And what do you suppose that "something" could be?' she asked, her tone turning supercilious.

'May I ask you a personal question?' Jason asked.

She giggled. 'You may ask. I may not tell.'

'What's your maiden name?'

Her eyes went cold. 'Is that relevant?'

'Does it start with a D?'

'My maiden name was Dryansky.' She pronounced it carefully, drawing out the syllables as if to flaunt how foreign and working-class it sounded.

Jason nodded and smiled slightly, and with that smile I suddenly felt the power dynamic shift. I held my breath.

What is he up to? Where is he going with this?

'When we spoke, you said you held on to the house for "sentimental reasons."'

Cindy nodded.

'You were the informant, weren't you? The one who told, you know . . .'

Although he spoke softly, and left the sentence dangling, her reaction was swift. She gulped down her drink, covered her mouth with her hand, then rose and started awkwardly toward the bar as if to pour herself another. Then, changing her mind, she turned and faced us.

'Excuse me. I'll be right back. Got to visit the loo.' And with that and a stricken look, she rushed out of the room.

I turned to Jason. 'What's going on?'

'Stab in the dark.'

'Seems you hit the bulls-eye. How'd you know?'

'Gut instinct. In the warrant application the confidential informant was designated C.D.'

We waited in silence for several minutes. When Cindy returned, her eyes were red but otherwise she seemed to have pulled herself together.

'You were saying?' she asked, this time stopping at the bar to pour herself a second Scotch.

'I believe you were the young woman in the house who recognized Courtney Cobb, then called the police.'

'It didn't exactly go down that way, but, yeah, basically, that's correct.'

'Want to talk about it?'

'Not really. But I will if we can talk about some other things first.' Jason motioned for her to go ahead. 'I take it you found something interesting in the house; otherwise, you wouldn't have sought out my accountant.'

'"Interesting" is a mild word for what I found. As you know, Hannah wasn't with me, but she's seen my photographs.'

'Was the place in decent condition? I ask because it's been years since I've been inside.'

'Not bad considering.'

'And the cupola?'

'Quite good, I'd say.'

'The murals intact?'

Jason nodded. 'Almost as if they'd been painted yesterday.'

She smiled. 'Well, that's a relief.'

'We think they're masterpieces,' I told her, 'or pretty close. As a check, I showed photos to Anna von Arx.'

'What did Anna say?'

'She pretty much agreed. Of course, I didn't tell her where they were from and she knew not to ask.'

Cindy nodded. 'Masterpieces? I recall them as a bit primitive, but I suppose they're quite good in their way.'

'Better than good, Cindy,' Jason said. 'This is what I don't get. Here you have a high-end gallery. You know good art when you see it. You own those murals because you own the house. They're painted on plywood. They can be easily removed. So why leave them up there where they're vulnerable to fire, rodents or a leak in the roof?'

She sat back. 'That's a long story. Which is what you came for, isn't it?'

'We're eager to hear whatever you feel comfortable telling us,' I said.

'I'll tell you what happened, but off the record. OK?'

We told her OK, and with that she started her tale. She spoke haltingly at first. It was clear she had some trouble getting it out. But then, lapsing into confessional mode, she spoke more rapidly the deeper she got into it.

Her mother and stepfather were alcoholics. There was violence and spousal abuse in the house. At age sixteen she was desperate to leave home. A counselor at her high school told her about the Schechtners, known as Dr Liz and Dr Ted, and their East Calista halfway house, A Caring Place. She went over there, met with them, liked them and was grateful when they invited her to stay. While she stood by the phone, Dr Liz called her mother who quickly gave her consent.

'She didn't give a damn about me, stopped caring soon as I reached my teens. I admit I was difficult. We fought a lot. Couple of times she slapped me around. She was more than receptive when Doctor Liz called, happy to foist me off on someone else.'

Everything went well the first few months. She got along with the kids in the house, transferred to the local high school, had twice-weekly psychotherapy sessions with Dr Liz, and group sessions with both docs and the other runaways. It didn't take her long to assume the role of house princess. Most importantly, she started to feel a lot better about herself and her future prospects.

Then two new girls moved in. They were introduced by phony names: Pam and Jen. The docs made a big fuss over them, and were cagey about their true identities. It was clear to most of the kids that the two new girls were VIPs. They had a bedroom to themselves on the third floor. They didn't socialize and didn't take part in group sessions. They were standoffish, spoke to each other in whispers and barely said a word to anyone else.

Cindy tried to befriend them. She'd noticed that both girls did a lot of sketching. She asked Pam if she'd be willing to draw her portrait. Pam shook her head, making it clear she preferred to keep her distance.

Within a few days of their arrival, the new girls started spending a lot of time in the cupola room, which the Schechtners called the attic, but which the kids dubbed 'the orgy room' because that was the room where they were encouraged to go when they needed to vent and let off steam.

'You know,' Cindy told us, 'a place where we were allowed to be angry, what Doctor Liz called an "orgy of strife."'

When Cindy and the other kids asked what the newcomers were doing up there, Dr Liz said they were engaged in a therapeutic art project. When asked for more details, she said they were working out their issues by painting on the walls, that the work was very personal, had to do with the girls' personal demons, and, no, it wasn't possible for anyone else to go up there even for just a peek.

This prohibition engendered discontent. Cindy was particularly upset. It was clear that she was no longer house princess. The new girls, whom she thought of as outsiders, were now clearly the Schechtners' favorites. She was resentful that they'd supplanted her. The Schechtners, she felt, acted oddly around them. Little by little she started to pick up hints that Pam and Jen were in hiding and that their presence in the house was covert. For example, they didn't eat at the communal table. They'd come downstairs, fetch food from the kitchen, then take it back up to their room to eat. They didn't help with housekeeping chores, didn't do the dishes, water the lawn, work in the garden, put out the garbage or sweep the porch. They rarely left the house, and then only in the company of one of the docs. They didn't go to school but spent all their time in the attic doing whatever they were doing up there. The fumes from their painting started drifting down to the lower floors. Cindy hated the smell.

One day in the cafeteria at school, she overheard several students talking about a pair of local best-friend girls who'd disappeared. Had they been kidnapped, murdered, or were they runaways? No one knew for sure.

After lunch she went to the school library to look through back issues of the *Times-Dispatch*. It didn't take her long to find an article about the girls. There was a picture of the girl she knew as Pam identified as Courtney Cobb, and the news that her family was offering a $50,000 reward for information leading to her return.

'Fifty thousand – that was huge! Back in those days it was

enough to cover four years of college. I took the newspaper into the ladies' room, cut out the article and put it in my pocket. *Could I – what's the expression? – drop a dime on them? Surely Courtney Cobb's parents deserved to get their kid back. Could I? Would I?* I didn't know. Doing so would be a huge move. There would surely be consequences for the girls, and also for me. For some reason it didn't occur to me that the gravest harm might fall upon the Schechtners. Greedy fool that I was, I never thought of that.'

She spent four full days thinking it over, then made her decision. The breaking point came when she again tried to talk to Pam, and was, she felt, rudely blown off.

OK, if that's how she wants it, she'll have to take what comes. This house will be a lot better off with both those girls out of here.

There was a phone booth at the school. She went into it, shut the door and called the number in the article. A woman answered. Cindy told her she was calling about the Cobb girl, that she knew her whereabouts and wanted to be sure that if she revealed it, she'd be eligible to receive the reward.

She was put on hold, then a man came on the line. He told her his name was Walter Loetz, that he was a police captain, and that if she really did know the whereabouts of Courtney Cobb, he'd very much like to talk to her. They arranged to meet on the corner of Robertson and Weybridge, two blocks from East Calista High. He said he'd drive right over there in a civilian car, park and wait for her. He assured her their meeting would be private and warned her not to mention it to anyone else.

She remembered Loetz well even after so many years. He was fairly good-looking, she said, with middle-parted black hair and what she called 'a thick cop mustache.' His manner was patient, his demeanor serious. Cleverly, he didn't start out asking where Courtney was. Instead, he asked Cindy about herself, why she'd decided to call in and what she'd do with the reward money if her information proved correct.

'I told him I wanted the money for college. Right away I could see he liked that. He pointed out that I was a minor, so if it turned out I did qualify for the reward, the best thing would be for the money to be set aside for me by the Cobb family attorney until I came of age. That way, Loetz said, the matter could be kept discreet and no one would ever know about my involvement. He asked me if that made sense. It was only after I told him it did that he asked me where Courtney was being kept.'

Cindy was cautious. She'd watched a lot of TV crime dramas. She told Loetz that although she was sure he was honorable, she also knew she couldn't rely solely on his word regarding the reward. She told him that since the money would be coming from the Cobb family, she also wanted assurances from them.

Loetz seemed taken aback by that, but also impressed by her intelligence and maturity. He suggested they go down to police headquarters, where she could meet with the Cobb family attorney, receive appropriate assurances, and then, once she was satisfied, tell them what she knew.

The attorney, Nathan Silver, turned out to be a friendly, sharply dressed middle-aged man. He assured her that if her information proved accurate, she would be entitled to the reward. His recommendation was that he keep it in an escrow account where it would earn interest. Then, once she entered college, he'd draw on it to pay her tuition.

'It would be like you were a trust fund kid,' he said, smiling. She liked that he was dapper and easy-going. 'How does that sound, young lady?'

She thought that sounded great.

'I thought it would be so easy,' Cindy told us. 'I'd just give them the address, 1160 Locust, tell them that Courtney and the other girl were staying there under assumed names, and that would be that. But after I told them, Loetz and Silver went out to the hall to confer. When Loetz came back, he told me he was going to bring in a stenographer and conduct a formal interview. He'd ask me questions and I should think carefully before I answered. He explained he needed more information to get a warrant to enter the house and remove the girls. He used the words "sharp info," the kind that would convince a judge. Did I understand what he was looking for?

'I told him I wasn't sure. He looked me straight in the eye, then lowered his voice. "I think you'll be able to tell from the way I phrase my questions that I'm looking for specific answers. But understand, I don't want someone to come around later and say I asked you leading questions. Know what leading questions are?" I nodded. "I'm not going to ask them in a leading way, but understand that your reward depends on how well you answer. We in sync on this?"

'After I nodded, he left the room, came back with the stenographer, introduced us, then sat down and started the interview. I picked up right away on the kind of answers he wanted. For example, he asked if the two girls were being kept in the house against their will. I knew the answer would have to be that I believed they were. He asked me about the Schechtners. How would I describe them? When I told him Doctor Ted was very charismatic, he asked me if he had a "cult leader personality." Again, I knew the answer to that was yes. In truth, there *was* something cult-leadership-like about Doctor Ted. He asked me about Doctor Liz's reference to the girls' "personal demons." What did she mean by that? By "demons," did she mean something satanic? By that time I understood where we were going. I told him yes, I believed the Schechtners might be leading a satanic cult, that in my opinion the two girls had been "brain-washed," and were now "confined" to the attic of the house in a room that those of us who lived there referred to as "the orgy room."'

In fact, she said, she believed some of what she'd said – it did seem at times that the girls were 'confined,' and there was a certain cult-like aspect to the way the docs ran the house. 'Satanic?' Well, that, she admitted, was more than a stretch. It was a lie. But in retrospect it struck her that in the end it wouldn't have made any difference what she said. Once Loetz had the address, he'd figure out a way to get the girls out of there. Better, she thought, to please Loetz and ensure she'd get the reward than hedge with her answers and risk losing out on the money.

She could tell Loetz was pleased with her answers. Meantime, the steno was taking everything down. She guessed later that the reason Loetz had brought in a steno rather than recording the interview was to disguise the fact that he was leading her responses. She was aware throughout that her words would have consequences, but convinced herself that everything she was saying was part of a commendable effort to return Pam and Jen to their folks. And always in the back of her mind was the $50,000 reward and how much it would mean for her future.

'I've never admitted this before to anyone: I was fully aware at the time that my cooperation was for personal gain. I wanted two things: the reward money and those two girls out of the house. At that point nothing else mattered to me. To this day I'm not ashamed I wanted those things, but, yes, I'm ashamed I exaggerated and lied in the interview. Loetz understood me. He sniffed out my greed. He knew exactly how to manipulate me, and I willingly went along. He got exactly what he wanted . . . and so did I.'

The raid took place that night. Cindy was surprised Loetz moved so fast. She was eating dinner with the others when there was loud banging on the door. Before Dr Ted could open it, a bunch of uniformed cops burst in, along with two male/female couples. Dr Ted shouted at them, 'Who the hell are you? What'd you want?' Dr Liz and the kids started to scream. There was chaos.

'I pretended I didn't know what was going on,' Cindy told us. 'I saw Loetz but didn't acknowledge him. He and two officers went storming up the stairs. About a minute later I heard screaming from the attic. Meantime Doctor Ted was freaking out. "You can't just bust in here! Get out!" He and Doctor Liz were handcuffed and taken outside. A woman came in to talk to us. She said she was from CPS. She told us there was a bus outside waiting to take us away. She told us the house was being shut down, but not to worry. We'd be processed, taken care of, placed in good foster care homes.

'A few minutes later, aboard the bus, I caught a glimpse of Pam and Jen as Loetz led them down the porch stairs. Both were handcuffed. Jen was emoting, but Pam looked like she was ready to collapse. Loetz placed them in separate cars, each with one of the civilian couples. Mr Silver and another man (I think he was Courtney's father) stood together watching. Then we were bused out. I never saw Pam or Jen again. I found out later that the docs were in a heap of trouble, that the cops had taken seriously what I'd said about a satanic cult and orgy room. Then I heard they were let off, left town, moved out west. The only person I saw again was Mr Silver. He kept his word, set up a trust for me, and when I was accepted at Mount Holyoke, where, it turned out, Courtney's mother had gone to college, all my tuition bills were paid and I received an additional two hundred a month to cover personal expenses.'

Cindy sat back. 'So, yes, I *was* the informant. Am I proud of that? Of course not! Am I ashamed? Only for one thing – that what I'd done may have ruined the Schechtners' lives. Fifteen or so years ago, after I bought this gallery from Lane Easton, I checked on the house on Locust, found it was in arrears for unpaid taxes, and that it was coming up at a city auction of abandoned properties. Jeff Meyers set up a dummy company and we placed a bid. I was the only bidder. Even though I got it cheap, Jeff thought I was crazy investing in a worthless property. I didn't care, I wanted it, and I wasn't interested in his opinion. After I bought it, I had it properly boarded up. I pay the taxes on it, and I pay Oscar at the observatory to keep an eye on it for me.'

'Did you ever go inside?'

'Just one time right after I bought it. Never went in again. Yes, I did go up to the attic, saw the murals, was impressed, but I certainly didn't see them as masterpieces. I found them threatening and belligerent, part and parcel of the whole crazy nightmare. I recall wondering about what must have been going through those girls' heads to have created pictures like that. I had seen enough of them to know they were both damaged, but it was only after I saw their murals that I realized how severely.' She paused. 'You ask why I haven't removed them. I guess because I think they're where they belong. They were made to fit the walls of that room. Also, there's something kind of amazing about coming up the ladder through the trap door and having them surround you as you emerge. You say they're powerful. I think the way you discovered them may explain that power. Frankly, I don't think they'd work very well on my gallery walls.

'After that one visit, I had the power turned off. No point in paying for gas and electricity. I remember going downstairs, sitting on that battered old couch and crying my eyes out. It was nostalgia for the months I spent there and the care I'd received. It truly was a "Caring Place." Also guilt for the harm I'd done, because that last day and night between my calling the cops and the raid was probably the worst day of my life.'

'Did you go into foster care?' I asked.

She shook her head. 'I moved back in with my mom. She stopped drinking, got rid of my stepfather and things were better at home. I finished high school, went on to college, got married, divorced, and now I have this gallery. All of which can be traced back to the afternoon I met up with Captain Loetz.'

'What about the Schechtners?' Jason asked. 'You went to a lot of trouble to acquire their house. Did you ever find out what happened to them?'

Cindy nodded. 'I hired a private detective. He tracked them down. Turns out they moved to Albuquerque. Soon as I got their address, I phoned, then went out there for a visit. It's a sad story. They tried to start again as therapists, but even though the charges here were dropped, seems those words "satanic cult" followed them out west. No one would touch them. As Doctor Liz told me, "We were stigmatized." She finally got a job running a house for indigent seniors for which, being a trained psychotherapist, she was way over-qualified. According to her, Doctor Ted never recovered. He began drinking heavily, they split up, and he moved up to Taos where he worked as a clerk in a feed store. A few years ago she wrote me that he'd passed away. She took the blame for what happened. "We had no right to take in those girls and not report it. From what Courtney and Penny told us, both family environments were awful. Still, their parents were entitled to know they were safe. We could have applied to become their guardians *ad litem*. We intended to do that, but hesitated because Courtney's family was so powerful. We made a huge mistake and we paid heavily for it." Just so you know, every month I send her a check to help her out with expenses.'

'Did you ever tell her you were the informer?' I asked.

Cindy hung her head. 'I didn't have the heart,' she said.

Or the courage.

So there it was: the backstory, at least Cindy's part of it. It was clear Loetz had lied to Joan, that he and Silver had cooked up a tale so they could mount a raid and snatch out Courtney Cobb. The whole thing was about her. Everyone else was, as Joan put it, 'collateral damage.' Loetz's warrant application was based on false responses to leading questions. Loetz had taken advantage of a teenage girl's envy and greed, then falsely sworn out a warrant application.

Later, when Jase and I talked it over, we agreed we couldn't blame Cindy for what she'd done. Loetz, it seemed to us, was the villain of the piece. We also agreed that since we'd given Cindy our word that what she told us would be off the record, we had no choice but to honor our pledge. We'd recount her story to Joan on 'background only.' Later, we hoped, Joan would be able to interview her and get her story direct.

We were moved by her tale. Acquiring the house and helping out Dr Liz struck us as her way of doing penance. She knew she couldn't take back what she'd done. Her visits to the house, sitting in her car outside, reliving her emotions – that had become her atonement.

She seemed relaxed after her confession, relieved to have told us a story that was so painful to remember and recount. Jase thanked her for her honesty. It was clear she appreciated that. The slick gallerist, who'd earlier dangled the possibility of exhibitions, now struck me as a human being in pain.

'What can I do for you?' she finally asked, after fixing herself a third drink.

'I'd like to see the murals again,' Jase said, 'and I'd like Hannah to see them with me. Also my partner, Tally. Maybe we're wrong, maybe they're not masterpieces, but there's something very compelling about them. I'd like to go in with battery-powered lamps and study them up close, re-photograph them in better light and see if I still feel as I did when I first stumbled upon them.'

'I'll arrange it,' Cindy said. 'Oscar has a key to the front door. But I won't go in with you.' She shook her head. 'I don't think I can ever go in there again.'

Tally Vaughan

I want to say something about Jason, why I like him, work with him and respect him. It goes back to the first day of his photo-journalism class. There were ten of us, cameras around our necks, expecting to hear him talk about equipment and technique. Instead, he said he wanted to start the course discussing 'the journalist's dilemma.'

'You see something happening, it's really bad, and maybe you can do something about it. So do you stand back and document it, or do you intervene?' he asked. 'In my view, there's no dilemma. You're there, you get involved. Sometimes documentation is the best way to go. Acting as a witness is an important form of involvement. Sometimes if you try to intervene, you risk being killed. You have to be acutely aware of your surroundings so you can weigh the odds and make a split-second decision.

'Here's an example from my own career. I was embedded in Iraq with a platoon of US Marines, with them as they swept through a village. Everyone was on edge. Shots were coming from nearby buildings. Four of them burst into a house from which shots had been fired from an upper floor. I went in with them. In a dark corner there was a family crouching in fear – old lady, young mother, two very young kids. One of the marines was trigger-happy. He saw those people, fired at them, slaughtered them before my eyes. I was shooting images fast, bang-bang-bang, almost as fast as he was firing bullets. Realizing his mistake, he was shocked by what he'd done. Also furious. His buddies tried to calm him. "It's war. Shit happens," one of them told him.

'OK, I have photographic evidence of a war crime and the guys know it. The sergeant asked me nicely to please erase the images and spare the shooter a court martial. I told him I couldn't do that. He got mad, got right into my face, informed me I *had* to do it. "That's an order!" he said. He and his men were armed. I wasn't. As they crowded me, the threat was clear. Marines kill people. That's their job. One of them just killed four innocents before my eyes.'

He stopped, let his story sink in, then went around the room asking each of us to put ourselves in that situation, and say what he or she would have done. We talked about it the full hour, got deeper and deeper into it. Jase just let us talk. Each of us had an opinion. There was a consensus among some that survival was the most important thing, that you could erase the images and live to shoot another day. Or you could give eye-witness testimony in a court martial trial even without the images. I remember saying that you could pretend to erase the images, though I admitted that would be risky. Finally, when class was nearly over, we sat there waiting for him to tell us what he'd done.

'I stood my ground in a non-confrontational way,' he told us, 'mumbled something about discussing the matter later after everyone had cooled down, then turned and exited the house. If they were going to shoot me, they were going to have to shoot me in the back. Obviously, they didn't. It was a calculated risk.

'Here's the thing – the kid who shot the family wasn't a homi-cidal maniac. He was a scared nineteen-year-old who'd have to live with what he did the rest of his life. Moreover, my images didn't say anything that hadn't already been said thousands of times. So I decided to keep them, but not release them or send them on to my agency. After I made that decision, I informed the sergeant, who accepted what I told him at face value. "I hope you get that kid some help," I said. He promised he would, and I heard later that he reported the incident and the kid was psyched-out of the corps.

'You do what you have to do,' Jase told us. 'Your camera can be more powerful than a machine gun. We're not bystanders. We're not artists who work coolly from a distance. We're witnesses. We go in close. We get involved. Our presence makes us part of the event. And as participants we do what we can to help people, especially when there's something we can actually do. Yes, we're conflict photographers, but first of all we're human beings. You see a war crime, you try to stop it. You don't just let it happen because it'll make a great shot that'll maybe win you a big prize. It's like you're in a hurry to get to the airport, you're running late, but a car hits the center strip, there's an accident and somebody's bleeding on the pavement. Do you keep going so as not to miss your flight, or do you stop and try to help? Think about that as you go out into the city with your cameras. I believe your gut will tell you if and when to step in. So what's the lesson? I believe that in many ways photojournalism is a test of character. Someone with poor character can take a great shot, capture a great moment. But so can someone with fine character, with compassion in his heart. Up to you to decide what kind of photographer you want to be.'

Whew! I never got over that first class. With that discussion, he set up the course. We took lots of pictures, put our work up for critique, everyone offering notes on everyone else's stuff. When Jase gave his critiques, he didn't comment much about lighting, framing, exposures, any of the technical stuff. He was looking for compassion, whether our eyes were connected to our hearts. So when he asked me to work on *Leavings* in what would amount to a secondary role, but with the understanding we'd equally share credit and revenue . . . well, how could I refuse? The man had a lot to teach and I was eager to continue to learn from him. And then when he found the murals and we started to concentrate on that, I have to say that even though the work didn't involve my taking pictures, I think it was the best professional experience of my life.

We went into the Locust Street house on a Sunday morning: me, Jason, Hannah and Joan. Old Oscar unlocked the front door for us, but didn't join us inside. We all wore headband lamps. Jase and I carried large battery-powered lights.

We didn't spend much time downstairs. The set-up there was just as he'd described: communal dining table, battered couch, dinner bell in the kitchen, huge 666 spray-painted on the living-room wall. We briefly checked out the subdivided bedrooms on the second and third floors: the bunk beds, shared bathrooms, and the roomy sitting-room/bedroom/bath suite which Jason said was likely where the Schechtners had lived.

I could feel Jason's tension as he pulled down the attic ladder. I was keyed up myself. I only knew the murals from photographs. Had Jase overstated their power or was I about to see something extraordinary?

I could tell Hannah was nervous, too. She took hold of my hand. Joan stayed cool. That was her thing. She pretended to be the dispassionate observer, but the more I got to know her, the more clearly I saw she wasn't. She's ambitious in the same way I imagine Jase was in his photojournalist days. She was eager to latch on to a great story and had high hopes that this could be the one. She felt as strongly as any of us that the story of the murals was important, no matter how it finally played out.

'This is it,' she whispered, as Jason started up the ladder.

He overheard her, turned. 'It *is*,' he said. 'Wait till I get in there, then you guys come up slowly one at a time.' With that, he ascended to the attic.

I'd been working for two weeks at his computer on a first cut of *Leavings*, with his model of the murals room set up on the table beside his desk. I thought I knew the murals pretty well, had internalized them along with everything he and Hannah had to say about them. Even so, I wasn't prepared for their impact as I climbed the ladder. The figures on the walls were familiar, but as I stepped into the room, looking at them first from floor level, then rising slowly until I was standing before them face to face, eyes to eyes, I felt I was seeing them anew. They were as I remembered them, but endowed with uncanny force, perhaps because the figures were life-size and the room was small. I remember feeling overwhelmed as I turned to face each of the walls. I felt the figures pressing in on me, their eyes confronting mine.

'I feel a little drunk,' Hannah whispered.

Jason turned to Joan. 'What about you?'

'I feel like I'm being judged by them,' she said.

'Tally?'

I told him they reminded me of a crowd of boys standing around me at middle school when I was in a schoolyard fight with another kid.

'Like an audience?' Jason asked.

'The kind of mean audience that enjoys watching a fight.'

'They make me feel naked,' Hannah said.

'Yeah, I think that's part of it,' Jason agreed. 'They're watching, judging, and they seem to relish the fact that they're intimidating us.'

'I think everyone who sees them will have their own reaction,' Joan said. 'You were right about the menace. There's something coldly curious in their faces. I'm feeling very uncomfortable. I want to turn away.' She turned. 'But I can't. They're surrounding us. There's no escaping them, no avoiding their eyes.'

We stood in silence for a while.

'I'm feeling better now,' Hannah finally said. 'I guess I'm getting used to being in the middle of another person's nightmare. These murals are very disturbing. I can't imagine anyone dismissing them.'

'Cindy said she found them a little primitive.'

'Doesn't matter,' Hannah said. 'Just like it doesn't matter when you look at a so-called work of primitive African art. The power here doesn't derive from painterly skill. It's about how these murals make you feel.'

We set up the lights so Jason could re-photograph them. I told him I didn't think that was necessary, that his first set of images had captured them well. He said he wanted to do it anyway.

'They'll look different under strong light. And photographing them again will help me see them better. I want to document the hell out of them . . . just in case something happens to them.'

We spent about an hour in the room, then packed up our gear.

'Anyone want to stay?' Jason asked.

We shook our heads.

'We may not be able to come up here again, so let's all take a good long look before we go.'

I don't remember how much longer we spent up there. Maybe just a couple of minutes. Then we descended in silence, waited while Jason pushed up the ladder, then went down to the first floor and out the door where Oscar was waiting on the stoop.

'Get your fill?' he asked.

Jason nodded. 'Thanks, Oscar.' When he tried to hand Oscar a hundred-dollar bill, the old man shook his head.

'Not necessary,' he said. 'Ms Broderick took care of me. She's good that way. A very fine lady.'

At Hannah's suggestion, the four of us went to Café K on Lucinda Road. We took a table outside, ordered espressos and pastries, and discussed our next step.

Café K's a cool place named for Franz Kafka. There's a huge poster of him on the wall inside. It has an aura of mid-European angst, and the house-baked sweets are named after Kafka titles: *The Amerika*, *The Trial*, *The Castle* and, Hannah's favorite, *The Metamorphosis* – a gooey mixture of chocolate fudge and caramel atop a round of strudel.

As we munched and sipped, Jason went over the various leads we hadn't yet explored: find the cult deprogrammers and hear their stories; find Penny Dawson in the Keys and hear hers; same with Elizabeth Schechtner in Albuquerque; see if the Cobb family attorney, Nathan Silver, is still around and try to interview him if he is; try to find art teachers who'd worked with Courtney and Penny, and see if they remembered them.

'I notice you've left out the Cobb brothers,' I said.

'I think we should approach them last. The more we know, the better our chances of being able to persuade them to tell us where Courtney is.'

'Or what happened to her.'

'Right, Tally. Because she seems to have fallen off the earth.'

Hannah sighed. 'I'm wondering . . . we keep talking about this as if the murals are totally Courtney's vision, that Penny was just her assistant. What if they worked it out together? Or if Penny played the bigger role. She didn't reveal much when you spoke to her, Joan. By not calling you back, she made it clear she didn't want to talk about the murals. I think we'll be missing a bet if we don't make a big effort to find her.'

Jason agreed. 'I keep asking myself what it is that we really want to know. Not just whether Courtney is still alive, and, if so, where we can find her. It's what the murals *mean*. For me that's the real mystery – what's the story? What's the message?'

We divided up the leads. Joan volunteered to try to find Nathan Silver. I volunteered to try to find the art teachers. Hannah was eager to go out to Albuquerque to see Elizabeth Schechtner, but thought it was probably too soon.

'I'll look for the deprogrammers,' Jason said. 'Even though the company's defunct, there ought to be a way to get their names.'

I'd been booked to cover a wedding that afternoon. Although that wasn't the kind of photography that interested me, I worked hard at it to build my reputation. Fine art photography's a tough game. Few can make a living at it. Jason encouraged me to do wedding work. 'Better to have a day job where you get to use your camera than flip burgers or take a night watchman's gig. Take it seriously,' he advised me. 'Commit yourself. Figure out ways to make the best wedding pictures anyone ever took. Give your clients more than they expect. Do that and word'll get around that Tally Vaughan delivers. Then you'll be able to pick and choose your gigs, and, when the time's right, devote yourself to personal work.'

He told me that when he started out, he never intended to go into conflict photography. 'I wanted to roam the world, shoot on city streets like Robert Frank did in *The Americans*. I didn't want to seek out the grotesque like Arbus, make cruel portraits like Avedon, or impeccable platinum-printed shots of cigarette butts like Irving Penn. My role models were Frank, Cartier-Bresson and William Klein. But I found I didn't get enough of a rush from street photography. Fighting, war – that was something else. They fulfilled my need. I wanted adventure, to go where it's tough, go in close, take big risks in the hope of emerging with big rewards. I wanted to be like Capa, Rosenthal, take definitive images like Nick Ut and Eddie Adams, make important social statements like Salgado and Don McCullin.'

He'd been very good at it, and then he got sick of it. His thing was always to engage with people – soldiers, victims, refugees. And the way he did that was to always go for their eyes. He turned his obsession with eyes into a personal style. This came up when I asked him what had gotten him hooked on the murals.

'I think it was the eyes,' he said. 'They spoke to me. I felt that they were engaged by someone else's pain. Not just cruelty, but also curiosity. Like "How much can this person take, how much further can we push her?"'

Anna von Arx

'd been less than candid with Hannah at our lunch. We'd been friends since our days at Ashley-Burnett, so I was open with her about my troubled relationship with Anders. I told her about the anonymous letter, and Anders's insistence that I resign my job at the museum. But I left out the part that was most troubling – how Anders, when asked by the CMA board chairman if we were involved in an affair, didn't merely laugh the question off. He looked the man straight in the eyes and lied to his face.

He was an excellent liar. He had a sincere manner that caused people to believe whatever he said, which most of the time was his best guess as to what he felt they wanted to hear. I'd caught him in a number of lies, the biggest of which was that he was eager to leave his wife and kids, and, after a decent interval, marry me. This was part of a plan he laid out – that we would both leave Calista, which he claimed he despised, move out to California and take up museum jobs there as a couple.

'Who wouldn't want to hire us?' he said. 'Two scholars, one a former director of a major museum and the other – you, my dear – an expert in *art brut*. We'd be irresistible.'

Yeah . . . right.

This was a problem I'd have to solve for myself. I thought I came up with a pretty good solution: break up with Anders, resign from CMA, move to New York and set up as an independent dealer in outsider art. I knew the field, had prospective clients and didn't doubt I could find more.

There was one other thing I didn't share with Hannah. I think it was partly because I wasn't sure, and also worried that I'd find myself in the middle of some sort of stink and end up antagonizing powerful people who'd lose confidence in me and possibly become enemies.

Hannah was cautious, too. She made it clear that she wasn't going to tell me where those murals were located, or anything more than that Jason had stumbled upon them on one of his nocturnal expeditions into the city's lower depths.

Thing is, I thought I recognized several of the faces. Again, I wasn't sure, so as soon as I got back to the museum, I went into the boardroom to check. There they were, in a joint portrait on the boardroom wall, two of the museum's most generous benefactors: Alfred and Florence Cobb.

No doubt in my mind that whoever painted those murals had caricatured them. So what were the faces of two of Calista's most important philanthropists doing wearing menacing expressions in a group of similarly menacing people on the painted walls of a cupola atop a boarded-up house?

Alfred and Florence had died in the late 1960s in a freak airplane accident. Their private plane, transporting them to their winter home in Palm Beach, went down in the Appalachians, a crash attributed to pilot error. Their only child, Horace Cobb, inherited Cobb Industries, and he and his wife, Elena, took his parents' places on the CMA board where they served for many years. According to rumor, their daughter, Courtney, who'd followed Hannah and me at Ashley-Burnett, had been abducted and initiated into a cult, although later it turned out she'd run away from home, and the so-called cult was actually a responsibly managed halfway house for runaway teens.

But there was something else I knew about Courtney Cobb: that she was one of the most talented artists ever to attend Ashley-Burnett. I knew this from Miss Edith Lardner, who taught art at AB. One alumni day she took me aside. 'You were my best student your year,' she told me. 'I want to show you something special.'

What she showed me were several of Courtney's drawings from her eleventh-grade art class – works I recognized as astonishingly good.

So, was the artist who created the mysterious murals which Hannah wanted me to evaluate the same Courtney Cobb whose work I'd been shown by my old high-school art teacher? The fact that those murals contained recognizable portraits of Courtney's grandparents seemed to clinch the case.

I could have told all this to Hannah, but by doing so I might later be exposed as abetting an investigation that Hannah made clear she and Jason were keen to undertake. The downside was that the current CMA chairman was Courtney's older brother, Jack Cobb – the very man to whom Anders had lied about our affair.

The Cobb family was prominent in Calista. Its members had

served on the CMA board for three generations. They'd donated
millions of dollars' worth of art to the museum, and Jack had
promised to leave it more works from his collection. Moreover,
Jack's wife, Mary, was one of the people I'd been encouraging to
purchase and donate works of outsider art to the museum. If I went
into business as a private dealer, she'd be a prime client prospect.

So . . . after my foray into the CMA boardroom, many possible
conflicts of interest swirled around in my brain. Maybe I was
wrong. Maybe those mural figures weren't portraits of Alfred and
Florence. Maybe Courtney hadn't painted those murals. Rightly
or wrongly, I felt I'd best keep my mouth shut and wait to see
how things panned out.

I did, however, call Hannah that evening to mention that there
was something in the back of my mind concerning the murals and
that I'd get back to her if/when I figured out what it was. I did
this as kind of a safety valve in case she confronted me later on.
'Oh, yes,' I'd tell her, 'don't you remember? I *did* tell you that
something bothered me.' In short, I covered my butt.

But then, a week or so later, something else flew into my brain:
the ragdolls.

I wasn't sure whether they really were connected to the murals,
and I was almost afraid to try to find out. In the end, I couldn't
stop myself. When I looked into it, I concluded the connection
was too strong to deny.

I became aware of those ragdolls the same time everyone did,
when they first appeared on the market, offered at the booth of
Galerie Susanne Weber at the Outsider Art Fair in New York. Weber
was a small *art brut* specialist located in Lucerne, Switzerland, who
was trying hard, so it seemed, to become a major player. The ragdolls
she showed that year were so extraordinary that they were soon the
talk of the fair – how wildly expressive yet superbly crafted they
were, and the aura of mystery concerning their nameless creator,
listed in the gallery brochure simply as 'The Ragdoll Artist.'

When asked for details, Susanne would only say that this artist
was a foreigner who'd lived for a long time in Switzerland and
who'd been diagnosed as deeply schizophrenic. She would say no
more, not even whether this person was young or old, male or
female. She had three of the dolls for sale that year, each priced
at forty thousand Euros – extremely high for a hitherto unknown

artist. They were all sold within the first two hours – one to a prominent American collector, another to a Russian, and the third to a Japanese gentleman who promised to donate it to the Setagaya Art Museum in Tokyo.

How best to describe these sculptures so as to convey their totemic power? Perhaps 'haunting,' 'mesmerizing' and 'darkly visionary' would be a start. Also 'obsessive,' 'gripping' and 'shamanic.' Let me be clear: they have nothing to do with so-called voodoo dolls in function or appearance. Another way to describe them would be to say that they seem to represent 'dark spirits,' human in form in that they have heads, torsos and limbs, but also otherworldly and frightening in that they seem to radiate malice. And if dramatically lit, say from beneath, they resembled the kind of creatures that might appear in a terrifying nightmare.

From a technical point of view, much outsider art is fairly primitive. Sculptural pieces tend to be poorly constructed and must be carefully handled lest they fall apart. The ragdolls exhibited by Susanne Weber were not in this category. They were extremely well made. Each was about twenty inches tall, give or take, constructed of tatters of various plain white and off-white fabrics, with the features artfully demarcated with thick black or scarlet thread in the manner of caricatures. The heads of the Ragdoll Artist's figures were somewhat larger than the bodies, and were stitched together as if sewn up by an untrained surgeon. The faces were scarred, their eyes were marbles or buttons, their lips were rendered in pink silk.

But it was the frontal positioning of these figures and their facial expressions that had the greatest effect on viewers. It was in these two respects that they reminded me of the mural figures Hannah showed me. The eyes of these dolls engage with yours, and they are all double-faced, with blank poker-face expressions on one side and unguarded expressions of derision, scorn, gloating, defiance and moral corruption on the other. Turn one around and you're viewing another portrait of the figure in which the face is etched with marks that reveal his or her corroded soul. I saw similar double portraits in the murals. These pieces brought to mind Oscar Wilde's *The Picture of Dorian Gray*.

If, indeed, it turned out that the Ragdoll Artist and the painter of the murals were one and the same, then Courtney Cobb might well be the creator of both.

Working in the field of outsider art, you get a sense of creators obsessively working through personal issues. Their artwork seems sourced in their inner demons. Although some outsider art is quite joyous, much of it is very dark. The darkest element in the ragdolls does not appear in the murals, but is so prominent in the work of the Ragdoll Artist that many viewers are repelled. This is the bulging of genitals against the tightly trousered groins of the male figures, and the use of pink cloth and deep red thread outlining the groin area clothing of the females – erotic motifs that attracted much discussion when the dolls were first put up for sale. Thus my quandary: should I reveal this likely connection to Hannah and by so doing assist her and Jason on their quest, or should I keep quiet lest I disrupt my own life and possibly damage my hoped-for career as an independent dealer?

It was a month after our lunch that I resolved the matter. Hannah phoned me to say she'd heard I was resigning from CMA. I confirmed the rumor and added that I had something I wanted to show her before I left the museum. I arranged for her to visit me there the following Monday, the day the museum is normally closed.

I waited for her at the front desk, signed her in, then guided her first into the Nineteenth-Century European Paintings Gallery where there's a terrific Camille Pissarro on the wall. The painting, a night view of Boulevard Montmartre in Paris, had been donated to CMA by Hannah's grandfather, David Sachs.

'I *so* used to love this one!' she said. 'Grandpa hung it in the living room just to the right of the fireplace. Pissarro painted the boulevard through the seasons from an upper-floor room at the Hôtel de Russie. I've been in the room. It's in someone's apartment now. The view from there is still amazing.' She turned to me. 'Thank you, Anna, for bringing me in to see it with no one else around.' She paused. 'But I don't think this is why you invited me.'

I nodded. 'We're going up to the top floor.'

'Sounds mysterious,' she said.

From the elevator I guided her to the boardroom, unlocked it with my passkey and beckoned her in. The room, long and narrow, smelled of wood polish. The only furniture was a magnificent Regency dining table surrounded by fourteen period chairs. On the walls were commissioned portraits by local artists of major museum benefactors and board chairpersons.

'Walk around, look at the portraits,' I told her. 'See if anyone looks familiar.'

I sat down in one of the board member chairs and watched as she slowly moved around the room, pausing in front of each painting.

She stopped in front of the double portrait of Alfred and Florence Cobb, gazed at it, squinted, then turned to me.

I nodded, then brought my finger to my lips. 'Let's go down to my office and discuss.'

She brought out her cellphone. 'May I?'

I nodded.

She took a snapshot of the painting, then close-ups of the senior Cobbs' faces.

'Seen enough?'

She nodded. I locked the boardroom, then escorted her down to my office on the basement level. Once inside, I shut the door.

'This what you meant when you told me something was nagging at you?' she asked.

I told her I noticed the resemblance when she showed me the model at the restaurant and confirmed it when I got back to the museum. When I explained why I didn't say anything then, she said she understood.

'But now that you're resigning . . .'

'Yes. But I'd rather not be sourced on this,' I told her. 'Since I'm going into business, I can't afford to burn my bridges here.' She accepted this as well.

She gave me a quizzical look when I told her there was something else. I handed her several pictures of ragdolls from Galerie Susanne Weber catalogs. She studied them, fascinated.

'Do you think . . .'

'There's a lot in common.'

'But a different medium. In fact, my own.'

'I thought these would intrigue you.'

'Do you see the same hand?'

I told her that I did, but couldn't be certain since there was not only a huge difference between life-size acrylic wall paintings and small textile sculptures, but also an interval of twenty-plus years. I told her that as most artists, such as herself, progress and forge a personal style, outsider creators tend to have a single set of obsessions which they proceed to work and rework throughout their lives. I told her that if the murals artist and the Ragdoll Artist turned out to be the same person, this would suggest some kind of devouring obsession – perhaps the result of an unresolved emotional trauma frozen deep inside.

'A kind of mental illness is what you mean.'

'That's where a lot of great outsider art comes from. I sense a lot of power in these dolls, something raw beneath the superb craftsmanship. The only thing we really know about the Ragdoll Artist is that he or she is schizophrenic.'

We discussed possible ways of learning the Ragdoll Artist's identity. I told her a number of people had already tried to discover it, and that an art journalist who did would achieve something of a scoop.

'For a long time people tried to discover the identity of the Italian writer Elena Ferrante. Finally, someone did. It's really a matter of detective work, a commitment by someone who is not going to stop until he solves the puzzle.'

Jason Poe

'Basically, Anna's saying we should hire a detective,' Hannah told me. 'Someone in Switzerland or here who we can send over.'

'Either way it'll cost a fortune,' I said.

Hannah said she'd cover it. I didn't want her to think I doubted her, but I felt I had to ask if she was serious.

'Totally,' she said. 'We gotta find out if Courtney's the Ragdoll Artist. I'll ask Noah,' she said, referring to her lawyer brother. 'He uses investigators. Maybe he can recommend a good one.' She smiled. 'I'm actually feeling good about this, Jase. The boardroom portrait – that's a huge clue. We're finally getting somewhere.'

I felt the same, especially after Tally came up with several internet leads on the deprogramming firm, Cult Intervention & Recovery Services in Buffalo, New York, which Joan discovered had filed for bankruptcy in 1998.

'I knew there had to be some record of it,' Tally said, handing me print-outs of articles from *The Buffalo Enquirer.*

The articles, which went back to the early 1980s, told quite a story. CIRS, as the firm was called, turned out to have been the offspring of Synanon, a California-based drug-treatment program that had morphed through the years into a scary cult. CIRS was founded by two former Synanon group leaders, Chuck McGrath and Libby Harmon. They moved to Buffalo where they set up as cult deprogrammers, applying methods they'd learned at Synanon to brainwash adolescent cult members.

CIRS filled a need. Parents of kids who'd been inducted into cults were willing to pay almost anything to people who promised to bring their children home. But as the CIRS owners pointed out, simply rescuing kids and bringing them home wouldn't solve their problems. First, the kids had to be deprogrammed. Otherwise, they were apt to run away again and return to a cult where they felt safe and loved.

McGrath and Harmon presented themselves as idealists. They printed up a glossy brochure filled with photos of them bear-hugging troubled kids, and of happy-looking young people practicing animal husbandry and crop cultivation in the fields of an idyllic working farm. The main house on the farm had been converted to a treatment center, and the outbuildings into boys' and girls' dorms. Fees ran high. The CIRS brochure didn't claim otherwise. But as one set of parents stated, in an appreciative letter excerpted in the brochure: 'No cost is too great when your child's future is at stake.'

In the first years of CIRS, articles recorded the organization's growth, acquisition of adjoining properties and additions to its therapeutic staff. Starting in 1992, though, there were reports of lawsuits in which CIRS was accused of employing coercive methods.

An article about one of these suits appeared in *The Buffalo Enquirer* on October 10, 1994:

LOCAL COMPANY EMBROILED IN NEW LAWSUIT
CLAIMING PHYSICAL AND EMOTIONAL ABUSE

In a lawsuit filed Monday by John and Sally Devigne of Scarsdale, N.Y., on behalf of their son, Paul, against Cult

Intervention & Recovery Services, a local therapeutic firm
specializing in deprogramming, reference is made to a proce-
dure called 'The Game' in which teenagers are forced to
stand in their underwear in front of peers while being
subjected to 'ruthlessly critical personal assessments which
inevitably cause the teen to break down in tears.'

Another form of abuse referred to in the lawsuit is called
'The Ring,' in which male and female teens, who refuse to
own up to infractions at the CIRS farm, are surrounded by
their peers in an 'improvised human boxing ring and then
pummeled by the group.'

Although, according to the suit, all participants in 'The
Ring' wear oversized boxing gloves, kids subjected to the
punishment rarely attempt to fight back. Rather, the suit
contends, they cover up to protect themselves, and are hit
until beaten to the ground.

The suit contends that both 'The Game' and 'The Ring'
are variations of 'totally discredited techniques previously
used at Synanon in California, where the CIRS founders were
formerly employed as group leaders.'

When asked for comment, CIRS CEO Libby Harmon
called the lawsuit 'garbage.'

'We at CIRS do not abuse the vulnerable young people
placed in our charge, nor do we condone abuse in any form,'
she said in a written statement. 'We are grateful to parents
for their trust and confidence in our treatment of their children.
Our sole aim is to deprogram troubled kids who have been
abused at cults, then return them to loving homes. This suit
was filed by disgruntled parents whose son we sadly couldn't
help despite our best efforts. Now they are demanding their
money back even though they signed an agreement in which
they acknowledged that CIRS does not guarantee success
with every child enrolled in its program.'

The Devigne lawsuit is the third of similar suits brought
against CIRS in the last two years.

By 1997 a total of five lawsuits had been filed, the number of teenage
residents at the CIRS farm had fallen from twenty-seven to eight,
numerous staff members had resigned, and institutions that had
bankrolled construction at the farm were calling in their loans. In

early 1998, when CIRS went belly-up, McGrath and Harmon left Buffalo and returned to California.

Just as I finished reading the *Enquirer* article, Tally suddenly let out with a yelp.

'Get this, Jase! There's a CIRS survivors' site!'

The site welcome page explained that, due to the highly personal nature of the material, access to content was restricted to bona fide former CIRS kids. There was an email address to which inquiries could be made, and to which former CIRS kids could apply for site membership.

I immediately wrote explaining who I was and why I wanted to know if anyone in the group recalled a Courtney Cobb and/or a Penny Dawson. Two days later I received a reply. The group leader, Saul, wrote that he'd asked around, and that one of the CIRS survivors, Kate, had a vague recollection of a girl named Penny.

'At the farm we didn't use last names,' Saul wrote, 'so she might not be the person you're asking about. Kate says this Penny didn't stay long, maybe five or six weeks, and that she didn't make much of an impression. Kate thinks she said she was an artist. This other girl you mentioned, Courtney – nobody remembers her, but Kate remembers there was a girl Penny talked about in group sessions. The way she spoke about her made Kate think the two of them had been close. Sorry, Jason, that's all I could come up with. Good luck with your quest.'

Hannah's brother, Noah Sachs, gave her the name of a New York private investigator he'd used, a former NYPD detective named Lou Dimona.

We called him together, got his voicemail. He had a no-nonsense New York accent: 'Hey! This is Lou. I'm out on the job. You know the drill. Leave word and I'll get back to you.'

From his accent, I figured Dimona for a tough outer-borough deez-dems-and-dose-type guy. The man who called us back on FaceTime fit the voice. He wore a tight black T-shirt and sported a bushy mustache.

Dimona looked disappointed when he discovered we weren't lawyers. He told us he was busy, but was willing to listen to our story.

'Let me get this straight,' he said, after we filled him in. 'There's this schizo in Switzerland who makes artsy ragdolls, and you don't know this person's name, age or gender. The only lead you can give me is the name of the gallery that sells the dolls. That about it?'

We told him it was.

'OK,' he said, 'here's my deal. Three grand per day plus expenses. If I travel, I fly business and stay in four-star hotels. Because I don't want to waste your money, I'll cut my daily fee to two if you agree to pay me a twenty-thousand-dollar bonus if I find and ID this Ragdoll Artist. One other thing. I'm pretty much booked up. Can't get to this till January. Give it some thought and get back to me if you want to go ahead.'

After we hung up, we looked at each other.

'I don't want to wait till January,' Hannah said.

'Why don't we take a crack at it?'

'You mean fly over there?'

'Why not? Maybe we'll find something. I think we should give it a try.'

Our first thought was that we would go there together, which led to an amusing discussion as to whether we'd share a room, and, if we did, whether sex would be optional. In the end, to limit expenses we decided it would be better if I went there alone.

Soon as I got to Lucerne, I took a taxi to Galerie Susanne Weber on Zuerichstrasse. Miracle of miracles, there was a hotel directly across the street. Hotel Metropol was only rated two-star, but for my purposes it couldn't have been better.

Bernice, the pleasant young lady at the front desk, tried to persuade me to take a room at the back.

'It will be much quieter facing the garden,' she advised.

I replied that I enjoyed listening to the pulse of a city.

She smiled knowingly, then offered me a room on one of the higher floors, but I insisted on one on the first or second.

'You're an interesting man,' she said, checking me in.

You have no idea, I thought.

The room was neat and clean: lumpy bed, small desk facing the window, shallow closet and tiny bath. What more did I need? The price was right – ninety-nine Swiss francs per night including continental breakfast. I figured Hannah would appreciate that.

I watched the gallery from my lookout for two days. There was a lot of foot traffic in front; some people stopped to peer in the window, but few, I noticed, actually ventured inside.

The street window display was intriguing – two framed pieces, a charcoal sketch of an intense young man holding his hand in front of his face, and a complex painting of tiny multicolored figures set between long German words. Resting between them, so as to engage passers-by, was one of the Ragdoll Artist's double-faced dolls.

I noted that just before closing time at six p.m., a young woman removed the doll from the window, and then, a couple of minutes later, came outside, cranked down the roller screen, padlocked it, checked to make sure the lock was secure, then walked briskly up the street. At nine fifty-five a.m., just before the ten a.m. opening, she reappeared in front, unlocked the screen, cranked it up, entered, and a couple of minutes later replaced the doll to its original position. All like Swiss clockwork.

Was she the gallerist? I doubted it. She had the bearing of an assistant.

On my third morning I decided to find out. I lingered for a time in front of the window, studying the three works with special attention to the doll. A bell tinkled when I opened the door. The young woman I'd been observing peered up at me from her desk and smiled. She was a bit on the plain side, but her brown eyes were lovely. She wore oversized hoop earrings and a Chinese knock-off Cartier tank watch on her wrist.

She addressed me in British-accented English.

'May I help you, sir?'

'Just browsing.' I asked if she was Ms Susanne Weber.

'Oh, no,' she giggled. 'My name's Constance. Frau Weber isn't here very much. Right now she's attending an art fair in Rome.'

'So you're in charge?'

She looked down. 'I wouldn't put it that way, sir. I'm just her assistant.'

I chatted her up. Was she British? Indeed she was. Had she lived here long? A little less than a year. Was she interested in outsider art? Oh, yes, she was fascinated by it. She viewed this job as an apprenticeship. She hoped someday to open a gallery of her own in Britain.

She asked if I was interested in outsider art. I told her I very much was. That pleased her, she said, because most people who stopped in did so merely out of curiosity. She told me she rarely sold anything to these drop-ins – tourists for the most part. She wished she could sell more, she said. Her salary was small, barely enough to get by. When she did manage to make a sale, Frau Weber kindly paid her a small commission.

As she showed me about, I drew her out, interspersing my questions between her explanations of the works. I asked permission to photograph pieces that interested me. She told me to go right ahead. Clearly she was hoping I'd make a purchase.

On the plane from New York I'd boned up on outsider art, enough to carry on a basic conversation. As she spoke, I threw in knowledgeable-sounding phrases to prove my bona fides: 'compulsive quality of the mark-making,' 'visualization of the artist's world-view' and, my favorite, 'projection of a troubled self.'

She asked if I was a collector. I told her the truth, that I taught photography for a living, which, I added, made it difficult to afford to purchase major pieces. I told her that I loved outsider art and enjoyed prowling galleries that offered it, occasionally picking up a piece here and there on behalf of a wealthy friend back home.

'She relies on what she calls my "good eye." I take photos, and if she decides to buy an artwork, I get a commission just like you.'

This fib had a bonding effect.

'Well, seems we're similar that way, aren't we?' she said. 'Like two peas in a pod.' She stuck out her hand. 'Please call me Connie.'

'Please call me Jason,' I said, handing her one of my cards.

She spent an hour and a half with me, showing me the gallery inventory. In that time she fielded two phone calls, both times speaking in German. After the second call she smiled at me.

'That was Frau Weber. She'll be back the day after tomorrow. She asked how things are going. I told her I was busy with a prospect.'

I assured her that I definitely was a prospect.

'Soon as I leave I'll send photos to my friend. If she's interested, I'll come back later and let you know.' I hesitated. 'It's such a pleasure to talk with you. I don't know anyone in Lucerne. You're the only person here I've had a real conversation with.' I paused again. 'Forgive me, Connie, if I'm being too brazen, but I'm wondering if I could take you out to dinner tonight?'

She gazed into my eyes as she made her decision.

'I would like that very much,' she said.

'Great!'

'I close at six. Come by then. There're some pieces in the backroom I'd love to show you. I'd take you back there now but I can't leave the front without first locking the street door.'

Ah, a secret stash! What wonders did she have? I thought.

Back in my hotel room, I phoned Hannah and filled her in. As we spoke, I emailed images of the pieces I'd photographed, all in the 2,500–3,000 Swiss Franc range, suggesting that if she saw one she liked, she'd authorize me to buy it.

'I think a purchase will help me move things along with Connie,' I told her.

'Do you intend to sleep with her?' she asked, amused.

'Only if I must,' I said. 'She seems a nice kid. Anyway, I doubt I'm her type.'

'Hey, you're on a mission, Jase. Do what you have to do,' she said. 'OK, your images just came through. You have a good eye. I guess we already knew that. I like one of them – the small mandala on silk. Buy it for me, please. I'll enjoy having it, and hopefully the purchase will, as you so nicely put it, *move* things along.'

Hannah could be pretty funny when she wanted to be.

I turned up at the gallery again just before six, prepared to buy and woo. Connie smiled when she saw me, checked her watch, locked the front door from inside, then beckoned me toward the backroom.

'Before we go further, I want you to know my friend wants to buy the mandala.'

'Terrific!' she exclaimed. 'May I kiss you for that?' And she did, so quickly I didn't even have time to consent.

'I'll write you a check right now. Are dollars OK?'

'Absolutely.' She quickly calculated the amount, then gazed again into my eyes. 'I am so happy!' she said, giving me a second kiss as I handed her my check. 'Now I'm going to show you some pieces few get to see. Please, not a word! Frau Weber would kill me if she knew,' she said, unlocking the backroom door.

I liked the way things were going. She'd not only initiated physical contact, but she'd shown a willingness to betray her boss. I had no idea what she was going to show me. When I saw it, I couldn't believe my luck.

'Erotic outsider art,' she said, opening a closet in the backroom.

'We have a client in Germany who's into this stuff.' She showed me a painting of numerous small penises-with-testicles arranged like notes on a blank sheet of music staff paper.

'How about this one?' she said, giggling, as she showed me an elaborate pen-and-ink drawing of a woman giving head to a horned priapic monster.

I didn't pay much attention to either of those works, or to the others she showed me. Rather, my eyes were fastened to a doll made in the Ragdoll Artist's style, but unlike any of that artist's other creations. This one differed in that the figure was naked, her legs were spread, showing oversized labia and other female parts depicted out of carefully cut and sewn scraps of pink silk.

'Isn't she the bomb!' Connie exclaimed. 'It's by the same artist who made the doll in the window.'

'Of course,' I said. 'The Ragdoll Artist.'

'You know about her?'

'*Her?*'

'Yes, the Ragdoll Artist is a woman,' Connie said.

'Ah! A secret!'

'It's really the only one I know.'

'You've never met her?'

Connie shook her head. 'Neither has Frau Weber.'

'Then how—'

'How do the dolls come to us?' Connie smiled. 'Sorry, I can't tell you that. But what I can tell you is that she created this one on commission. As I understand it, this is the only fully naked doll she's ever made. Our German collector was desperate to have it. It's going to cost him plenty. Probably double the price of her other dolls, and that's a lot of money.'

'So I understand.'

She studied me. 'Seems you know quite a lot. I'm impressed.'

'I think everyone into outsider art knows about the Ragdoll Artist.'

I asked her if it would be OK if I photographed the erotic doll.

'You really shouldn't. Frau Weber would positively slay me if she found out.' She shrugged. 'Promise you won't show it to anyone?'

'I promise,' I lied, clicking off three shots.

She peered at me again. 'You're the kind who does pretty much what he wants, aren't you, Jason?' she asked, smiling. 'I like that in a man. Give me a couple of minutes to lock up, then we'll go have dinner.'

I waited for her out on the street, watching as she took the dressed doll from the window, carried it to the backroom, locked that door, then came out, locked down the roller screen and took hold of my arm.

Things are moving almost too quickly, I thought. Not only had she kissed me twice, betrayed her boss, showed me erotic art, revealed confidential information, but she'd declared that she liked a man who wasn't afraid to go for what he wanted – all signals that she harbored expectations for the evening which I was a little hesitant to fulfill.

You're on a mission, Jase, so do what you have to do, Hannah had said. *OK*, I thought, *if that's what it's going to take, I'll do it.*

She guided me to an upscale restaurant several blocks up Zuerichstrasse. Outside, she scanned the menu, described the house specialties and asked if I found any appealing.

'All of them,' I told her.

'This place is kind of expensive.'

'Fine with me,' I said. 'I like good food.'

'Oh, I can tell,' she said, lightly patting my belly. 'Am I being too familiar?'

'Familiar's great,' I assured her as we stepped inside.

We spent a good part of the meal discussing outsider art. When I asked her why she was so keen on it, she gave a credible answer.

'It's so earthy. And the artists are so different. They're not locked into movements or periods. I love their unschooled self-expression. Yes, some have had training, but most are self-taught. For example, I believe the Ragdoll Artist's work represents deeply personal obsessions. Difficult to know what drives her, what she's trying to say. I really like art that's mysterious.'

'Seems to me she's expressing the double-sided nature of people, the masks they show the world and faces that betray their inner selves.'

'Of course, on one level, but I think it may go deeper.'

'To something in her childhood perhaps?'

'Perhaps some trauma she feels compelled to relive and deal with.'

'Dolls are for children. Perhaps that's a key.'

'You keep surprising me, Jason.'

'How so?'

'You're a very perceptive guy.'

'I'm not sure how to take all these nice things you keep saying about me.'

'Take them at face value,' she said, then looked down shyly at her lobster bisque.

I had a pretty good hunch as to what she had planned, but she surprised me as we were finishing dessert.

'I'd like it if you'd take me home,' she said, 'but I don't want you to get the wrong idea. I don't really enjoy intercourse. I know that statement's almost certain to turn a man off. And we are out on a date, aren't we?' I nodded. 'There is something I do enjoy doing with a guy, and if you're game, I'd like to do it with you.' She grinned at me. 'Curious?'

'Very,' I told her.

She lowered her eyes. 'Cuddling. Do you think you'd like to do that?'

Relieved, I told her that I would like that very much.

She acted surprised. 'Really?'

'Actually, it's one of my favorite things,' I told her. 'Anyone can have sex. Cuddling – that's special.'

'Then we're still on the same track, two peas in a pod.'

Yeah, two peas in a pod, I thought. *She's a nice young woman, and, like everyone, she has her needs. This time, fortunately, I don't have to suss hers out.*

She lived in what she called a 'bedsit,' a bedroom/sitting-room combo in a rooming house fifteen minutes from the town center, equipped with a hotplate, tiny fridge and small linoleum-lined bathroom. Art books were neatly arranged on one shelf, family photos on another. Two framed posters for outsider art exhibitions hung on the wall. The bedspread was fluffy, the pillows encased in frilly shams.

I won't go into detail about the cuddling. It was fairly innocent. She didn't get naked, simply took off her watch, earrings and blouse, then lay back on the bed still wearing jeans and bra. I took off my jacket and lay down beside her, took her in my arms and gently stroked her back.

She explained herself when, after we'd engaged this way for a while, she revealed that more than anything she enjoyed being held.

'I know it's neurotic,' she said, 'but I'm not going to apologize for needing it. I'm so glad to meet someone who understands. Most guys expect sex. I hate the hook-up culture. Guess I'm too old-fashioned for people my age.'

'Don't knock yourself,' I told her. 'You've had boyfriends?'

'I have,' she admitted.

She told me about her high-school boyfriend, and the one she had at her university, Bristol; the ups and downs of these relationships. As we spoke in whispers, I sensed her drifting off.

I couldn't let her do that, couldn't leave without finding out what else she knew about the Ragdoll Artist.

When I told her I had to get back to my hotel, she reached down, brushed her hand lightly across the front of my pants, felt my hardness and smiled to herself.

I read this gesture as vampish. Seemed Connie wasn't as pure as she let on. Watching her as she got off the bed and heated water for tea, I vowed not to let our hour of cuddling go to waste.

'There's something I've been dying to ask you,' I said, as we sat opposite one another in the sitting area, sipping and winding down. 'I'm a little apprehensive about how you'll react.'

'Go ahead,' she said, 'ask me anything.'

'It's about the Ragdoll Artist.'

'Ha! Well, I really don't know much about her,' she said. 'And neither does Frau Weber, though, of course, she knows more than me. You see, there's a middleman, intermediary, whatever you want to call him – a middle-aged man with a short-pointed beard. Maybe older than middle-aged, like late fifties. I'm guessing because I only saw him once. Monday's normally my day off. That's the day the gallery's closed, and that's the day he comes by. I happened to be there one Monday catching up on paperwork when I saw him arrive. He was hauling a suitcase, the roller type. He rang the bell, Frau Weber let him in, then turned to me and suggested I go out to a café for an hour so she and the gentleman could transact business. The man nodded kindly at me but Frau Weber didn't introduce us. When I got back, he was gone, but later there was a new ragdoll in the backroom. Frau Weber wanted me to see it. "Isn't this one a beauty!" she said. I agreed that it was. "Is he the artist?" I asked, referring to the man. She laughed. "No, he's the go-between," she said. And that's all I know . . . except for one thing. He comes like clockwork on the first Monday of every month. I know because every first Tuesday when I come into work, there's a new doll in the backroom.'

'So the Ragdoll Artist makes twelve a year?'

'Evidently, but Frau Weber doesn't sell them all. She holds some back. She says this is how a gallerist creates rarity.' She paused. 'Frau Weber's taught me a lot.'

Certain I'd found out everything Connie knew, it was time for me to go. Although I recognized that the seduction (such as it was) had been hers, I felt kind of bad about deceiving her. Each of us wanted something from the other. In the end, each of us achieved his/her desired goal. And isn't that the best kind of deal, the kind when both parties leave satisfied?

I phoned Hannah from the airport, filled her in. 'First Monday of the month – that's three weeks off. I'll come back then if it's OK with you, and if the kindly middle-aged man with the roller case shows up, I'll follow him.'

'Oh, it's more than all right,' she said. 'In fact, I'll come with you. As for following, I think we'll need some help with that. So, Jase – who knew you'd be such an excellent detective, a regular Sherlock Holmes? I just hope you didn't have to do anything contrary to your moral code.'

My cuddling story delighted her. 'That's just so *sweet*,' she said. 'And innocent. Lucky girl to get to cuddle with the great Jason Poe.'

Joan Nguyen

The police corruption story was at a standstill, as long-term investigations often are, and so far I hadn't heard anything new from Tony Delgado on the secret CFD arson investigation. I called around, told various fire department officials I'd heard an arson specialist named Gallagher was running a special unit, and to please tell him I'd like to talk to him and pass on my name and number.

I got stonewalled. No one would admit there was such a unit or that anyone named Gallagher had been brought in to run it.

That is, until I got the CFD commissioner's assistant on the line. She didn't bother to hide her annoyance. 'We're busy here. I'm not running a damn relay station. Call him yourself.' She rattled off a number and hung up.

I dialed the number, got Gallagher's voicemail, left him a message. When he didn't call me back, I called him again the following day, and again the next, leaving the same message each time, expressing varying degrees of pleading, disappointment and fervor. OK, he didn't want to give me an interview. I could understand that, but I resolved not to get discouraged. I wanted the summer fires story so much I decided I'd call him every single day until eventually he or someone called me back.

With time on my hands, I decided to try to locate Nathan Silver, the Cobb family attorney who'd negotiated the deal with Cindy Broderick.

He wasn't listed in the attorneys register, but the *Times-Dispatch*, being an old-fashioned newspaper, has a room full of old city phonebooks. In the 2005 book I found a listing for a Nathan A. Silver, Esq., at the firm Kline, Krechner, Silver & Wales located in the Doubleton Building on East Ninth. The firm was now just Kline & Wales, but figuring someone there might be able to tell me how to reach Silver, I phoned the office, asked to speak to the firm manager, and was pleased to find him helpful.

'Sure, I remember Nate. He was a name partner when I started here. He retired a dozen or so years ago, but kept an "Of Counsel" office for a while. At first he'd come in three, four times a week, then less and less. When his wife passed, he closed up shop. That was maybe six years back. I hear he's now in assisted living at Desmond House out on Yarrow. Give him a call. I bet he's still plenty sharp. And I bet he'll be darn pleased to be contacted by a reporter. Give him my best too, will ya? Tell him I miss the old dog.'

I called Silver, arranged to see him that afternoon, then drove out to nearly the end of Yarrow. I could tell at once that Desmond House was a posh facility. It had been converted from the estate mansion of General Taylor Desmond, founder of Desmond Steel, a long-abandoned mill in the Calista Valley. It was the huge kind of house the robber barons built between the end of the First World War and the market crash of 1929, when contractors would swarm a site with skilled immigrant Italian carpenters and masons. Constructed in the English Tudor style, it had six chimneys, intersecting slate roofs, and a long cobblestone drive that ended in a turn-about in front of a massive front door with a phony coat of arms above, a nouveau riche industrialist's fantasy of old wealth and nobility.

Walking from my car to the entrance, I heard classical music pouring through the open first-floor windows. Entering, I discovered a youthful string quartet playing Schubert in the main lobby. The audience consisted of fourteen elderly men and women seated in a semi-circle on recliners. I recognized the music, 'Death and the Maiden,' perhaps not really appropriate for an assisted living facility, but I could tell by their expressions that the old folks were taking the music in.

As I stood listening, a dignified-looking man, who I guessed was the facility manager, approached, brought his finger to his lips, gestured me aside and in a whisper asked what he could do for me. I told him I had an appointment with Nate Silver. He nodded, led me to the visitors' room off the lobby, asked me to sign the guestbook and wait until he retrieved Mr Silver the next time the quartet took a break.

'Meantime,' he said, 'enjoy the music. Our residents love it when young people come out here to play. This group, performance students at the Calista Institute of Music, are regulars, so I think they like coming out here too.'

I've always loved the energy of that particular quartet, and I thought the students played it well. If this concert was a sample of events provided for residents, I couldn't think of a better place in Calista at which to spend one's declining years.

There was a short pause at the end of the Andante. That's when Nate Silver appeared.

'Very pleased to meet you,' he said, offering his hand. With his fine courtesy, thick silver hair and brilliant blue eyes, he exuded an aura of class and ease. The way he was dressed added to the effect – cashmere sports jacket, silk shirt with silk ascot, mirror-polished black loafers. He didn't come across as a man who required assisted living. When I asked him how he liked Desmond House, he smiled and told me he loved it.

'The suites are luxurious, the food's great and the people here are lovely. Costs a fortune and it's worth it. When I used to visit friends here, I knew this was the place for me. After my wife passed, I put my name on the wait-list. Took three years before someone died and freed up a suite. No regrets. I think moving out here was the best decision I ever made.'

He explained that even though he was retired, and his clients, Horace and Elena Cobb, had passed away, he still felt constrained by attorney–client privilege.

'I'm happy to go on the record so long as you understand there're things I can't talk about. And forgive me if you ask me something and I take a moment to recollect.'

After I agreed to his ground rules, he permitted me to set my phone to record.

'Of course I remember Cindy. Very grown-up and serious even when she was just sixteen. How many young women that age would ask for money to pay for college? Most would want to spend it on a car, clothes and vacations. During her Mount Holyoke years she'd stop in to see me whenever she returned to town. I paid her bills and doled out her allowance. She always brought me a little gift to express her gratitude. That was the deal, and I kept to it, even though my clients had reservations. The reward was supposed to be fifty K, not the ninety-plus this was costing them. I told them if it weren't for Cindy calling in when she did, they might well have had to face Courtney in court. Was that really what they wanted? Of course not! So wasn't it worth it to help a nice, smart, under-privileged young woman gain a foothold in life? And wasn't the money really just a pittance to them? They had no good answer for that and didn't complain again.

'I was the old-fashioned type of lawyer you don't see much of these days – a general practitioner who actually *counseled* his clients. Lawyers today, they just do the client's bidding. And the clients today, they don't want counseling. They just want to know how to get away with stuff.

'You know the club downtown, the Mayfair, the one on Main with the big pillars out front that looks like a Greek temple? Now they'll let in most anyone who can afford the dues, but when I started out in practice, there were no Jews in the Mayfair, and certainly no blacks. God forbid that the Jewish attorney who advised you, counseled you, knew all the intricacies of your personal and financial life, should be allowed to enter that hallowed space! So one day after I dealt with a very personal matter having to do with the Cobb boys, I turned to Horace and asked him point-blank if he'd put me up for membership. Know what he said? That a few years before another member put up David Sachs, one of the most elegant men in the city, owner of a ball-bearing factory, a guy who had a Pissarro and a Chagall in his living room. "They black-balled him," Horace told me. "If I put you up, they'll do the same. They're just not ready to let in a Jew. It's wrong, Nate. It shouldn't be that way, but that's the way it is." And you know what I thought? "Horace, you're a coward. So fuck you! Funny, all this time I thought we were friends. Now I understand we're not."'

Listening to him, it didn't escape me that the black-balled David Sachs was Hannah Sachs's grandfather.

He went on, 'Why am I telling you this? Because of what happened later. Near the end of his life, Horace called me, asked if we could get together. I'd retired, wasn't his lawyer anymore, but I said, "Sure, come on over, we'll chat." He said, "No, let's meet at the Mayfair. They have a nice bar. I'll leave your name at the front desk." "OK," I said, "fine, we'll meet there."

'This wasn't the first time I'd been invited by a member for a drink, but it was the first time Horace Cobb invited me. So, all right, we have a drink, then he says he wants to show me around. So he takes me on the grand tour – main dining room, private rooms upstairs, library, gym, glass-enclosed pool on the roof, then down to the wine cellar in the basement. So I tell him, "Thanks for showing me the club, Horace." And he gives me this intense look. "You don't get it, do you, Nate?" "What don't I get?" I ask. "I'm going to put you up for membership," he says. "You'll be the first Jew in the Mayfair." So I look at him. He's got this stupid grin on his face. I peer right into his eyes. "I won't be black-balled?" I ask. "Not now you won't. They wouldn't dare, not if *I* put you up," he says. And you know what I told him? "Not interested, Horace. Too little too late." And those were the last words we ever spoke.' Nate nodded. 'I didn't bother to attend his funeral.'

Like wow! This was the kind of delicious revelation I lived for, the kind that told me I had a source with a grievance. Nate Silver was not only a man aggrieved; he was a man who loved to hear himself talk. 'Nothing better than that when you're hot on a story,' my old journalism professor used to say. So I did what I'd been trained to do and took full advantage. *Time*, I told myself, *to go in for the kill.*

Here's the essence of what he told me:

Regarding the warrant: 'Horace Cobb was not only close to

Commissioner Jim Hawkes. Judge Neville Brown had served as in-house counsel at his company, and Horace had been a major contributor to the campaign of Judge Stephanie Johnson Bates. On account of that, Horace pretty much had both judges in his pocket. No way in a case involving his daughter would Brown turn down a request for a warrant or pose questions to the applying officer.'

Regarding Loetz: 'He was Hawkes's protégé, an ambitious guy who'd do anything to please his boss. The only issue: Could he locate the girl? Once Cindy called, everything fell neatly into place. Was Loetz rewarded? Financially, no. He was a straight arrow and that would have been corrupt. But that caper put him on the fast track for promotion. He ended up second in command of the department. He had a good clean career, far as I know. After he retired, he was hired as chief of security at Cobb Industries . . . so, though long-delayed, he got his pay-off. More power to him, I say.'

Regarding Courtney Cobb: 'She was a troubled soul. Gave her parents a lot of grief. She was artistic, talented at drawing, and, like a lot of precociously talented kids, a real pain to deal with. She was a bit off too, somewhere on the autism spectrum, probably at the Asperger's end. She had this weird way of looking at people. She'd get too close to you, right in your face, then instead of looking at you head-on, she'd turn and peer at you from an angle. All three Cobb kids were spoiled rotten. Riding lessons, tennis lessons, luxury vacations, fancy private schools, you name it. As for Court, I heard after the rescue she had a complete mental breakdown. Not surprising. She was always unstable.'

Regarding rumors of abuse within the Cobb family: 'I remember that columnist, Waldo Channing, wrote something to that effect. Give me a break! The Cobbs were uptight WASPS. Al, the old man, was a hard-ass. And his wife Flo was a piece of work. Horace was slick. They sent him East to boarding school and college. Wanted to polish him up. It took. He came back with the proper glow. I liked Elena. She was a Mount Holyoke grad. She put in a good word for Cindy, which was nice. Now that I think about it, Elena was the only one showed any warmth. You know those WASP types – they act nice, have fine manners, but you never know what they really think of you.'

Regarding Courtney's brothers: 'Talk about slick! Kevin Cobb's slick as a beaver's tail. And Jack, he's as hard-ass as his grandpa, except he's got this phony soft manner that covers it up. He talks to you in this whispery voice. You have to bend in close to hear what he's saying. That's when he sticks the shiv in your belly.

'They've made a huge success out of Cobb Industries. Unlike a lot of folks who inherit family companies, the Cobb boys understood theirs had to change. They got out of steel and into chemicals and paint. Now they got more money than God.' He paused, some bitterness creeping into his eyes. 'Soon as they took over from Horace, Jack fired me. Not brutally, but in that soft whispery way of his: "Don't you agree, Nate, it would be better now for us to turn the page, assemble our own team?" They wanted their own lawyers, guys closer to them in age, guys who'd be beholden to them. Understandable. They didn't want to hear "Well, that's not the way your dad would've handled it." "So, OK," I told him, "I agree. There're some excellent young people in my firm who'd be more than happy to handle the account." In the end, they chose to leave Kline, Krechner, and go over to the hotshots at Darcy, Paul and Clift. Some of my partners blamed me for losing the Cobb account. That's when they started to ease me out.'

More about Courtney: 'Come to think of it, she used to whisper too, even quieter than Jack. Sometimes she'd just plain refuse to speak. Horace told me sometimes weeks'd go by without her saying a word. They were worried about her. She really seemed unbalanced. Then when she ran away, they were frightened out of their minds.'

Regarding the 'very personal matter' having to do with Kevin and Jack: 'Sorry, I'm constrained from discussing it. Let's just say there was some disgusting behavior that could have resulted in major consequences. Horace was all steamed up about it. "They're just college kids," he told me. "Boys'll be boys." That kind of crap. He asked me to clean up their mess, and I did. Got them out of a serious jam. Billed him plenty for it, too. Come to think of it, that's probably why the boys wanted me out. They knew I knew something unpleasant about them, which made it difficult for them to look me in the eye.'

Regarding the Drs Schechtner: 'Yeah, turned out they were legit. So what? What's that got to do with anything? By encouraging Courtney to become a liberated minor, they became Cobb family enemies, and were treated as such. You say Loetz calls them "collateral damage." Oh, I see, that was *your* term. Still, I'd say that's a fairly accurate description of how we viewed them. The object of the exercise was to bring the kid home. Far as Horace was concerned, anyone in the way . . .' Nate shrugged. 'To this day I don't know what they were thinking, keeping those girls virtual prisoners in that house. They knew better. They certainly knew who Courtney was. They had to know you don't go up against people like the Cobbs and get away with it. Calling their house A Caring Place – what a hoot! Like everyone else, they cared about what they could get out of it. In the end, they got a pretty good deal.'

Regarding the Schechtners' lawyer, Spencer Addams: 'The guy was a scoundrel, but, I gotta admit, very good on his feet. He'd go into court and mesmerize a jury. I don't know how, but he did. He was not the kind you wanted to go up against at trial. So I counseled Horace: "Forget the Schechtners, don't sue them, just let 'em go. They can't do you any more harm. To hell with them! They're ruined here anyway. They'll have to go someplace new and start over again."'

Regarding what happened to Courtney after the rescue: 'That's a strange tale. All I know is what Horace told me. Fact is, I never saw her again. That deprogramming couple from Buffalo took her away to a safe house – I guess you'd call it – that Horace rented out on Taylor Road. She clammed up, wouldn't say a word, wouldn't even look at them, covered her ears when they spoke to her, shook her head violently when they asked if she'd like to see her parents. After a few days they told Horace they couldn't help her – that she needed a psychiatrist – then went back to Buffalo to deal with the other kid. Horace flew in a high-powered female shrink from Boston. He didn't want a local one involved. Didn't want any gossip. This woman – can't remember her name – even she couldn't get Courtney to talk. Tried to give her some tests. Courtney refused to take them. The shrink told Horace and Elena their daughter needed long-term psychiatric care, so they arranged for her to be moved to a clinic. They never told me where she was, except that she was in a good safe place overseas. I know Elena wanted to visit her, but I'm not sure how that worked out.'

Nate was a sly old fox, but something about the way he claimed he didn't know where Courtney was didn't ring true to me. Still, I wasn't about to pursue it and interrupt his flow – he was giving me too much good stuff.

Regarding the other girl: 'What was her name? Penny

something. Don't know much about her, just that she and Courtney got close. Not sure how they met. Anyway, Courtney told Elena she wanted to take after-school art classes like her friend at the Community Center in Danzig Heights. Elena didn't see the need, but Courtney wore her mother down. Turned out it was because Penny was enrolled there and she wanted to be with her BFF. I was never clear about whose idea it was to run away. Could be they came up with it together. Horace and Elena were pretty sure it was Penny's idea, that she had some connection to the Schechtners, or had heard about them somehow.'

Whew!

My head was reeling two hours later, when Nate Silver, being a well-mannered gent, accompanied me out to my car. Visiting hours were over. It was time for me to go.

'Great meeting you, Joan,' he said. 'Was good to talk to you about all this. Brought back lots of memories – some of them, I admit, not all that sweet. Anyway, call me if you think of something we didn't cover. Meanwhile, you take care.'

I could barely contain my exuberance as I drove down the long cobblestone drive from Desmond House to Yarrow. Nate Silver had given me far more than I could have hoped.

Tally Vaughan

Florence Baker, the cheery manager at the Danzig Heights Community Center, had promised Joan she'd check if anyone on her staff remembered the names of teachers who'd taught kids' art classes back in the day.

Mrs Baker kept her promise and came up with a name: Kathy Zevin.

'Kathy doesn't teach anymore,' she told me, 'but I hear she still makes art. She had a studio in a converted industrial building on West 66th. It's set up as a city-subsidized artists' collective, apartments upstairs and studios beneath. I'm sure she's still there. Terrific place. Can't imagine anyone lucky enough to get one of those units voluntarily moving out.'

* * *

I called Ms Zevin. When she heard I wanted to interview her about Courtney and Penny, she kindly invited me over for a visit. I found the building, a sprawling block-long two-story edifice with glass brick windows facing the street. There was an archway in the middle that led to a courtyard. Here there were huge plate-glass windows, some draped shut, others open to the sunlight.

Through the open ones I saw men and women in first-floor studios painting, sculpting, making ceramics. In one I saw a man and woman rehearsing ballet steps, in another a space set up as a photo studio. I never knew such a place existed in Calista. City-subsidized – was that possible? If so, how could I wangle myself a studio there?

A wall register showed the names of the occupants listed alphabetically along with their respective métiers. I saw listings for people who identified themselves as *Painter, Potter, Sculptor, Dancer, Photographer, Composer, Singer, Cellist.* The last name on this list was *Katherine Zevin, Painter.*

I rang her on the intercom.

'Come on up,' she said. 'Unit fourteen.' The buzzer sounded, I opened the door and entered.

I was greeted by a rail-thin woman with kindly features. She wore a shapeless garment, the kind my mom used to call a 'house dress.' Her face was deeply lined, her head bobbed slightly and, I noticed, her hands shook.

'Don't mind the tremors. I've got Parkinson's with a touch of Lewy's Bodies . . . or maybe it's the other way around. The bad part is that my painting hand shakes unless I hold my brushes tight. I've had to adjust my style, learn to use the shaking as a plus. Then there's the fun part – the hallucinations. Sometimes I'll see a cat dash across the room, or an iguana crouching in the corner. I like seeing visions. They spice up my life. So, young man, let's have tea and talk.'

She had clear memories of Courtney and Penny.

'Two of the most talented kids I ever taught,' she said. 'Summers I used to teach at Red Raven, a summer arts camp west of Cleveland. That's where the girls met. They were cabin mates and soon became great pals. Pen had been taking classes with me over at the Danzig Center. Come autumn, Court wanted to do the same. I remember she had a hard time convincing her mom. She was going to that snobby school, Ashley-Burnett, and her mom thought the art instruction there was good enough. Anyway, her mom finally gave in. The girls did wonderful work, dark work. I believe both of them saw the world the same way. They had one of those special friendships too, sealed by devotion to art-making. You know, like Picasso and Matisse.' She chuckled. 'Hardly on that level, of course. They were kids. But it was like they fed off each other, reacted to each other's work. I had them do critiques, and that was fun. First they'd hem and haw, then they'd get into it. "I don't get where you're going with this one, Court." "Hey, Pen, you're going to have to reverse the whole thing to make it work."'

We were sitting in the living space of her loft. The ceiling was twelve feet high. The walls were covered with her art work, unframed canvasses of various sizes, filled with stylized imagery. In one I saw pieces of chairs piled into what looked like a canoe. In another the naked muscular back of a man, cut off at the neck and waist, filled the foreground against a red sky.

I asked her what she meant by 'dark work.' She thought about it.

'They were similar in some ways, different in others. Court was great at rendering a likeness. She could do it from memory. Even at that age, she could have made it as a street portraitist. But her vision was dark. Even in life-drawing class, she'd twist the models' features or put some malice into their eyes. She didn't have much use for color, so I'd say her primary talent was draftsmanship – or "draftspersonship" as some call it these days. Pen – her approach was more conceptual. Court would start with a figure or a face, go in close and build out from there. Pen would start with an idea, sketch it out in broad strokes, then fill it in. Her ideas were as dark as Court's vision. She liked the idea of making paintings that would oppress the viewer. "I hate pretty!" – she'd repeat that like a mantra. "If it's pretty, it's telling a lie," she'd say. The interesting thing was that even taking opposite approaches she and Court would end up with fairly similar works.' She paused. 'I was so worried for them when they ran off together. I'm not religious but I prayed they'd stay safe.'

I asked her if she had any inkling they were planning to run.

'I used to ask myself that,' she said. 'There was something conspiratorial going on with them – a lot of nudging and whispering. You know what teens are like. But those girls weren't whispering about boys or clothes, they were whispering about art. It was as if they were living in their own private bubble.'

She paused. 'They left behind a couple of sketchbooks. After they went missing, this detective came around to the center asking to see their work. He said there might be clues in it about where they'd gone. I handed over the sketchbooks and never saw them again. I never believed for a second they'd been kidnapped. I figured they'd made a run for it, which was hard for most people to understand. Especially with Court, who led such a privileged life. Neither one was happy at home. I knew they had family issues, but had no idea what they were. I had a hunch they'd taken off for New York or San Francisco, some place where they could live out their dream of being artists. I was pretty surprised when it turned out they were in a cult house over on Locust.'

Her eyes teared up. 'Excuse me,' she said, 'I can't help myself. Those kids meant a lot to me. They were so passionate, so intensely into art-making, the way only young people can be. You teach for years, young people come and go. Most have some talent – some more, others less. Then along come two girls with talents that are huge. You want to help them, guide them, show them ways to develop, forge their own styles. Then they run off. Except for one brief visit from Pen, I never saw them again. For years I thought I'd hear about them, that they'd emerge, exhibit, show work that would astound the world. Never happened. Some kids show talent that burns white hot, then burns out when they become adults. Makes me sad this probably happened with them.'

'You say Penny came by to see you?'

'Just one time. She was living in San Francisco, attending SFAI, home for a few days to visit her folks. One day, out of the blue, she stopped in to see me. I asked her if she was still making art. "I stopped painting for a while," she said. "Lately I've been fooling around with abstract sculpture." *Fooling around* – words I never imagined would pass her lips. But what struck me most were her insistent questions about Court. Did I know what happened to her? Where she might be found? Her family, she said, refused to tell her anything. They admonished her: "You two are not supposed to see each other again." Pen said they blamed her for pushing Court to run away. They told her she'd damaged Court enough, and warned her not to try to find her.

'I was astonished by this. She said after the police broke into the house and dragged her and Court out, they split the girls up. She, Pen, had been taken to a so-called deprogramming farm out

of state, which was ironic, she said, because though the house on
Locust wasn't anything like a cult, the deprogramming place literally was. She told me it was brutal. Luckily, she said, she didn't
have to stay there long. Her dad came for her and took her home.
"I have friends now," she told me, "but none as close as Court.
I'll always remember working here side by side with her, and then
later at the house."'

Ms Zevin's eyes lit up when I told her about the murals they'd
painted in that house. When I asked if she'd like to see some
photos of them on my phone, she nodded vigorously and sat up
straight.

'Wonderful, wonderful . . . yes, these are terrific,' she said as
I flicked through Jase's images. 'Their work for sure. Thrilling to
see it. Just wonderful, wonderful . . .'

Again I saw tears forming in her eyes. I could see she was
getting tired. But when I stood to leave, she insisted I stay a while
longer and tell her about myself. I told her that I'd studied fine
art photography at CAI, and now was eking out a living doing
wedding photography in the black community.

'We all had to take jobs like that. I have artist friends, terrific
painters, who had to do house painting to get by. I was fortunate
to find teaching positions. At least your day job's in your field.
I'd love to see your work, Tally. Please come visit me again and
bring along your portfolio.'

There was a meeting that night at Hannah's loft, the four of us
– Hannah, Jase, Joan and me. We started out pooling everything
we'd discovered. Joan had hit the jackpot with Nate Silver. And
Jase had found out a lot about the Ragdoll Artist.

He showed us the photo he'd snapped of the erotic ragdoll. We
all found this doll perplexing.

'Why would she make an X-rated doll to please some German
erotica collector?' I asked.

Hannah announced that she and Jase were going back to Lucerne
to wait for the go-between to turn up.

'Our hope is the guy'll lead us to the Ragdoll Artist. Then we'll
know for sure,' she said.

Jason said he didn't buy Nate Silver's claim that the Cobbs,
being uptight WASPS, were incapable of doing weird stuff.

'You don't run away for no reason,' he said. 'To me, the murals tell a story of something traumatic. Like the grown-ups are performing some kind of satanic rite, witnessed surreptitiously by the little girl in the corner with her dog.'

He said it was clear now that we *had* to find Penny Dawson.

'I'm sure I can find her,' Joan said.

Jase also thought it was important to interview Elizabeth Schechtner. 'She could be the key to the whole thing.' He turned to Hannah. 'Why don't the two of us fly out to Albuquerque? Cindy could set her up for us.'

'Then we play good cop/bad cop?' Hannah asked.

'Maybe something like that. Listen, guys,' Jason said, 'I feel we're closing in. We're starting to understand these kids. But there's still a lot we don't know. How did a couple of disturbed teenagers create something so powerful? And, big question, what's the story *behind* the murals? Do they depict something real or is the whole thing some weird fantasy they had? If it's a fantasy, then there's no story. Me, I'm betting there *is* a story.'

Johnny Baldwin

id I like Dr DeJonghe? I did at first. I found him compassionate, intrigued by my case, interested in me as a person. Later, of course, I changed my mind. That happened when I realized how manipulative he was, not with me so much (though it's fair to say I was 'used'), but with the patient everyone called Agnès . . . whose real name, it turned out, was something else.

'Befriend her,' Doc DJ urged me. 'She needs a buddy. Becoming her friend will help you as much as it will her. Don't misunderstand me, Johnny. I'm not proposing a romantic relationship, and certainly not intimacy [chuckle-chuckle, haha!]. Only that you become platonic friends. I think some bonding would do you both a lot of good.'

Well, now, wasn't that nice!

'Is this like a prescription?' I asked him.

'You can view it that way. Why not give it a try, see how things develop.'

OK, so here I am, gay, randy-as-hell, nineteen years old, queer-as-an-ostrich, an English fruit, one everyone in my family thinks is nutso, and I'm supposed to 'bond' with a forty-two-year-old American lady who barely speaks, doesn't bother to acknowledge a friendly 'good morning,' refuses to make eye contact, and who spends most of her time in her studio making weird rag dolls out of fabric scraps.

Give me a break!

On the other hand, it's not like there's much to do around here in this ultra-luxurious clinic for the deeply disturbed. The clear, crisp air and restful Alpine environment are supposed to salve our psychic wounds. Hang out in the day room with the other nutters. Play chess with that stick-up-his-ass Kraut, Heinz, who gloats when he wins, which is always. Put together huge jigsaw puzzles of pastoral scenes, which, when completed, are inferior to the lake view out the window. Curl up on one of the leather couches in the library and reread *The Odyssey* and assorted other classics. Scribble in my journal. Listen to the birds and the bees on boring walks about the grounds. Lounge around the pool. Watch videos of old movies selected for their positive effects on disturbed minds. Make goo-goo eyes at the cute mustachioed gardener. Jerk off in my bedroom when I know nurse Thérèse will be coming in with my medications. Etcetera.

So, why not give old Agnès a try? She has intelligent eyes when she bothers to show them. She's got lovely long braided hair and appears to practice good hygiene. She smiles sometimes, though it seems only at her own thoughts. 'Lost in her own world,' the nurses say. *Sa tête est à la lune.*

So, tell me, how the hell am I supposed to bond with such a creature?

Gerald, my first love, my teacher and seducer, taught me that few can resist the look of longing in a handsome lad's eyes. You want to seduce someone, make yourself vulnerable, he taught me, exhibit your neediness, let your eyes be your magnets. Blah, blah, blah . . .

Gerald was full of crappy life lessons such as that, his oh-so-precious pearls of wisdom. Now he's in prison for messing around with minors. Still, the old pedophile may have had a point.

OK, I thought, let's turn Doc DJ's prescription into a game. Let's see if I *can* bond with this very peculiar lady.

Gotta tell you, it wasn't easy.

I started off ignoring her don't-mess-with-me signals. I decided to show her I wouldn't accept her refusal to respond to my cheerful 'good morning!' I repeated the greeting, and, the next day, repeated it three times in a row. On the fourth day, she nodded at me, probably because she couldn't stand hearing me repeat it four times. So on the fifth morning I added, 'So how are you today, Agnès?' To which she gave a very quick nod, then abruptly turned away.

Hmmm. We seem to be getting somewhere. Perhaps we're on the path to an actual relationship.

On the following days I added phrases, as per: 'Good morning. How are you today, Agnès? Sleep well? As for me, I know you're not going to ask, but I'm happy to report that I slept quite well and to my surprise am feeling quite good actually.'

This produced an ironic Mona Lisa smile, which I understood could be interpreted one of two ways: (1) *You really are an annoying little shit* or (2) *I'm faintly amused by your pathetic attempts to engage with me.*

Either way would be fine, I thought. At least she's showing that she hears me.

Your mission, young sir, I told myself, *should you choose to accept it, is to make her acknowledge your existence without making yourself obnoxious in the process.*

I approached her in the dining room during breakfast. She always chose to dine alone. I asked if I could join her, and, before she could either nod or shake her head, took the chair opposite.

'Look,' I said, 'I know you like to keep to yourself, and that I'm barely half your age. You should know that I'm irreversibly homosexual, and thus have no designs on you other than friendship. I know that you don't like to talk very much, but I have a feeling you won't mind listening to me talk . . . providing I don't bore you. I need someone to listen to me, or at least pretend to. Sure, Doc DJ listens, but since he's a shrink he does so as a duty, not because he much cares about what I have to say. I just want to leave you with this thought: if you find me at all annoying, please so indicate by word or gesture, and I shan't bother you again. If, on the other hand, you find me even the slightest bit amusing, and wouldn't mind if we invested lightly in getting to know one another, please let me know, again by word or gesture, and I will proceed to show you more of my . . . er . . . charming self.'

At which I stood, bowed chivalrously to her, met her eyes, which to my surprise, were gazing into mine, then turned to go.

I hadn't taken but two steps when she spoke to me for the first time. Her voice was weak, barely above a whisper.

'I don't mind,' she said.

I turned. 'Wonderful! I was so hoping you'd say that. In truth, my heart was in my mouth for fear you'd turn away.' I met her gaze. 'We'll talk later, OK? May I come visit you in your studio at tea-time this afternoon?'

She nodded. I nodded back, then, smiling to myself, strode briskly away.

Doc DJ had a twinkle in his eyes.

'You seem to have made an impression on Agnès.'

'Good or bad?'

'Good, of course. Why would you think otherwise?'

'I often feel people dislike me. I got that feeling from my family for so long that I find myself in a state of wonderment when the opposite turns out to be the case.'

'Most everyone here likes you, Johnny. You must know that.'

'I think they feel sorry for me if you want to know the truth.'

'Why would they feel sorry for you?'

'Because I'm a messed-up kid, a worthless faggot, who couldn't cut it at university. Because my wealthy parents are storing me here so as not to have to deal with me and be reminded of my repulsive perversities.'

'I like the clear way you express yourself, Johnny. There's no subterfuge with you. Back to Agnès – how do you feel about her?'

'Against my better judgment, I'm finding that I like her. By which I mean there's no particular reason that I should. She's one weird lady, but her silence intrigues me. Also, I feel she doesn't judge me, no matter what I say, and therefore I'm free to say most anything. Something liberating in that. Of course it's a one-way street. She's what my aunt used to call "a dark study" – a person of unfathomable depths. As for me, what you see is pretty much what you get. No secrets hiding in my psyche. Maybe that explains why we get along. We're opposites, and opposites attract . . . or so they say.'

If truth be told (and I think it always should be), I did enjoy hanging out with Agnès. I tried not to babble too much. I certainly didn't want her to tire of me. So sometimes when I spoke, I had the feeling she heard me with half an ear, the way one might listen to background music. Other times, I simply sat silent beside her, watching her work with her scissors, threads and needles.

She was marvelously dexterous. She seemed to have a magical way with fabric, cutting and sewing, turning a mess of light-colored scraps into those amazing characters. She seemed to create them out of her head, improvising as she worked. She didn't sketch her dolls in advance, would just cut and sew, cut and sew, and though it looked as if she wasn't going anywhere, suddenly something recognizable would emerge, a double-faced human creature with eyes, nose, mouth, ears, and then neck, torso, arms and legs.

It was quite amazing to observe her at work, expressing whatever it was she was striving to express, cutting and sewing, cutting and sewing, rarely hesitating, although sometimes she'd stop, tear two pieces apart, then set to work again in an almost feverish state.

'Are they about hypocrisy – your dolls, I mean? The two-facedness of our fellow humans? The public face and the Janus face?'

She shrugged.

'Perhaps they're about virtue and deceit? Or the tragic and comedic sides of what we laughingly refer to collectively as "folks"?'

She shrugged again.

'I believe you may be struggling to reconcile the opposites in people? By putting two faces on their heads, you attempt to combine their irreconcilable qualities?'

This time she stopped work, turned to me and met my eyes. 'They can mean whatever you want them to mean,' she whispered, then set back to sewing a jagged cut in a male figure's cheek.

'You have beautiful eyes. You know that, Agnès?'

She shook her head with derision. 'Pooh!'

'Well, you do. And I'm a sucker for lovely eyes.'

She ignored this remark. She was much more interested in the button eyes she was sewing on to the doll's face.

I put the question to Doc DJ point-blank: 'Did my parents send me here for gay conversion therapy?'

He sat back in his chair. 'We know that doesn't work.'

'Do *they* know it?'

'I would hope so. Why would you think they'd send you here for that? And, more to the point, why would you believe I'd take on a patient for such a purpose?'

'I didn't say I believed you would. I asked if that's why they sent me here. In another era they'd send off the queer son to some exotic locale such as Tangier, where he could plunge unnoticed into his personal pit of perversity. These days they're more likely to send him to a shrink to get him straightened out, sometimes by connecting electrodes to his penis and giving him shocks when he gets hard looking at gay pornography.'

I looked straight into Doc DJ's eyes. 'I notice,' I added, 'you don't deny it.'

He harrumphed.

I continued: 'As for why they would want to put me through such a useless exercise, I can only say that they so despise the way their progeny turned out that they'd do most anything to turn me vanilla. They feel cheated. They didn't expect this outcome. At first they put all the blame on Gerald North, "that vile pederast of a schoolmaster" (as my father always referred to him), as if he alone, by virtue of his meticulous grooming, cologne and devilish guile, could turn an upstanding straight boy such as I once was into the slithering worm of a sodomite that I've become. I know, I know, speaking this way reeks of self-hatred. Please understand that I'm simply putting myself into their heads. It's not self-hatred I'm expressing; it's *their* hatred of *me*. Surely you understand that.'

'Do you speak of yourself this way when you're with Agnès?' he asked.

'I try to avoid it. I think it upsets her.' I leaned forward. 'Has she complained about me?'

'She enjoys your company, Johnny. She's told me so several times.'

'Did you tell her you put me up to it?'

'Why would I tell her that?'

'You probably wouldn't,' I mumbled. 'I just want to be certain.'

'What do you think of her artwork?' he asked, gesturing toward a doll she'd recently made that sat on top of his bookcase loaded with German-language texts by Carl Jung.

'I think it's pretty damn amazing. But I'm not sure what she's trying to say. Whatever it is, she's saying it again and again. Like she's locked into a kind of cul-de-sac.'

'But there are slight variations. Each doll is different. Each has its own personality.'

'I haven't seen that, because I haven't seen enough of her dolls together to compare. When they're finished, what does she do with them?'

He shrugged. 'She gave me the one on the bookcase. Once she's finished one, she loses interest in it. It's on to the next, and so on.' He paused. 'You mentioned her being locked.'

'I was pretending to be a psychologist.'

'I think you're right. She is in a cul-de-sac. Schizophrenic artists often are.'

'Wait a sec, Doc! Schizophrenic? That seems a bit harsh. Is that really your diagnosis?'

'Do you think she's in touch with the real world?'

'That depends on what you think "the real world" is?'

'You're much too clever for me today, Johnny. I'm sure you can see she's deeply disturbed. What I'm getting at is that perhaps you could help her find her way out of this dead-end she's in.'

'How would I manage that? And why should I? She seems quite content with things as they are.'

'I believe a new approach would release her. You yourself said she seems locked in. The purpose would be to unlock her, free her from the prison of her pathology. As to how – that's a difficult question. You have a relationship with her – really the only one she's had here in years. I believe that one sincere friend can help another. And I believe that by helping her you might also greatly help yourself.'

Oh dear! How manipulative he was! I didn't see it then. I thought of him as a healer. But now I see him for what he really was and is – a deceitful, greedy spider.

A marvelous surprise! When I went to see Agnès later that day, she was wearing a tight-lipped I'm-quite-pleased-with-myself smile.

'Something rather smug about you today,' I said. 'So tell me, what's up?'

She picked up a sketch pad from the floor, opened it, turned it around and showed me what she'd drawn.

I was amazed. It was a totally flattering portrait of me in which I appeared far more handsome than I am. She'd removed those disgusting spots from my face, and exaggerated the shock of hair that falls slantways across my forehead.

'Oh my God, I want to kiss you . . . but don't worry, I won't.

I know you wouldn't like it. Still, I have that feeling. You've made me look so poetic, a regular Rupert Brooke.'

She stared at me, confused.

'You don't know who he was? Not surprising since you're American. He was this fabulously talented poet, a kind of Lord Byron type, who died tragically very young from an infection while serving in the First World War. He was described by Yeats as "the handsomest young man in England." Oh dear, you don't know about Yeats? He was the outstanding Irish poet of his time. But never mind, sweet Agnès. Your portrait of me is fabulous. I just hope I can live up to it.'

'I believe you will,' she whispered, then went back to work on her doll-in-progress.

A little later, for no particular reason I can think of, I asked her if she'd ever drawn a portrait of Doc DJ. She stopped sewing and stared at me, then grinned. There was cunning in her eyes.

'Come!' she whispered, beckoning me into her bedroom. This was the first time I'd been invited in. Her inner sanctum was sparsely furnished, elegant and austere, with a little balcony over-looking the lake. She walked to one of her closets, knelt down, pulled out a cardboard box from beneath a pile of sketchbooks. She then beckoned me to kneel beside her as she opened the box, unwrapped a doll swaddled in tissue paper and held it up for me to see.

Oh my God!

It was Doc DJ in doll form, instantly recognizable, quite horri-fying, too. On one side of his head she'd perfectly captured his phony expression of empathy, the one he always shows when I confide my deepest troubles. On the other side, the obverse, she depicted what she imagined lay beneath his mask, a visage that reeked of spite and contempt.

'You don't like him?' I asked, quite disingenuously since her doll made that abundantly clear.

She crinkled her nose.

'Did he do something to you, something I should know about?'

She waved her hand in front of her face, as she often did when she had enough of a topic. She wrapped the doll back in tissue, stowed it back in its box, hid it again in her closet, then led me back to her sitting room.

'I hope someday you'll confide in me,' I told her as she resumed cutting and sewing. 'I'm in his hands. We both are. We're in his care, taking his medications. I'd hate to think we shouldn't be.'

She stopped working, sat silent, then finally she blurted in the fiercest whisper I'd ever heard her use: 'I try *not* to take them, but can't help myself. He's got me addicted.'

Jason Poe

On the flight to New Mexico, Hannah snuggled against me, which, I admit, felt pretty damn good. We hadn't engaged in any lovemaking (which she still insists on calling, ironically, 'mercy fucks') in a while, and that was fine with both of us. I felt our friendship deepened once we took on the murals project, and I told her so on the plane. I also told her how grateful I was to her for underwriting the Ragdoll Artist investigation.

She shook her head when I said that. 'That's my contribution. You, me, Joan and Tally – we're a team. Each of us does what he can.'

I liked that she didn't plead the usual rich person's rejoinder: 'I can afford it; that's what money's for.' But I didn't tell her that, only that I felt fortunate to have her in my life, that I'd loved her since the day we met, and that I always would.

That's when she snuggled against me.

'I like it when you show me your soft side, Jase.'

'I'm sure it's a change from my phony Hemingway front.'

'Dare I say I was beginning to worry about you the last few months before you found the murals?'

'Because I was so bogged down in *Leavings*?'

'Because I thought you had *Leavings* nailed and were unnecessarily spinning your wheels. Like you were afraid to wrap it up.'

'Tally says he was worried about that too. As a matter of fact, I was worried about it myself,' I confessed.

Elizabeth ('Dr Liz') Schechtner, having retired from her job with the State of New Mexico, had moved north from Santa Fe to a small town, Abiquiú, famous for being the location of Georgia O'Keeffe's Ghost Ranch, where the artist had lived and painted for many years.

Cindy Broderick had set us up with Dr Liz, introducing us via telephone. Hannah and I spoke to her twice, so she was fully aware of why we wanted to talk to her. She'd been resistant at first.

'I don't see why you need to come all this way. We can communicate perfectly well like this.'

I explained it was important for us to interview her in person. She finally relented, gave us the name of a nearby inn and invited us to come see her 'on the mesa' (as she described her house) as soon as we checked in and unpacked.

Her little house on the mesa couldn't have been more different from her old Gothic-style residence on Locust. It was up at the end of a rutted bone-dry dirt road, no more than fifty feet from the edge of a thousand-foot-deep chasm, a simple one-story three-room adobe structure with solar panels mounted on the roof. She was waiting for us in front: a short, stout woman with long iron-gray hair framing a lined sunburnt face. She wore a prairie skirt, a linen blouse and a native-style turquoise necklace.

She greeted us warmly, hugged us both, then immediately led us to the ledge overlooking the chasm and observed us as we took in the drama of the drop.

The cliffs opposite were multicolored. She told us there were petroglyphs cut into them. She pointed to a ranch down in the valley, which, she told us, belonged to an aging female movie star.

'Most of us up here, we live simply and we're loners,' she told us. 'I used to go down to Santa Fe once a week. I don't go there now except to see my dentist. And, no – not that you asked – I don't miss Calista. Haven't been back since they ran us out of town. Like most folks who move to the south-west, I can't imagine living anyplace else.'

She had put out a bowl of thick taco chips and two home-made salsas. The house was lined with bookcases, and the few empty spaces on the walls were crowded with paintings by local artists. A pair of cats wandered around, one black, the other calico.

'Meet Ulysses and Penelope,' she said. 'They're complicated felines. Penelope likes to curl up and play dead, and Ulysses is deep into string theory. A ball of yarn will occupy him for hours. I let them roam outdoors so they can chase away the mice. Far as I know, they haven't killed any . . . which is fine with me.'

There was something good-humored about Dr Liz, a warmth I found hard to resist. She possessed the kind of natural compassion that must have served her well as a therapist. She and Dr Ted had been treated poorly, but except for her throwaway remark about being run out of town, she didn't seem to harbor resentment against Calista or the people there who'd made it impossible for them to stay.

'Ted was the charismatic one,' she told us. 'He probably could have led a cult if he'd wanted to. He had the qualities of a leader and an almost hypnotic effect on the kids. Some worshipped him. I know Courtney and Penny did. They liked me fine, but they were devoted to Ted. He was the one who worked with them. Did he take advantage of that?' She shrugged. 'Maybe, maybe not. Anyway, you say those attic murals are a kind of masterpiece. I hope you brought the model. I want very much to see it.'

She'd never seen the murals! That surprised us. She explained that Ted had worked exclusively with the two girls and was the only one who visited them in the attic. When he described the murals to her, it was clear he didn't value them as art, but as expressions of emotion.

'He said they were wild,' she told us, 'but he never used words like "masterpiece."'

I went out to the car, brought back the model, opened it up for her, and studied her as she examined it.

She appeared stunned. 'I see what you mean about powerful,' she finally said. 'I knew those girls were talented, but I had no idea they were capable of something as strong as this.'

She said she had no idea what the murals meant, who the figures were or why they seemed so intense and demonic.

'Could they be imaginary?' she asked. 'Hard to believe they knew people who looked like this.'

That remark, coming from a trained psychologist, struck me as willfully dense. Maybe, I thought, Dr Liz knew more about the murals than she was letting on. Exchanging a quick glance with Hannah, I could see she was wondering the same.

Dr Liz was happy to tell us how the girls had come to Locust Street. Penny, she told us, had been seeing Ted for sessions. He'd been the consulting psychologist at her high school, which specialized in artistic kids, the only public school of its kind in Calista.

'Penny was troubled and had problems at home . . . like all the kids we were caring for. I don't remember Ted telling me what her problems were, just that she was very talented and that her teachers had high hopes for her. He found her likeable and not

bottled-up about her issues. I also remember him saying something
about her being jilted by her boyfriend and that she was under-
standably depressed about that. These were the kinds of problems
we often faced in our practices. Anyway, it was through their
sessions at the school that she learned about our halfway house,
A Caring Place.

'She spent the summer before her senior year at Red Raven art
camp. That's where she and Courtney met. They became fast
friends, and in autumn, when each went back to her respective
school, they missed one another and so arranged to get together
at the after-school arts program where Penny was enrolled. At this
point Penny had stopped seeing Ted, so he was surprised when
one day she turned up at our house. She seemed desperate. She
told us she and a friend, who turned out to be Courtney Cobb,
were miserable in their home situations, and she begged us to take
them in. Ted told her to bring her friend around; he'd talk to them
both and see what could be done.'

Liz sighed. 'They turned up the next afternoon, arriving by bus
without any baggage directly from their art class. There was clearly
something distraught about Courtney. She was monosyllabic. She
had this droopiness about her. I remember thinking she looked
beaten down and depressed. The two of them gazed at us with
beseeching eyes. You know what kids are like, how manipulative
they can be. Two pairs of eyes like that are pretty hard to resist.
I guess we were seduced by their neediness and our belief in the
efficacy of what we had to offer. So we made a big mistake. At
least Ted did. He took Courtney into our little office on the first
floor, interviewed her privately, and when they came back out, he
told them both we'd take them in, but without mentioning that
we'd first need their parents' consent. We both knew perfectly well
we needed that. After they left, I reminded Ted of this, and he
promised to take care of it.

'As you know, he didn't. And I became complicit in that failure.
I kept telling him we had to call their folks, if only to assure them
their kids were safe. He responded that if we did, he was certain
their parents would refuse to let them stay. He'd recognized the
Cobb name. He knew she was from a wealthy, socially prominent
family. Maybe he was seduced by that, the possibility of working
with a kid from such a background. He insisted he'd seen something injured in Courtney, some part of her that was deeply

wounded, and that in the half-hour he'd spent with her, he'd learned very disturbing things about her home life. He reminded me that when girls that age are messed-up, there's a ninety-nine percent chance there's something bad going on within the family. And, he reminded me, he already knew stuff about Penny's home life. "We can't deny them," he said, insisting that it was our duty to give them shelter. "They're almost eighteen. In a few months they'll be adults. Right now, they qualify to become liberated minors." Ted could be very persuasive. Even now, I'm not sure why he was so intent on breaking the rules, putting our reputations and liveli-hoods at risk. For me, the issue is why did I go along with him? I still can't answer that.'

She stared at my model of the murals, then bent to examine it closely.

'I guess the reason's in here. Having them paint on the walls was Ted's idea. He had the windows boarded up so they'd have an unobstructed surface. He was a great believer in getting patients to visually express their issues, while I was more of a classical talk-therapy type.'

I told her that Cindy said she used to speak of dealing with personal demons.

Liz smiled. 'That's true. I'd tell the kids to wrestle with them, pin them down, vanquish them.'

'Doesn't sound much like classical talk therapy,' Hannah said.

'Well, maybe not. Ted influenced me. I adopted some of his methods, the ones I thought worked, and in return I kept him (his word) "grounded." We worked well together for quite a few years. I believe we did productive work, helping kids deal with their pain. But then it all blew up, and afterwards we were never able to get our mojo back. Plus nobody would touch us. Our reputations were in tatters. And all because we arrogantly believed we could get away with something we both knew was absolutely wrong.'

'You say you were complicit. Is that because you failed to "ground" him on this?' I asked.

'Yes, I failed him, I failed us both.' She paused. 'We paid a very heavy price for that.'

The sun was setting. Suddenly, the little room was aglow. The uneven cream-colored stucco walls danced with orange light. Liz brightened up at that. She told us that she'd had the house built so that the sun would set inside her living room.

'It'll start getting cold soon. I'll light the fire.'

She went over to the kiva built into the corner and lit the kindling. We sat in silence for a while, watching as the light seeped out of the room and the sunset faded from the sky. Soon there was no light except the glow of the kiva. I stood up.

'This has been intense. Let's call it a night, talk more tomorrow.'

Liz nodded. 'I'll try to think back. Maybe in the morning I'll remember more.'

Hannah and I had dinner at a restaurant Liz recommended in Ojo Caliente, a hot-springs resort twenty miles north-east of Abiquiú. It was a lovely place with a series of open-air spring-fed pools.

Over our meal we discussed Liz, the things she told us and the things she hadn't.

'I saw you were surprised when she claimed she'd never gone up to the attic,' Hannah said.

'Yeah, and that Ted never discussed the girls' problems. I'd think that psychologists who practiced together would consult on their cases all the time. These two were married, with each other twenty-four/seven. How could they *not* have discussed the girls' issues?'

'She says she blames herself for not insisting they call the parents. Not sure I buy her rap that Ted was "seduced" by Courtney's status, and that she still can't figure out why she went along with him on not calling them. I have a hunch they were both equally seduced. They saw an opportunity and unwisely took advantage of it.'

'Could be,' I said. 'But what kind of opportunity? Maybe a chance to be at the center of a major case, expose a scandal involving prominent wealthy people, or, maybe, *not* exposing it . . . for a price.'

'Hard to believe.'

'But not impossible. Which brings us back to the girls. I think she knows very well what their issues were, and that's what made them think they were on to something.'

'Not sure what you mean,' Hannah said.

I took a couple of bites then ventured a theory.

'Suppose Courtney's troubles were so explosive – maybe Penny's too – so explosive that the Schechtners believed that justified their risking so much by breaking a basic rule of their profession.'

'But—'

'Yeah, I know – if they had info that explosive, why didn't they offer it in their defense? Well, maybe they did. Suddenly, the prosecutors drop their complaints, and the Schechtners get off and leave town. Maybe there was some sort of deal – "we'll keep quiet about what we know about certain things in return for you dropping all the charges and the Cobb family throwing in some money to sweeten the pot so we can start over someplace else."'

'You really think the Cobbs paid them off?'

'We know they paid Cindy and Loetz. That's what rich people do.'

Hannah gulped. 'Sure, but taking money from them would've been a huge betrayal of the girls. Would they really do something that nefarious?'

'Their hands were dirty. No matter how things went at trial, they were certain to lose their licenses. Anyway, the Cobb girl was back under her family's control. They had no idea where she'd been taken and no way to communicate with her. If it was a choice between fighting an unwinnable battle and losing their licenses, or abandoning the girls and saving their own skins, I can imagine them doing what I said.'

'That's speculation.'

'Sure, but now that we're here, maybe we can get to the bottom of it.'

'She's such a nice lady. I'd find it hard to crowd her.'

'We don't have to crowd her, Hannah. Just draw her out. Remember how good Cindy felt after she confessed? I think Liz would feel good too if she told us the truth.'

'Seems like this is turning into a story about what was going on with those girls, what was in their heads.'

'That's exactly what it is. Because that's the key to the murals.'

The next morning things didn't go as we expected. Dr Liz changed tack. After listening to our thanks for her suggesting we dine at Ojo Caliente, she tried to turn the tables on me. Seemed she was done playing the *mea culpa* card.

'Forgive me for prying, Jason, but I have to ask – what is it about those murals that has you so riled up? Why are you so fascinated by them?'

I was affronted. 'You think I have an ulterior motive?'

'As a psychologist, I always seek to understand what drives

people – not their ostensible reasons but the deeper ones they may not be aware of.'

I stared at her. 'How can I answer if I'm unaware?'

'Oh dear, I see I've offended you. I was just putting my thoughts out there. I didn't realize you'd be so touchy.'

She stood, excused herself, went into the kitchen to fetch more coffee. As soon as she left the room, Hannah shook her head.

'Calm down,' she whispered. 'Let her play the psychologist. Show her some respect.'

When Liz came back with a steaming pot, I apologized for acting defensive. 'You touched a nerve. I've been wondering myself why the murals mean so much to me.'

She nodded, relaxed, smiled at me. 'Thanks for saying that. Clearly, the murals are important to you both. I agree they're powerful. But when something is so powerful that it drives an obsession, we must ask ourselves why.'

I let her carry on in this vein, knowing sooner or later she'd run out of steam. I had a hunch her attempt to take control of the dialogue was her way to distract us from probing into matters she didn't wish to discuss.

'Do you still have your case files on the girls?' Hannah asked.

'Oh, no!' she said. 'Ted shredded everything before we left. He said we owed that to our patients. He didn't want our files to fall into the wrong hands.'

Hannah leaned forward. 'Here's what's bothering us, Liz – you and Ted were married and in practice together, yet he didn't confide in you regarding these girls beyond the obvious fact that they were troubled.'

'I'm sure you've heard of patient confidentiality.'

'Between a husband and wife – that seems a bit far-fetched.'

I understood Hannah had meant to speak gently, but her words cut hard at Liz. She began to tear up, then turned away and let out with a convulsive moan.

'I'm sorry,' Hannah said. 'I didn't mean to upset you. It's just—'

'I know, I know . . .' Liz shook her head as if to clear it. 'It *is* far-fetched. I realize that. Of course it is! I mean, how could it *not* seem so?'

Suddenly, the story spewed out of her: how difficult Ted had been even back when they were living on Locust, how secretive and proprietary he'd been about his patients, ignoring her questions, deflecting them, demanding to know why she asked them, suggesting that she wanted to invade his clinical relationships in order to disparage his unorthodox techniques and/or because of envy at his successes.

'He was always paranoid. When we moved out here, his paranoia became worse. It got to the point when I couldn't stand it anymore, when we couldn't stand each other. That's when we parted ways. I don't know what he was doing with those girls. He refused to tell me, refused even to describe their issues. All he'd say was "They're working it out. You should see what they're painting in the attic. You wouldn't believe it." But when I asked if I could go up to there and see for myself what he was talking about, he became agitated. "Don't you dare go up there! That'll ruin everything! You'll upset them, pull them back. They'll lose their momentum and never regain it." It was crazy talk.' She shook her head. 'I've never told this to anyone, not even to Ted, but when the cops burst in and dragged the girls away, I was actually relieved. *Finally, it's over*, I thought. *Whatever he's been up to with them is finished now.*'

After she calmed down, she muttered something to the effect that our coming out to New Mexico had been a fool's errand.

'I should have warned you,' she said, 'admitted I didn't know anything, not even the symptomology. Looking at your model, I'm even more confused. What did Ted think these paintings meant? What did they mean to the girls? Why was he so secretive? Why were the three of them so conspiratorial? What was the purpose? The treatment plan?' Liz spread her arms. 'Truth is, I have no fucking idea!'

'Well, holy shit!' Hannah said, as we rumbled down the road and off the mesa. 'Where does this leave us? Back to zero. We never got around to asking if there was a deal with the Cobbs.'

'Still, we learned something.'

'What?'

'How much we still don't know.'

Hannah glanced at me. 'She may have had a point, asking why you're so invested in this.'

'I thought we were equally invested.'

'We are! So *why*, Jase? Why do these murals painted a quarter of a century ago by a pair of troubled adolescents speak so powerfully to us? I think we owe it to ourselves to get to the bottom of that.'

Unsettling questions, which unsettled our relationship. We weren't so cuddly on the flight back east. We didn't speak much on the plane. It was only in the taxi, driving from Calista Airport to the Capehart, that Hannah said something that struck me.

'I think we may have learned more on this jaunt than I thought.'

'What's that?' I asked.

'It's always "the girls," "the two of them," "what were they doing up there together?" We've assumed all along that Courtney was the lead artist, and Penny was her assistant. But what if it was the other way around? Or, more interesting, what if the two of them played equal roles.'

'You mean like a *folie à deux*?'

'Yeah, a *folie à deux.*'

Joan Nguyen

To explain why I became so obsessed with what everyone was calling 'the summer fires,' let me speak about my feelings toward Calista. Despite my initial negative reaction to the city, I found it was a pretty cool place. But there's also something moody about it, an overlay of grit, injustice and gloom that I find haunting and which I can neither explain nor escape.

Perhaps it's the pervasive corruption, particularly in the CPD, which I deal with as junior member of the *Times-Dispatch* investigative team. Also the endless litany of irrational crimes reported daily to our newsroom. Someone holds up a liquor store; he's doing it because he wants money. But a white cop who shoots a ten-year-old black boy dead because he claims he thought the kid's cap pistol was a weapon – race seems the only explanation. Jase touched on this kind of irrationality when he described the notorious crimes that had been committed on Locust Street, crimes that caused print and TV reporters to refer to Locust as 'Street of Horror.'

My first year in town, there'd been panic over a sniper who was taking pot-shots at supermarket shoppers wheeling grocery carts to their cars. Three people were killed in these attacks. The sniping started, the city went into panic mode, then three weeks later it suddenly stopped. To this day the case remains unsolved.

Then there was the triple killing in upscale Danzig Heights – the result of a love triangle. And the tornado that seemed to come out of nowhere, swept through the rundown neighborhood called Gunktown, ripped the roofs off a row of houses, then dispersed over the lake as suddenly as it had arrived. Calista has some of the most elegant suburbs in the Midwest, yet large portions of the city are derelict, providing Jase with numerous places to explore for his *Leavings* series. And then came the summer fires. No wonder people (myself included) starting walking around in T-shirts inscribed with the hopeful slogan: *Calista Strong*.

The fires started breaking out in late May, at least one major blaze per night. Some were ordinary: kids playing with matches, a stove left on, a bad electrical connection. But others were more serious and of mysterious origin – cats and dogs doused with gasoline and then set aflame, homeless people set on fire, fires breaking out in the upper floors of office buildings, a mosque burned to the ground, a synagogue burned, two upscale homes deliberately torched.

These were signs that a crazy firebug was at work, or perhaps more than one. Firemen were on edge. I heard sirens every night as the fire trucks screamed their way to conflagrations. The city was on edge. Who was doing this? What was the purpose? Was he or she a serial arsonist? The worst fire of all, because the smoke was so toxic, was the chemical blaze on Watomi Lake – long the dump for putrid and, as it turned out, highly flammable run-offs from the Wheaton district industrial complex – that decimated an entire neighborhood of working-class homes built along the lake shore.

I badly wanted this story. I felt it could be huge. Thanks to my fireman informant, Tony Delgado, I learned something that no other reporter on the *Times-Dispatch* seemed to know – that an ace arson specialist named Nick Gallagher had been brought in from the state capital to investigate the Calista summer fires.

Early one morning I received a text from Tony: *Meet same place 6 p.m.* I texted back: *CU there.*

I drove to the same far corner of the Haggerty Mall parking lot. Tony must have been watching for me, because he pulled up a few seconds later.

He ran down his window. He looked excited. 'Last night Gallagher's peeps arrested a fireman,' he said. 'Guy name of Norm Hicks. They're saying he's firebug zero.'

'What does that mean?'

'He rigged out a drone to drop Molotov cocktails. The union got him a lawyer, but I'm hearing he's the guy.'

'Why call him "firebug zero"?'

'When there's a disease going around, like Ebola, "patient zero" is what they call the first one catches the infection.'

'You're telling me there's contagion?'

He nodded. 'Firebug zero starts fires, then other people get infected by the bug. People jump on the bandwagon. Yeah, they got Hicks, but that's far from the end of it.'

'This is great info.'

'Check it out. Anyone asks where you heard it, don't mention my name. You and me – we never met.'

'Never!' I assured him.

I told him I'd left a ton of messages on Gallagher's voicemail, but he didn't bother to return my calls.

'Tell him you know about firebug zero. I bet he gets back to you then.'

Before I could thank him, he closed his car window and took off. I waited five minutes, then took off myself.

It made sense to check out Tony's tip. I went back to the office and looked up Norm Hicks. I found a Norman J. Hicks at a West Side address. I drove over to the house. It was in a row of older homes in a well-kept middle-class neighborhood. The downstairs blinds were drawn but I saw light ribbons at the edges. I rang the doorbell. A fortyish woman with a sour face answered, peering at me from behind the screen door.

'Who the hell are you?'

I introduced myself as a reporter. I asked if Norm was home.

'Senior or Junior?'

'Not sure.'

'Well, Junior got arrested. You already know that. That's why you came around. As for Senior, he's upstairs probably crying his eyes out.'

'I'm sorry, ma'am. Didn't mean to disturb you. I heard a rumor and had to check it out. What can you tell me? How old is Junior? Did he start the fires?'

'I'll tell you this, Missy – this is an honest house. My brother Norman – Norm's dad – is a fireman. Our dad was, too. When Norman heard they nabbed Junior, he went into a funk. Doesn't want to go into work. Canceled all his shifts. Junior's twenty. I don't know what he did or didn't do. That's all I gotta say.'

She drilled her eyes into mine, then firmly shut the door.

In some of the numerous messages I left for Gallagher I expressed my severe disappointment he never saw fit to call me back. In others I pleaded for him to do so. I told him that the public had a right to know what was going on, that an elite team was working hard on the fires. In one message I bluffed that the *Times-Dispatch* was prepared to conduct its own investigation and then we'd see which team cracked the case.

I felt kind of dumb making such an empty threat, but Josh Tilly, my editor, told me to go ahead. Again no response.

Soon as I got home from the Hicks house, I left Gallagher a new, more somber message: 'I hear there's been an arrest – firebug zero. I need to hear back from you, Nick. Otherwise, we'll have to go with what we got.'

The next morning I found his message on my office voicemail: 'Hey, Joan, Nick Gallagher here. Sorry about the phone tag. Gimme a call back, will ya?'

His voice was deep, authoritative, confident. I called back, and, to my astonishment, he immediately picked up.

'Guess you think I've been avoiding you,' he said.

'Crossed my mind,' I told him.

'This is a highly confidential investigation. How'd you find out about FB-zero?'

'An informant.'

'I know better than to ask who.'

'So don't. What made you finally decide to get back to me? That I know about Hicks?'

'That and because I admire persistence. My dad used to tell me: "Listen up, son – persistence is the secret to success."'

'Your dad sounds like my kind of guy. Are we going to meet?'

'Yeah, on background only.' He gave me the address. 'Noon.

No recordings. I'll fill you in. If we get along, I'll dole out more news to you from time to time.'

'By that you mean you'll deign to use me as your mouthpiece?'

'How 'bout we use each other, Joan. Isn't that how it's supposed to work?'

The address he gave was an old city building on West 4th, which, according to a plaque, was an out-of-use property belonging to the Calista Board of Education. There was a state-of-the-art security system installed just inside the outer door. I rang the buzzer. The responding voice was female.

'Name?' I told her. 'Hold your ID up to the camera.' I did. 'Purpose?'

'Appointment with Mr Gallagher.'

'Second floor. Take the stairs. Meet you at the top.'

The woman waiting for me was a grim-faced, brawny, kick-ass uniformed cop sporting a sidearm.

'Follow me,' she ordered, leading me down a corridor lined with unmarked frosted glass doors.

She showed me into a room that contained nothing except a small bare table, two wooden school chairs and a large black mirror at one end.

'Is this the interrogation room?' I asked.

She wasn't amused. 'Take a seat facing the mirror,' she ordered. I figured the mirror was a pane of one-way glass.

A couple of minutes later, Gallagher appeared – intelligent eyes, pencil-line mustache, curly graying hair. I figured him for early forties. My first thought was that he was movie-star-handsome because his mustache reminded me of Errol Flynn's.

'Finally we meet,' he said, pulling up a chair beside me, then placing a device that looked like a TV remote on the table.

'You're a hard man to get to see.'

'This is a tough town, Joan, and I'm working a tough case.'

'Tell me about it?'

He exhaled. 'Most summers over the last several years there've been forty to fifty major fires here – most accidental, caused by gas explosions, kids messing around with matches, that sort of thing. Less than ten percent were labeled suspicious. So far this summer there've been one hundred twenty-four major blazes, about half of which we can attribute to arson. The thing about arson is that there can be lots of different motives. Some do it because they get off on it. They're excited by flames and their power to create them. Then there're highly motivated arsonists. They burn down a building to collect the insurance, or to destroy a competitor's business or an enemy's house. Regrettably, there're also firefighter arsonists – men like Hicks who become firemen because they're so fascinated by fires they end up setting them. When there's an eruption of fires like we're having here now, it's usually a mix. Our job is to investigate each one, determine its origin and, if it's suspicious, look into possible motives.'

He picked up his device and clicked it, causing a large map of the city to appear on the black mirror at the end of the room.

'As you can see, we've charted every major fire. You can also see there're clusters, but no discernible geographic pattern. There've been big fires in nearly every neighborhood – commercial, industrial, residential. We believe many were set by people taking advantage of rumors that there's a psychopathic arsonist at work. Say I want to collect insurance on my failing business. I pay a guy to burn it down and make it look like it was set by the psychopath. The more fires that break out, the more imitators emerge to take advantage. The forensics are difficult and the analysis is complex. I was brought in to supervise the effort to identify and arrest the one who started it all, the key arsonist, the one we call firebug zero.'

'That's Hicks.'

He nodded. 'So far he hasn't confessed, but he will. Firebugs tend to be boastful.'

'Hicks is a third-generation fireman.'

He gave me a quick look. 'How do you know that?'

'Last night I interviewed his aunt.'

Gallagher raised his eyebrows as if to signal he may have underestimated me.

'I came here with eight of my best investigators. We set up here so there wouldn't be any leaks. Because we suspected there was at least one uniformed firefighter involved, we had to work apart from CFD.' He paused. 'Is Hicks a psycho arsonist? We believe so, as there've been a number of fires set by his drone device. Those were the fires we were looking at most closely. As for the others, the ones set by copycats, we've gotten some tips. We're watching some people. Are we close to making arrests? Not yet. The one thing I'd like you to get across to your readers is that every fire is being investigated to the max, and the ones that look to be motivated by insurance fraud or vindictiveness . . . those folks'd better watch out. We're coming for them, and when we find them, they'll be prosecuted to the full extent of the law.'

I asked him how much of what he said I could use.

'Everything except my name, where we're located, the number of investigators, and that a firefighter arsonist started it. For obvious reasons, we want that kept quiet.'

'I can't *not* write about Hicks. I didn't hear about him from you.'

'Will you name him?' I nodded. 'I wish you'd wait.'

'I can't. Unless you let me interview him. In that case I'll hold off a couple of days.'

'Sorry, Joan – no can do. We're still interviewing him ourselves.'

By the set of our months, we acknowledged we were at an impasse.

He studied me a while, then he squinted. 'Here's a tip to encourage you to hold off. Go over to the Wheaton district and take a look at the fire damage around Watomi Lake. If you see anything interesting, write about it. When we're ready to go public with Hicks, I'll give you advance notice. How's that?'

I told him I'd think about it if his tip paid off.

'I'll call you when I have more to say. And if you hear anything, call me.' He smiled. 'Now that we've met, I'll make a point of returning your calls.'

I called Josh Tilly, told him what I had, and that I was headed out to Wheaton. It took me nearly an hour to get there. Years before, most of the area had been set aside for heavy industry. It was regarded as the most heavily polluted part of town. 'The Shit Hole' was what they called it in our newsroom – a mix of factories, refineries and miscellaneous industrial works, surrounding a cluster of funky old workers' houses along the edge of Watomi Lake. If the Locust Street area was in decay, the houses in Wheaton were decrepit even before the fire. It was an awful place to live due to the chemical stink that came off the lake.

A huge fire had raged there in June, wiping out the lakeside community. It had started on the lake itself, when the chemical run off on the surface caught fire. If reporters called Locust Street

'Street of Horror,' they now called the Wheaton fire 'The Fire on Shit Hole Lake.' That a body of water, once sacred to native Americans, had spontaneously burst into flames became a national joke and a huge stain on the reputation of the city. But it hadn't been funny to the people who were burned out. Several were killed and everyone in the torched community lost everything.

As I drove around looking at the damage, I wondered what Gallagher expected me to see. The residential destruction had been well covered on TV news. I found that much of the debris from the fire had already been bulldozed into piles.

What does he think I'll find that's so 'interesting'?

I circled the area a couple of times, then drove around the industrial sector. I asked myself what could have been the motive to create a toxic combustible slick on the surface of the lake and then set it afire. Perhaps, I thought, one of the companies wanted to expand into the residential area. In that case, it would be a lot quicker and cheaper to burn the houses down than to buy up each one, tear it down and then go through the laborious process of having the property re-zoned.

So which bad-actor industrial company could have done such an awful heartless deed? As I drove around, I read the signs. One company, Cobb Industries, dominated the Wheaton sector. I was already aware of this, but it hadn't previously registered with me in connection with the Watomi fire. Now I noticed that the burned-out residential neighborhood sat directly between two large Cobb paint factories. So . . . if they could get possession of that neighborhood and bribe their way through the permit process, they could build a new paint works and connect it to their existing complex at both ends.

It was just a theory, but it hit me hard in view of the Cobb connection to the murals. Of course, there was no way Gallagher could know about the murals or that its story was bound up with the Cobb family. But I couldn't help but feel thrilled by the notion that, by chance, my fire story and the murals story just might be linked.

It would have been a big scoop for me if I wrote up the Norm Hicks Jr arrest. But maybe if I waited, there'd be an even bigger scoop ahead. I phoned Gallagher on my way back to the city.

'OK,' I told him, 'I went out to Wheaton and looked around.'

I told him my theory that an industrial firm, such as Cobb Industries, had maybe started the Watomi Lake fire to burn out the community there, then acquire the land cheap.

'You're good, Joan. I continue to be impressed. We're thinking along the same lines. We're investigating the inflammables. A number of companies out there have been dumping into the lake at night.'

'Will you keep me up to date?'

'Will you hold off on firebug zero until we go in for an indictment?'

'Will you give me exclusive advance notice?'

'I promise you'll be the first to hear.'

I told him I'd have to check with my editor, but I was fairly sure he'd approve.

'I'm glad, Joan. Soon as we met, I knew we could work together.'

That afternoon, with Josh's approval, I wrote an article, the gist of which was that the summer fires were under intense investigation, that outside investigators had been brought in and that they were working from a secret location.

I wrote that the team was looking closely at the destructive Watomi Lake fire, which, according to a high-ranking member of the investigative unit, may have been set to look like the work of a psychotic arsonist, but in fact may have been started for financial reasons.

With Gallagher's permission, I quoted him as follows, identifying him as the same high-ranking source who, for security reasons, did not wish to be named:

> We are particularly distressed by Watomi and other fires we believe were set by people using the summer fires as a cover. For example, two fires were deliberately set at the homes of environmental activists. It seems there's an egregious element here that's taking advantage of the rash of summer fires to target people they don't like for political and ideological reasons. We're looking very hard at people who might harbor such motives.

When I turned in my piece, Josh loved it.

'Since this guy, Gallagher, admires persistence, stay persistent,' he advised. 'You're on to a major story, Joan. Don't let it get away.'

My piece ran the next morning, three columns wide on the front page below the fold:

CITY TERRORIZED BY SUMMER FIRES WHILE ARSON
INVESTIGATORS EXAMINE MULTIPLE MOTIVES

An Investigative Report by
JOAN NGUYEN

Congratulations poured in all day, including from Jase, Hannah and Tally. And, yes, I admit, I was thrilled!

Hannah Sachs

Jase and I checked into the Metropol on a Sunday afternoon, having booked the same room Jase stayed in before. The view of the front of Galerie Susanne Weber was even better than I expected. If all went as we hoped, the kindly go-between would turn up at the gallery the next day, pulling his roller-wheel suitcase with a new ragdoll inside.

As we settled in, I kidded Jase about whether he was planning to meet up with his gallery assistant friend.

'I expect you'll want to spend the evening with your old snuggle-bunny,' I taunted.

'Connie's a sweet kid,' he said. 'I still feel bad about deceiving her.' He smiled at me. 'No need since we're here together.'

Hmmm. I shrugged, even as I was looking forward to him making a move on me. Things had been kind of strained between us since our visit to Abiquiú, but so far on this trip our relations seemed to have improved.

Meantime, we had business to transact. We knew we needed professional help if we were to follow the go-between successfully. Through my brother, I'd contacted a local detective agency, Privatdetektiv Matthias Becker, about hiring a car and driver skilled in vehicle-to-vehicle surveillance. Herr Becker himself agreed to take on the job. That evening we were set to meet him for drinks to discuss what we had in mind.

He turned out to be a retired military officer who'd worked in Swiss Army CID. He was a big bear of a guy with granite-blue eyes, short-cropped gray hair and an excellent command of English. At a café-bar up the street, he told us that most of his work consisted of domestic investigations initiated by client spouses suspicious of their mates. This involved discovering whether the other spouse was engaged in extramarital activity and/or determining his/her financial assets in preparation for a divorce.

'It's ugly work, but, as I tell my wife, someone needs to do it. I've been threatened numerous times by angry men resentful that I've pried into their affairs. I laugh at the ones who make threats. It's the ones who eye me quietly I find dangerous.'

Jase told him that working with us would not be dangerous.

'It's a straightforward shadow job, right?' Becker asked.

I nodded, told him about the Ragdoll Artist and our belief that her go-between would turn up at Galerie Susanne Weber the following morning.

'The object,' Jase explained, 'is not only to identify her, but to obtain a photograph to compare with this one taken twenty-five years ago.'

Jase showed him the old *Times-Dispatch* photo of Courtney Cobb.

'You're probably wondering why we think it's the same person,' I said.

He nodded. 'I am, but I make a point of not prying into my clients' business. Unless, of course, I think there's something illegal involved.'

'Nothing illegal,' I assured him. Then I explained why, based on her artwork, we believed the Ragdoll Artist and an American girl might be one and the same.

I liked the way he perked up at that. Jase and I had discussed how much of our search we would disclose, agreeing that the more confidence we placed in Herr Becker, the more likely he'd do a good job for us. We agreed that we'd describe our quarry, but not reveal the identity of our informant, the snuggle-bunny, from whom Jase had found out about the go-between.

'Interesting case,' Becker said when I finished. 'You're hoping this go-between will lead you directly to the artist. It occurs to me that if there's an exchange involving cash, he may take it straight to a bank. Or he may wait a while before contacting the artist. What's your plan if he doesn't go straight to her?'

'We'll improvise, make a quick decision,' Jase explained. 'I've done a lot of that in my career.'

'Let's use first names, if that's all right,' I said. 'I'm Hannah. He's Jason.'

Herr Becker grinned. 'Call me Matthias. And don't worry. Even if we lose him, and I'll do my damnedest to see we don't, I'll have his plate number. Then it's an easy matter to run it through the Federal databank.'

We agreed to meet again early the following morning. Matthias and a female operative (I loved that he used that term) would park in front of the Metropol. I'd get into the backseat. Meanwhile, Jase would observe from our room. If/when the go-between showed up, Jase would record his arrival on video, then join us in the car. If the go-between set off on foot, the operative, named Hilda, would follow him. If the go-between hailed a cab or stepped into a parked vehicle, we'd drop Hilda off, then follow the gentleman to wherever he went.

In the best Swiss tradition, things proceeded as planned. Matthias and Hilda were waiting for me in a nondescript car. Hilda turned out to be a pretty brunette who looked about sixteen years old. When I asked her age, she proudly told me she was twenty-two.

'She's my niece,' Matthias said. 'The kind of young woman you'd see walking on the street around here.'

At ten a.m. a kindly-looking middle-aged man with a pointed beard and a roller-wheel suitcase stepped out of a taxi and rang the bell beside the gallery door. A middle-aged woman, evidently Frau Weber, opened the door, gestured him inside, then peered up and down Zuerichstrasse in a surreptitious manner, like a character in a crime show satire. Apparently satisfied no one was watching, she followed him inside and latched the door.

Jase, observing them through the zoom lens of his video camera, recorded their encounter, or as much of it as he could see through the front window of the gallery.

'Based on their gestures, I got the impression that they might have had something of a spat,' he told us when he came down to

the car. 'Perhaps the kindly gentleman tried to up his price or the
lady tried to lower hers.'

The go-between looked calm when he appeared in the doorway.
He and Frau Weber exchanged air kisses, then he walked with his
suitcase up the block as if looking for a cab. Hilda got out of the
car and started to follow him. Meantime, Frau Weber again peered
suspiciously up and down the street, an obvious signal she'd been
up to no good. Satisfied as before, she nodded to herself and went
back inside.

The three of us chuckled at her absurd behavior.

'That's what we call "a tell,"' Jase said.

When a cab stopped and the go-between got in, Matthias signaled
Hilda to return to the office.

We followed the cab to a garage on the edge of town, waited in
our vehicle while he paid off the driver and went inside. A couple
of minutes later he reappeared in the driver's seat of a big silver
sedan.

'For sure our go-between's not just a courier,' Matthias said.
'That's a Maybach S-650, one of the most expensive cars in
Europe.'

The go-between sped off. We followed him.

'He's heading to Zurich,' Matthias told us. 'The car's from there
and we're on A-14 which connects to A-4 then goes straight to
the city. It's about a forty-minute drive.' He activated his dashboard
speaker phone, called Hilda and instructed her to run the plate. A
couple of minutes later the answer came back.

'The car's registered to a Doctor Franz DeJonghe d'Ardoye of
the Privatklinik DeJonghe, situated between Männedorf and Meilen
on the eastern shore of Lake Zurich,' Hilda said. 'Please hold
while I check the internet.'

'We call that shore the Gold Coast,' Matthias explained, 'because
it's bathed in sunlight all winter long, and because of the very
high price of properties there.'

Hilda came back on. 'OK, I found it. Privatklinik DeJonghe
specializes in long-term psychiatric care.'

Jason grinned at me. 'Bingo!'

We followed the Maybach to the gate of a walled villa on the lake
side of Seestrasse. The gate swung open, the Maybach drove in,

and the gate closed immediately behind. Impossible to see in from the road. The wall was high and the vegetation dense. Matthias pulled over, brought out his laptop and accessed a satellite image of the property. We made out a compound consisting of a large main house, outbuildings, rectangular pool, tennis court, small woods and, down at the lake, a marina and boats.

'Quite the luxurious clinic,' Matthias said. 'Switzerland is famous for places like this, where rich people can stash disturbed family members.'

'And then forget about them?' I asked.

'Sometimes that too,' Matthias said.

We asked him to find out what he could about the clinic. He agreed, drove us back to Meilen, then stopped at the centrally located café.

'In a small town, this is always the best place to make inquiries.'

We waited in the car while Matthias went in to speak with the cashier. He was smiling when he came out.

'Most of the clinic personnel live here in town. After work they hang out at a tavern called Schwarze Katzenbar, The Black Cat. It's just a couple blocks away.'

'A bar's a good place to meet people and get them to talk,' Jase said.

'The best place,' Matthias agreed. 'Let's go there and see what we can find out.'

The sign above the door of Schwarze Katzenbar showed the silhouette of a black cat on patrol. The tavern was nearly empty. We went to the bar, ordered sandwiches and beers. I peered around while Matthias chatted with the bartender.

I wouldn't describe it as a dive. It struck me as more of a cozy neighborhood pub, complete with dartboard, booths, and a wall sporting a dozen large taxidermy-mounted freshwater game fish interspersed with assorted Lake Zurich memorabilia.

Matthias introduced us to the bartender. 'This is Peter. He owns the place. He named it the Black Cat after he saw that name on a bar in an American movie.' We shook hands. 'He says the clinic people usually come in after six. He's heard a couple of them complaining about the head doctor. If I come back then, he'll introduce me around. As I'm sure you know, discontented employees make excellent sources.'

*   *   *

Matthias helped us check into the Beau Séjour au Lac, a luxury hotel famous, he told us, for its excellent cuisine. We sat around the lobby listening to his private-eye war stories, then, once the sky began to darken, headed back to Schwarze Katzenbar.

The place had filled up. There was a convivial hum. We took a booth against a wall, then Matthias excused himself.

'Sit tight while I work the room,' he said. 'If I find a good source, I'll bring him or her back.' He winked at me. 'I think a her would be better, don't you. Hannah?'

'They usually are,' I agreed.

We watched, impressed by his light-footed moves as he worked his way down the bar, evidently introduced by Peter to likely prospects, exchanging friendly greetings, finally taking a stool beside a forty-something woman and engaging her in what looked to be light-hearted banter. After a while they both turned toward the booth. Matthias pointed us out. We waved, and the woman waved back. They spoke a while longer, then he guided her to our table.

'This is Frau Zellweger. She speaks excellent English.'

'You can call me Thérèse,' she said, showing us a smile. She was blond, had big blue eyes and a soft, lightly accented voice.

'Thérèse knows the Ragdoll Artist,' Matthias said. 'She sees her every day.'

Jase showed her our photo of Courtney. 'Yes, that's her,' she said. 'We call her Agnès.'

When I asked if she'd be willing to take some pictures of Agnès, Thérèse said she'd be glad to.

'Great!' Jase said. 'Can we pay you something for your trouble?'

She shook her head. 'I'm happy to help. I don't believe Agnès is her real name, but that's the name she answers to. She's American and, I believe, a sad soul. I'm happy someone's interested in her. This gives me hope that someday she may be rescued.'

I seized on that. 'You think she needs rescuing?'

'I do,' Thérèse said. 'She's been in the clinic a long time. I've worked there seven years and she was there long before I came.'

'Thérèse says the man driving the Maybach was Doctor DeJonghe,' Matthias said.

'He never lets anyone else drive that car,' Thérèse confirmed.

Her distaste for the doctor was unmistakable. But to be sure and to make her complicit, I asked her point-blank what she thought of him.

'He's a scoundrel,' she said, tightening her lips, 'a despicable man. As I know all too well,' she added, suggesting severe disillusionment, perhaps prior intimacy gone bad. 'Anything you can do to help dear Agnès escape his claws, please count on me to assist.'

She spoke with such force that I didn't doubt she meant every word.

'I'm here with friends,' she told us. 'I must get back to them.'

We arranged to meet during her lunch hour the following day. She'd take photographs in the morning and bring them to our hotel.

'What do you think?' Matthias asked as we watched her drift back to the bar.

'It's been an amazing day,' Jase told him. 'Everything fell into place. We couldn't have done any of it without you, Matthias. Hilda, too. You've been terrific.'

'It's been fun for me too, Jason. Finally, an interesting case. Don't hesitate to call me if you need anything else.'

He dropped us at the Beau Séjour au Lac, we embraced, then watched him as he drove off, heading back to Lucerne.

That night Jase and I made love. It had been a while. It felt good to again be in his arms.

'Your snuggle-bunny really came through for you,' I told him later as we rehashed the day. 'The guy turned up just as she said. Evidently, you give great cuddle.'

'Do you really think?' he asked.

'Why don't you give me a sample?'

He did. As he held me, we giggled together over the door antics of gallerist Susanne Weber.

Thérèse showed up as promised just after noon with a half dozen photos on her cellphone, which we transferred to ours. We then invited her to lunch with us in the hotel dining room where we ordered the house specialties: Lake Zurich fish soup followed by delicious pike-perch fillets in potato crust.

As we ate, Jase placed his phone on the table to record, with her permission, everything she cared to tell us about Dr DeJonghe, the patient named Agnès, and another patient named Johnny who had recently befriended Agnès.

Thérèse Zellweger

D r DeJ – I despise the man! Reasons? Many! For one thing, he's a selfish lover. Back in the days when we were involved, he was solely interested in his own pleasure and cared not a whit for mine. Oh, he pretended to! He's quite the actor! But when I complained, he'd twist things around and put the blame on me.

'Your fault,' he'd tell me. 'You're denying yourself pleasure. Many neurotic women are like that.'

Typical! But what else should I expect from such a Great Psychiatrist!

This was four years ago. We haven't touched one another since. He's moved on to other clinic employees – Nora, Noemi, and probably others I don't even know about.

Not that I care! Let's be clear about that!

For another thing, the man's a phony – false right down to his core. I could give you plenty of examples, but I can see you're really interested in this business with Agnès. Even there he showed himself false. He told her he was keeping her dolls safe for her, that he was concerned that if she left them around, someone would steal one and give it to his kid, and clearly her dolls weren't meant for kids. Ha!

I know what he did with them. We all knew. He sold them, for quite a pretty penny too, is what I heard. One day Nora's boyfriend, Hans, searched on the internet and found they were being sold at a Lucerne gallery for tens of thousands of Euros.

He was the Great Docteur DeJonghe d'Ardoye, of high Belgium nobility, trained in Jungian psychoanalytic practice, owner and proprietor of the exclusive Privatklinik DeJonghe. What a hoot! I think the name's as phony as he is. We all call him Dr DeJ. As for his Jungian training, Nora and I did some research on that. Turns out he was dismissed from the Jung Institute for – guess what? – inappropriate sexual comments and non-consensual touching. Women there regarded him as a serial predator.

So why, you may ask, do we continue to work for an employer

for whom we have so little respect? One reason only: he pays better than anyone else on the lake. In return, he expects loyalty and 'amorous availability.' I'm sure you know what that means.

So, are we sluts? Some call us that in order to shame us. In truth, we're keen to see how this charade of his plays out. We await the debacle.

Two things you should know. First, the charges for residential treatment at the clinic are exorbitant, far higher than at comparable facilities. The monthly rate can exceed forty thousand Swiss francs. Can you believe it?

I don't know what Agnès's family pays. She's been there for years, the most senior long-term resident. Her fee arrangement is probably less, perhaps 250,000 Francs per year. What does she get for that? Twice-a-week psychotherapy sessions with the Great Man, customized drug treatment, special macrobiotic diet, lovely two-room suite with a lake view on the second floor of the main chalet, and all the bits and pieces of fabric rags she needs to create those bizarre dolls of hers.

Here's something else you should know. I have been working there for seven years, and never once in all that time has she had a visitor. Not one! Nurses who've been there longer report the same. It's possible she hasn't had a visitor in decades! I don't know the exact number of years she's been there. All the patient files are locked. Only the Great Doctor can access them. But, yes, decades seems about right. I hear that before she started making the dolls, she did a lot of sketching. There's a big stack of sketchbooks in one of her closets. I expect they represent many years of work.

She rarely speaks. When she does, it's usually in a whisper. She doesn't fraternize with other patients, yet she doesn't appear to be lonely. She seems to live very much in her own world. I'd describe her as gentle, but then those dolls she makes aren't gentle at all. She doesn't require much care from us. She pretty much takes care of herself in terms of dressing, bathing, that sort of thing. Basically, she's being stored. In certain ways I'd describe Privatklinik DeJonghe as less a psychiatric facility than a place to store difficult people about whose very existences their families would just as soon forget.

But then along came Johnny!

He's nineteen, still has adolescent spots on his face, is brilliant and also quite disturbed. Like several patients there, he says his family doesn't care for him. At least he talks about it, which is more than Agnès does. In fact, that boy will talk on and on, even if no one's listening.

I'm not sure why he started coming on to Agnès. She's more than twice his age. Now they're inseparable. This strange, silent American woman, who couldn't abide the company of anyone, now hangs out a good part of every day with this gay English lad.

None of us can explain it. When I asked Johnny, he shrugged.

'I like her, plain and simple,' he told me. 'Does there always have to be an effing explanation?'

He likes to throw curse words into conversations. He thinks they shock us. They don't.

Maybe he's right: there is no way to explain it, except to view them as two lost souls who found one another in the crazy little hot-house world of the clinic.

I'll tell you something else about Johnny. He's kind. He feels a lot of pain, I think, on account of rejection by his family. Far as I know, his only visitor has been his older sister. He worships her. Maybe that's why he's bonded with Agnès. Even though he's gay, he likes strong older women. Agnès, being so self-sufficient, could appeal to that need. He told me once that he was 'honored' by her acceptance of him. The fact that she opened herself to friendship with him, while rejecting interaction with everyone else, tells him he has value in her eyes. Also, he admires her artwork.

Back to the Great Doctor. He's got everyone there, including Agnès and Johnny, on serious drug regimes, capsules he has specially made up by a German compounding lab. He claims these drugs are both antidepressant and antipsychotic. When I asked him what was in them, he said it was a custom combination similar to a mix of Zyprexa, Celexa and Tranxilium and a few other things. Sounds nutty to me, but I'm just a psychiatric nurse.

I don't know where things are going with Agnès. I've detected changes in her since she's gotten close to Johnny. There's something conspiratorial about them of late – whisperings and knowing glances, that sort of thing. Dr DeJ has noticed too. He's asked me about it several times. 'I have a feeling they're cooking something up,' he said. 'Any idea what it could be?'

I shrug. Even if I knew, I wouldn't tell him. We'll just have to see, won't we? Personally, I think it would be good if they did cook something up and actually saw it through . . .

Jason Poe

'd been more upset than I let on by Elizabeth Schechtner's query: *What is it about those murals, Jason, that has you so riled?*

Yes, she wanted to deflect us from inquiring too deeply into the odd way she and Dr Ted had behaved. Still, she had a point. I knew my obsession with the murals was based on something more than their visual power. They had reached me on a subconscious level, probably because I read them as being about trauma and pain. Was that what drove my obsession? Was my quest to solve the mystery of the murals actually a quest to understand myself? I couldn't help wonder about that even as so much new info poured in.

Hannah and I had not only located the Ragdoll Artist, we also had photos which left no doubt that she and Courtney Cobb were one and the same. And then there was our recording of the rant of the nurse, Thérèse, a bizarre tale to the effect that Courtney, friendless and alone, had been sealed up for decades by her family in an ultra-expensive Swiss sanatorium where a Svengali-like psychiatrist kept her on a drug regime while covertly selling her much-coveted rag dolls, apparently for his own account.

I had a lot of trouble grappling with that, and it infuriated Hannah. She saw evil and wanted us to do something about it.

'What *can* we do?' I asked.

'Try to get her out of there.'

'How? And to what end? She's clearly disturbed. From everything we discovered, she's been that way most of her life.'

'But to be abandoned by her family, locked away in a foreign country under another name, unvisited for decades – truthfully, Jase, don't you think that's a scandal?'

Of course it was a scandal! But how could we get her out of that clinic? What standing did we have to do so? And if we did get her out, where would she go? In spite of her circumstances, she'd continued to make art. In fact, I suggested, maybe her situation wasn't all that awful. She was, I reminded Hannah, a permanent resident at one of the most luxurious private clinics in Europe.

That's when Hannah got really pissed. She knew what I'd said was true, but felt that we, as artists, had a responsibility. A fellow artist was in trouble. Didn't we have an obligation to do something about it?

'When you acquiesce to something like this, you become an accomplice,' she told me angrily. 'Think about that, Jase.' And with that she returned to her loft.

I *did* think about it. I asked myself if indeed we did have that responsibility. The longer I thought about it, the more clearly I saw that Hannah was right. I think what got to me most was Courtney's loneliness. I couldn't bear the thought that she'd been living in that clinic for decades without having once been visited by anyone. In effect, she'd been left behind, discarded the same way those objects I photographed for *Leavings* had been – abandoned and forsaken.

Hannah's sense of indignation was one of the things I loved best about her. I phoned her, told her how much I regretted not immediately seeing her point.

'Yes, we have to try to get her out,' I said.

'I knew you'd come around, Jase. I'm going to see my brother tomorrow, get his advice. Maybe there's nothing we can do for Courtney, but I don't want to give up without giving it a shot.'

Hannah's brother, Noah Sachs, was a prominent Calista attorney. His firm, Conway & Sachs, specialized in the representation of white-collar defendants. Noah, Hannah told me, would be the first to admit that he often represented unpleasant people. To compensate, he undertook carefully selected pro bono cases representing illegally fired whistleblowers, victims of lawyers who'd weaponized the legal system, people whose reputations had been damaged by slanderous and libelous statements. So perhaps, Hannah reasoned, Noah would take on a pro bono case on behalf of Courtney Cobb.

I asked to come along.

'Of course!' she said. 'We're in this together.'

Noah always struck me as headstrong, rigid in his convictions. Hannah assured me that was just the front he presented to the world.

'He takes after our grandfather,' she said.

Hannah had told me a lot about David Sachs, a tough businessman who'd built a small bicycle company into the country's largest manufacturer of ball bearings. He'd made a fortune on government contracts during World War II, built himself a Tudor-style lakeside mansion where he resided in baronial splendor surrounded by paintings by his beloved artists of what he called the 'Jewish School of Paris' – Pissarro, Chagal, Soutine, Kisling, Sonia Delaunay, Max Jacob, Leopold Gottlieb and Louis Marcoussis.

'Noah, like Grandpa, wears a hard mask, but he's got a gentle heart. If we can interest him in Courtney, he'll think of a way to help her.'

The offices of Conway & Sachs were on the fortieth floor of the Tower of the Great Lakes, one of Calista's landmark twin skyscrapers. The firm's reception area was done up in high modern – sleek black leather couches, marble table for the receptionist, one of Hannah's large abstract weavings displayed on the wall behind.

We were greeted by a well-groomed brunette. She introduced herself as Kim Barnes and escorted us back to Noah's office. Noah, whose features resembled Hannah's, had grown a goatee since I'd last seen him. When I admired his office view, he led me to one of the floor-to-ceiling windows.

'Gorgeous, isn't it?' he said, 'The city, I mean. It even looks good on miserable rainy days. From here, you'd never know what a dump it is.' He turned to Hannah. 'Shouldn't say that, should I, Sis? This town's been good to us.' He took a seat behind his desk. 'I'm glad the Swiss detective worked out. What can I do for you today?'

Hannah did most of the talking, with me throwing in a detail here and there. She laid out Courtney's situation with accuracy and passion. Watching Noah, I could see him getting hooked.

'Holy shit!' he said when she finished. He turned to me. 'All this because you happened to stumble into some murals in the attic of an abandoned house!'

Hannah brought out our portable model of the murals to show him what we were talking about.

He studied them. 'Fascinating,' he said. 'Also strange. I can see why you got into this.' He sat back. 'So, twenty-five years ago this girl was abducted. Now she's a middle-aged woman living in a Swiss clinic. Even if she needs care, I doubt you can commit an adult without consent to a mental facility in a foreign country. Here's how I see the issues: Did she give consent? Does she understand where she is and why she's there? Has her family forgotten her, or are they fully aware of her situation? Is this shrink actually selling her artwork for his own account or is he applying the money to her maintenance at his clinic? If she's the heiress to a fortune, who controls her money? And the big one: Was there family abuse, and, if there was, is she capable of coming back and giving coherent testimony to that effect?'

He pushed a button on his intercom. 'Kim, find out if there's a statute of limitations on family abuse.'

He turned back to us. 'Way I see it, *if* she's been abandoned in this clinic without her consent, and *if* her doctor is stealing from her, and *if* her inherited funds are being illegally kept from her, and *if* a provable case can be made for past abuse, then, *if* she wants to leave, there's an excellent chance she can be rescued.'

He paused. 'You know how powerful the Cobbs are. If I get into this, they won't like it. I knew them slightly at school. Never liked them. I've heard lots of unsavory stories over the years about their business practices and personal lives. All that makes me inclined to take this on. Let's say we go to war on Courtney's behalf. Let's say we get her free of the clinic with her funds restored. What then? Where does she go? Is she capable of living on her own? If not, who'll take care of her? Have you considered all that?'

Hannah told him that we had. One of our ideas was that she could voluntarily commit herself to a top-notch American institution where she could continue making art.

'There's this famous Japanese artist, Yayoi Kusama, now nearly ninety,' she said, 'More than forty years ago she committed herself to the Seiwa Hospital for the Mentally Ill. She's lived there ever since.'

'The one who makes the polka-dot stuff?'

Hannah nodded. 'I think she'd be a good model for Courtney, if Courtney wants to go that way.'

'That's the underlying issue. What *does* Courtney want? Suppose she's happy where she is and doesn't want to leave? Moving after all these years could be traumatic. And it's possible she's designated this shrink as her agent.'

'Good questions,' Hannah told him. 'We don't know the answers.'

The intercom buzzed. Noah switched it on.

'The limitation's twenty years,' Kim said.

He turned back to us. 'That settles it as far as making this a criminal matter. But we could still bring a civil action if we could prove abuse.'

He peered at Hannah. 'I had no idea you were bringing me something like this. Believe me, I'm appalled. I suspect her money's in trust and the trust is paying the clinic. I'll look into that. Something tells me the Cobb boys may have written her off since their parents' deaths. That no one's ever visited her in all the years – that could make for a good argument that someone outside the family should take over as legal guardian. But you two are going to have to find stuff out. It won't be easy. Someone's gotta talk to her, hear her side of this. Most important, find out what she wants. As for the shrink, if he refuses to let anyone talk to her, that would suggest she's being held against her will. In that case, the dirty deal you taped in Lucerne could give you leverage. I can't imagine he'd be happy to be exposed for stealing and selling a patient's artwork. Finally, if you can get some evidence of child-hood abuse, that would help a lot. Think about it. Meantime, I'll do my part. This'll be pro bono. Aside from the considerable merits of the case, I can't tell you how much I'd love to take the Cobb boys down.'

We left his office totally wired. There was a ritzy restaurant-bar, Comme Chez Soi, on the ground floor of the Tower of the Great Lakes.

I peered in through the window. 'Looks like they're having a happy hour. How 'bout we have ourselves a quiet drink?'

Hannah said she thought that was an excellent idea.

'I'm starting to like your brother,' I told her after we sat down and ordered. 'He *is* smart. And your idea of Courtney following the example of Yayoi Kusama is brilliant. But proving abuse twenty-five years after the fact – how can we possibly do that? We don't even know if she actually was abused. If she testifies that she was, it'll be her word against theirs. Still, I doubt they'd want to answer to that in a public trial.'

'Noah made it obvious that he despises them.'

'Any idea why?'

'They went to Richmond when it was still an all-boys school. Maybe something happened there. Back then Richmond only went through eighth grade, then the kids went east to boarding schools. Noah went to Exeter. I think the Cobb boys went on to St Pauls.'

'So you think it could be an old rivalry thing?'

'More likely it's about those unsavory stories he's heard. Noah's always been a moralist.'

'Whatever the reason, he's motivated. To me, that's really all that matters.'

Something was gnawing at me. What if I was wrong and the Cobbs didn't care if they went to trial? What if they said, 'Go ahead, put her on the stand, she's schizo, no one'll believe her.' How the hell do you prove abuse so long after the fact?

I was deep into sleep that night . . . then suddenly woke up.

The bedrolls!

I checked the clock. Two a.m.

Those fucking bedrolls – why didn't I think to look inside?

I waited until eight to call Cindy.

'I need to go back in,' I told her. 'This time I hope you'll come in with me.'

'Not sure I'm up for that,' she said.

'I think you owe it to yourself to really look at the murals. There're on your walls. You own them. Maybe you can put aside your feelings about betraying the Schechtners and look at them as a work of art.'

'You sound edgy, Jason.'

'I *am* edgy. I need to get in there.'

'What's the big deal?'

'The girls' bedrolls. There're still up there. Maybe there's something inside them. Sketches, notebooks, a diary . . . or maybe nothing. Won't know till I look.'

She went silent. I heard her breathing rapidly. Then she meekly agreed to meet me at the house at noon.

When I got there, I found her sitting in her car. I got in beside her.

'I'm nervous,' she said. 'Not sure I want to do this.'

'What're you afraid of?'

'I don't like to cry,' she said.

'Look,' I told her, 'I'm not a therapist. Not my role to give you advice. But if I were you, I'd want to face my feelings and try to overcome them. By staying here in the car, staring at the house, you're giving it too much power. You'll feel better if you come inside and, you know, face your demons.'

She smiled. 'I like that! Reminds me of Doc Liz. So – OK,' she nodded, 'let's do this.'

I stayed with her as she peered around the first floor. I'd given her a flashlight so she could explore on her own, but she seemed reluctant to leave my side. As eager as I was to rush up to the attic, I thought it best to stay with her as she slowly made her way around. She stood in the dining area a while, likely recalling the night the cops burst in during dinner on account of her betrayal.

She touched the back of one of the dining chairs. 'I don't think I'm going to cry this time,' she whispered. 'Thanks, Jason, for bringing me in.'

She pointed at the huge 666 spray-painted on the wall.

'Phony!' she said. 'That was never there. The cops must have sprayed it on.'

On the second floor, she showed me her old room. 'That's my bunk,' she said, pointing to an upper berth. 'I wonder . . .' She looked at the mess of clothing strewn about. 'Some of that stuff is probably mine.'

On the third floor, standing with me as I pulled down the ladder, she asked if she could go up first.

'Of course,' I said. I fitted her with a headband lamp. 'Go on up. Take your time. I'll wait here until you call me.'

She nodded, started up the ladder. She paused halfway up. 'I see them. This is exciting!'

From the bottom of the ladder I could hear her exclaim. 'Wow! Jesus! Holy shit! I can't believe this!' she said. 'Come up, Jason. Help me look at them.'

When I got up there and stood beside her, she grasped my hand and mumbled something to the effect that the murals were so strong she could hardly bear to meet the eyes of the people in them. 'But there's no turning away from them, is there? Those eyes are on you, no matter which way you turn.' She glanced at me. 'The murals envelop you. That's their power, isn't it? We're in here with these people and there's no escape.'

This was my third visit to the attic, my third viewing of the murals. I stared at them, awestruck. They struck me with the same power as they had the night I first stumbled upon them.

After a while I left her side, went to the wall, knelt and felt the bedrolls. I didn't want to open them in the attic, but I squeezed them hoping to feel something solid inside. I couldn't feel anything, but that didn't mean there wasn't anything there.

'OK if I leave you here and take these downstairs?' I asked.

'Go,' she said. 'I'll stay a while. There's more power up here than in the whole rest of the house. I think these murals are what I've been afraid of facing all along.'

I carried the bedrolls out to the front stoop, laid them down on the planking, unraveled the first and unzipped it. Nothing inside but padding and a musty smell. The second one was thicker. I found a cardboard tube inside. Excited, I pulled it out and extracted a bundle of yellowed papers. *Sketches!* There were a dozen or so preliminary drawings for the murals – and, even more interesting, a schematic diagram showing all four walls with initials inscribed above stick drawings of the figures.

It was easy to decode the initials of Cobb family members: 'A' and 'F' (Courtney's grandparents, Alfred and Florence Cobb); 'H' and 'E' (her parents, Horace and Elena); 'J' and 'K' (her brothers, Jack and Kevin). Each of these six appeared twice, on opposing walls. The little girl and the puppy were designated 'Me' and 'Bonnie.'

There were other initials representing people on the other two opposing walls. Some were captioned with question marks. Perhaps these were figures from Penny Dawson's life.

I was taking all this in when Cindy emerged from the house. No longer tense, she wore the same expression of relief I'd seen on her after she'd made her confession in her gallery.

'What do you think?' I asked.

'I felt I was looking at the kind of evil people you'd see if you visited hell. But since the figures' faces are cold and blank, my reading that into them probably says a lot about me.'

'What are you reading into them?'

'Violence, violation, despoiling, defilement, malevolence.' She shook her head as if to shake off the horror. 'Looks like you found something in the bedrolls,' she said.

I showed her the sketches and the schematic.

'This is a key,' I told her. 'We already knew about the grand-parents. I don't think the identities of the others matter much. The Cobb family – they're the principals.'

'It's more what they represent than who they were, isn't it?' she said. 'Anyway, when I was up there, I made a decision.'

'A wise one, I hope.'

She nodded. 'I agree with you and Hannah – the murals are important and should be preserved. I'm going to bring in a conservator to see what can be done about removing and salvaging them. The plywood panels are fitted tight. That could be a problem. There could be some loss of paint when they're taken off the walls. It would have to be done carefully by experts. One good thing – they painted with acrylic. That holds up well.' She smiled at me. 'So . . . wise enough for you, Jason?'

Noah Sachs

L istening to Joan Nguyen's recorded interview with Nate Silver, I had a feeling he'd held a lot back. He'd been well known around the State Bar as old man Cobb's *consigliere*. Impossible he didn't know where the family had stashed Courtney and the details of her trust.

I called him, set up an appointment.

'Sure, Noah – come on out. Be nice to see you. Wanna tell me what this is about?'

'I'll tell you when I see you,' I said.

The part in Joan's interview about the Mayfair Club rang true. Our dad knew Nate through business. In the old days of genteel anti-Semitism, they'd stood out in Calista as the kind of Jews you wouldn't mind bringing into the Mayfair as guests, and possibly, to demonstrate your open-mindedness, putting up for membership, even though you knew they'd be black-balled.

It was a lovely day. I liked getting out of the city. On the way out to Desmond House, I listed to Bach on my car CD player.

Nate was waiting in the lobby. He guided me to the visitors' room where he and Joan had talked. He looked dapper, dressed in a tan-and-green window-pane sports jacket with one of his trademark silk ascots around his neck.

His manner struck me as obsequious. I declined when he offered to show me around. I'd come out there for information, so I got straight to the point.

'I listened to the recording of your interview with Joan Nguyen.'

'Good-looking Asian girl. Clever, too. She didn't mention she was working with you.'

'Back then she wasn't. Now we're on the same team. Some things you said raised red flags.'

'What team are you both now on, if I may be so bold?'

'A team that has located Courtney Cobb and intends to help her regain her rights.'

For a moment he looked stricken. Then he regained his poise. 'Sorry, Noah, I can't talk to you about this, attorney–client privilege and all.'

'You'll talk to me now or when I put you under oath. Your choice, Nate. You're hiding something. I can feel it. Frankly, I'm surprised you're willing to protect the Cobb brothers after the way they dumped you when the old man died, and turned their business over to those douchebags at Kline Krechner.'

'You're serious.'

'I am.'

'What do you want to know?'

'Four things. What's the deal with Courtney's money? Second, who put her in that Swiss clinic where the psychiatrist-proprietor sells her artwork and keeps the money for himself? Third, what's the deal with Courtney's problems with her family? I don't believe Courtney didn't talk about that to the "high-powered shrink" Horace brought in from Boston. Fourth, why'd she run away from home?'

Nate sighed. 'Horace never said much about that, just that he thought his daughter was off her rocker and he wasn't about to let her ruin the boys' lives.'

'Ruin how?'

'No idea.'

'This Boston shrink – what's her name?'

'No idea on that either. Anyway, I doubt she's still around.'

'You know the law, Nate. When a patient tells a shrink about a crime, the shrink must report it. Did Horace pay her off?'

He shrugged. 'Could have. He certainly didn't want Courtney's story getting out.'

'What story?'

'Beats me.'

'What's the deal with her money?'

'Horace and Elena were the trustees. When they died, the trusteeship was taken over by the Boston wealth management firm that was handling Elena's family's money.'

'Who's Courtney's guardian? Who has power of attorney?'

'I guess I do.'

'*You guess?*'

'I haven't thought about it in years.'

'Let me get this straight, Nate. Her parents stick her in this posh private clinic in Switzerland, they pass away, control of her money goes to some wealth management folks who never met her, you have custodial and fiduciary responsibility . . . and yet you never considered that as such you were and still are responsible for her welfare? Sounds like Courtney's the proverbial "forgotten child."'

'I had no idea anyone was stealing from her.'

'And, of course, you didn't know she makes art dolls that sell for tens of thousands of dollars.'

He shook his head. I could see he was scared. I moved to take advantage of his fear.

'I'm hiring you.' I pulled out my wallet, handed him a ten-dollar bill. 'Here's your fee.'

He laughed. 'TV show bullshit, Noah. You know that.'

'The Cobbs aren't to hear about this conversation.'

He smirked, took the ten, folded it neatly and placed it behind his pocket square.

'They won't hear about it. Surprised?'

'Actually, I'm not. That's the smart move, Nate. Dad always said you were a smart cookie.'

'I liked your dad.'

'He liked you too. Now, here's what I want you to do . . .'

I instructed him to demand a full statement of Courtney's assets from the Boston firm, and a list of all expenditures paid on her behalf for the past ten years, including management fees. If Courtney owned stock in Cobb Industries, as I assumed she did, I wanted to know how many shares and what voting rights she had. Finally, in future I wanted him to take instruction from me in regard to his custodial and fiduciary responsibilities. I made it clear that if he didn't go along, I'd take him to court where I'd show he'd done zip on Courtney's behalf and for that should be stripped of his guardianship.

He grinned to himself. 'Then Kevin and Jack will take control. That what you want?'

'They won't get control if they abused her.'

'Best of luck proving that!' Then he said he'd do as I'd asked.

He saw me to the front entrance of Desmond House, where we shook hands like the gentlemen we both wished we were.

'Nice to see you, Noah,' he said. 'Let's play golf one of these days.'

'Don't like golf. Tennis is my game,' I told him.

His grin sagged, then he looked away. He started toward the front door of Desmond House. Then he turned again and walked back to where I stood.

'On that proof thing – I've got a suggestion. Don't know why I'm giving you this, but here it is. See if you can dig up old Spencer Addams. I heard there was some kind of deal. If he's still around, maybe he'll remember what it was.'

I knew why Nate had offered that suggestion. It was because I'd reminded him how he'd been screwed, how Jack and Kevin had fired him and turned over the Cobb business account to a rival firm. Just the kind of thing you never forgive.

I put Vivaldi's *Four Seasons* on the CD player as I drove back to the city, eager to tell Jason and Hannah that the Courtney Cobb matter was now in play.

Joan Nguyen

S uddenly, the focus was on Penny Dawson.

'You've got to find her, Joan,' Hannah told me. 'You know she's down in the Keys. She's the only one who knows the full story. Find her – please!'

I'd made contact, spoken briefly with her, then she'd hung up. If she was really living on the Florida Keys, finding her shouldn't be that difficult.

There were no Dawsons in the Keys directory.

Penny might be her given name, or her nickname if her first name was actually Penelope. Or she might be listed as P-something, or not listed at all. She'd gotten her BFA at the San Francisco Art Institute. She was enrolled there in 1989. I suggested to Hannah that she get her contact address through CAI administration.

'I'll ask Rob Kraus first thing in the morning,' Hannah said.

She called me the next day. She had Penny's new name, Penelope Ruiz, c/o The Ruiz Gallery on Catherine Street in Key West. I looked it up, jotted down the phone number, then Googled the address. The satellite view showed a small white-roofed structure set back from the street. The street view showed just the barest glimmer of the building submerged in what looked like a tropical jungle.

She'd hung up on me once. Jason said I'd probably get just one more shot at her. He wanted me to travel down there, sniff around, then figure out the best way to approach her. If she balked or got pissed off, I'd lose my chance.

'First step is gain her confidence,' Jason advised. 'Once you do that, you can start asking her stuff. If she acts skittish, give her room, make it clear you're not trying to corner her and you're not in a rush.'

Like I needed him to explain how to approach a reluctant source!

'I have a master's from Columbia School of Journalism,' I reminded him.

I flew down to Miami, picked up a rental car and drove down to the Keys. It's an amazing four-hour, one-hundred-thirteen-mile, forty-two-bridges-long drive on a two-lane causeway with water on either side. US Route One, known by some as the Magic Carpet. The islands slip by – Key Largo, Plantation, Islamorada, Duck, Marathon, Big Pine, Sugarloaf and numerous small mangrove islands in between. Then at the end of the line, Key West, south-ernmost point of the continental USA.

I saw plenty of hurricane damage en route – smashed-up boats, collapsed motels, battered bait shops. At one point I passed a gas station ripped in three.

It was late afternoon when I pulled into Key West. Leaving the highway, weaving my way through quiet shady streets, I felt as if I'd entered another world. The tropical air carried an aroma of rotting flowers. The streets were lined with old wooden buildings – shacks, houses, mansions all mixed together, some decaying, others well kept. There was an aura of decadence and also seduction. I loved the plantings: jacarandas, hibiscus, fountains of bougainvillea pouring off the balconies.

I stopped near the Ruiz Gallery, parked, got out and walked slowly by the place. The vegetation was so dense it was difficult to see in, but I did catch a glimpse of a woman standing in front of a large table. There was a simple waist-high gate and an uneven stone walk leading to the front door, also a sign designating the gallery as a framing shop, and a poster mounted on a board attached to the fence showing an image of a watercolor seascape and the caption *Paintings by Penny*.

The watercolor was slickly executed, the kind of cheap artwork a tourist might buy as a souvenir. Nothing like the murals, or even something a grad of a first-rate art school would produce, unless she was just turning stuff out to pay for rent and groceries.

I strode up to the corner, turned and thought about how to approach her. A black-and-white cat scampered by, then slid under a fence and disappeared. I peered around. Two old men, possibly Cuban, were sitting on a veranda, playing checkers and sipping drinks. A woman the same age sat apart, knitting. It was starting to get dark and I hadn't yet found a place to sleep. Would I be better off waiting until the next day, scoping the place out, maybe waiting for Penny to leave, then following her as she made her rounds? Or might I do better to go into the gallery and introduce myself right now, then ask her advice on a place to stay, and see if she'd meet with me in the morning?

Go for it! And so I did.

She smiled when I told her my name.

'Well, here you are! You found me! I'm glad,' she said without any irony.

She was a good-looking middle-aged woman with a handsome sunburnt triangular face, large intense blue-gray eyes and thick graying hair cut into a rough shag. Her features matched the old newspaper photo I'd dug up in the *Times-Dispatch* morgue – older, of course, showing wear, but unquestionably the woman I'd come to meet.

I could detect no trace of vanity. Her body was thin and angular.

She wore jeans and a blue denim work shirt, bare feet with unpol-
ished nails shod in a pair of worn flip-flops. There was an amulet
of some sort hanging from a thong around her neck. There was
something a bit butch about her, but I wasn't ready yet to regard
her as lesbian.

'You were expecting me?' I asked. '*Really?*'

'Not expecting exactly, but wondering if you'd track me down.
Not that I'm hard to find. I've been living down here fifteen years,
had the gallery for ten.'

'So you're not surprised?'

'Should I be?'

'You said you'd call me back.'

She grinned. 'I believe I said I'd think about it.'

'But you didn't.'

'Guess I figured if there was something important on your mind,
you'd either call or turn up here in person.'

'Can we talk now, or should I come back another time?'

'Now's fine,' she said.

She asked where I was staying and seemed lightly surprised I
hadn't yet settled in. She told me about a woman's guesthouse
several blocks away, called the owner, booked me a room, drew
me a little map so I'd have no trouble finding it, then wrote down
the name of a small Cuban restaurant not too far away.

'Rest up,' she said, 'then meet me there at seven. They make
a good daiquiri, an even better mojito, and a superb Bahama Mama.
Good food, too – great *ropa vieja* with black beans and yellow
rice and their *lechon asado* is to die for!'

I couldn't get over how friendly she was, how warm and helpful.
Perhaps I'd been wrong to think of her as resistant simply because
she hadn't called me back. I decided my best strategy was to
conceal my expectation that she'd be difficult.

Let her set the mood. Don't drill in like you did with Loetz.

The guesthouse, Sue's, was decent enough. Sue, a stout fifty-
something with gray bangs, referred to herself as 'an old broad.'
She showed me to a pleasant room, told me the pool in back was
clothing-optional, and made a point of assuring me that her house
catered to both cis- and trans-females of any possible variety and
orientation.

'From girls to xirls – we get all kinds of womyn here. First time in KW?' she asked. I nodded. 'I tell people, you can have a good time or a lousy time in Cayo Hueso. You can party it up, get stoned or go into seclusion and write your novel. The only rule in this house is "Conch Republic Rules." That means respect everybody, don't impinge or infringe, and you'll get along fine. You need anything, give me a holler.'

I thanked her, shut my door, unpacked, and lay down to rest.

I knew La Caja China was going to be good even before I came through the door. The arousing aroma of roasted pork surrounded the restaurant like a halo. It was crowded and noisy, filled with a variety of island types – old guys and gals with gray pigtails, gay boys in muscle shirts, college girls in halter tops, a faux-Hemingway type sporting a scrubby beard. I spotted Penny perched at the bar nursing a salty dog. I sat down beside her, ordered a mojito, and listened as she told me how she came to settle in KW.

She'd been living on the Florida panhandle, teaching art to middle schoolers, working on her own stuff when she could. She was married to a chief petty officer named Pepe Ruiz, stationed at the Naval Surface Warfare Center in Panama City. They had a good life together, or so she thought, until it turned out to be not so good. She and Pepe were part of a group of sailors and their spouses who worked hard during the week and played hard on the weekends. This weekend play often consisted of partner-swap parties.

'All of us, guys and gals, were sluts to a fare-thee-well. Predictably, things got tense, folks got jealous, and, as you might expect with warriors, one night our idyllic life turned violent. There was a fight. Pepe got beat up pretty bad. Couple of days later he drowned in a diving accident. I was devastated. I never found out if one of the guys caused it. There was an investigation and our unsavory social life was revealed. So there I was, a twenty-five-year-old widow, and, when the story came out about the parties, fired from my teaching job. So I packed up the car and headed down here, as far away from P City as I could get in Florida. I thought the beaches would be as good as the ones on the panhandle. Not true! The beaches down here are shit. But there's an arts community – painters, potters and craft folks. I liked it and settled in, waitressed for a while, taught life-drawing classes, then used my naval widow's settlement money to buy the house on Catherine, set up as a gallery/frame shop, started knocking out the kind of watercolors tourists like to buy, and, when I have the time, work on my own stuff in the back room.'

She grinned when I asked her to tell me about her own stuff. She told me it was pretty far out.

'Like the murals in the Locust Street house?'

She shook her head. 'That was a one-time project. For years my personal work's been abstract. By the way, I notice you keep calling them "the murals." Court and I never thought of them in such grand terms. To us they were simply "the walls."'

After half an hour of chit-chat, we took a table in a quiet room off the bar, ordered dinner – big slabs of roast pork cooked in the house style, in a foil-lined plywood box which Cubans call a *caja China*. I didn't push her on the murals, but did ask her why they referred to them as 'the walls.'

'Because that's what they were – walls,' she said. 'Blank walls that beckoned to us, dared us to mark them up. There was another reason.' She smiled. 'We'd been reading a lot of Sartre. I doubt teenagers are much into him these days, but back then we regarded him as a literary god. At Red Raven I played Inèz in a workshop reading of *No Exit*. That's the play with the famous line: "Hell is other people." We loved that line. Also one from Oscar Wilde: "We are each our own devil and we make the world our hell." That's what we were after when we decided to mark up those walls. Other people and hell! That's what you could say the walls were all about.'

She didn't want to tell me more, explain what she meant. First, she wanted to hear how I got involved and how much of the story I'd uncovered. I told her I was just one member of a team working on it, then what we'd learned from Cindy Dryansky ('Yeah, I remember her. Kind of a psycho bitch as I recall'); Loetz ('Never heard of him'); Elizabeth Schechtner ('Sure, Doctor Liz!'); Katherine Zevin ('Terrific teacher! When I taught, I modeled myself after her').

I described the other members of the team: Jason, famous conflict photographer turned photography teacher at CAI, who'd stumbled on the murals and was bowled over by them; Tally, Jason's former student, now his assistant; Hannah, a textile artist, Jason's former girlfriend and colleague at CAI, who also thought the murals were amazing; and me, who'd gotten to know Jason

when there was an exhibition of his work, and to whom he
turned when he was trying to figure out who'd lived in the
Locust Street house and, specifically, who'd created the murals
there.

Penny listened attentively, but I sensed her impatience. Finally,
she spoke up.

'You've mentioned all these people who I know nothing about.
But so far you haven't told me anything about Doctor Ted and
Court.'

Her face fell when I told her Dr Ted had passed away.

'Oh, crap!' she said. 'I really loved the guy. We both did.' She
gazed into my eyes. 'Court – I hope you're not going to tell me
she's dead, too?'

I told her Courtney was very much alive, a long-term resident
in a psychiatric clinic in Switzerland. I told her we'd IDed her as
the mysterious Ragdoll Artist, and showed her some shots of the
dolls I had stored on my phone.

She studied them for a long time. I asked her if she saw a
connection.

'The two-sided faces look like her work,' she said, 'but Court
wasn't the only one who ever painted doubles. I remember
suggesting it to her, based on some paintings I'd seen in a book
of Schiele's portraits. We called them "ghosts." She painted them
like auras hovering above the characters' heads, reflecting their
true nature. Not everyone on the walls rated a ghost aura. Just
special people. Another thing, I never knew Court to work with
cloth, or that she even knew how to sew. But artists go through
stages before they find their voice.' She paused. 'Not sure if I've
found mine yet. Though I may be getting there . . .'

It was getting late. I offered to pick up the check, but she insisted
we split it. She may have felt that if she let me pay, she'd be
beholden to me, and it was clear that she was not a woman to
be beholden to anyone.

Out on the street, she unlocked a rusty old bike chained to a
lamp post.

'Don't have a car,' she told me. 'Sold mine years ago. Bike's
all I need here on the island.' She mounted it. 'Come by tomorrow.
Any time after ten. We'll talk some more.'

She pedaled off into the gloom.

*   *   *

I phoned Jason soon as I got back to Sue's, filled him in on all I'd learned. He was impressed at how easy it had been for me to get Penny talking, including that bit about sex parties in Panama City and her husband drowning.

'For me, the most interesting thing,' he said, 'is about the walls *daring* them to mark them up.'

I agreed; I'd also been struck by her comment that the subject of the walls was Sartre's notion that hell is other people.

'Figures. See if you can get her to talk about that.' He paused. 'Tell me about her seascapes?'

'You'd hate them,' I told him. 'Kind of stuff you find on a motel room wall.'

'You're doing good, Joan,' he said. 'Sorry I patronized you with dumb advice.'

The next morning, when I walked into the Ruiz Gallery, I found Penny working at the big table in the center of the room, framing up a huge French cinema poster for *L'Alibi*, an old Erich von Stroheim film.

'We can talk while I work,' she said. 'I promised I'd finish this by the end of the day. The client owns Bar Jean Cocteau off Duval.' She glanced at me. 'Check out von Stroheim's expression, so stern and *serioso*, kinda like those faces Court and I painted on the walls.'

I took it as a promising sign that she'd brought up the murals without my prompting her. I was about to follow up when she started questioning me.

'Tell me about yourself, Joan. What kind of writing do you do, and how'd you get into journalism?'

OK, fair enough, she wants to know who she's talking to.

I told her my story: born and brought up in Orange County, daughter of Vietnamese boat people, the youngest of six kids. My dad an architect who specializes in designing public schools, my mom who worked her way up from teller to the vice-presidency of a local bank. Writing for my high-school paper, then at UC Santa Barbara where I wrote for *The Daily Nexus*.

That was when, I told her, I got interested in investigative reporting, starting with a series I wrote on teacher/student sexual harassment.

'I ran this ad: "Email Joan if you've been harassed." Lots of responses. Spent months following them up. Campus exploded when my pieces started coming out, leading to the forced resignation of two TAs. That's when I understood the power of journalism, which led to my going for an MFA.'

She asked how I ended up working on the *Times-Dispatch*. I told her that decent journalism jobs are hard to come by these days, so when the *Times-Dispatch* editor said he'd let me work on investigative pieces as long as I understood my main job was to write feature stories for the culture page, I jumped at the chance. I added that I discovered that Calista, despite its reputation as a dead-end rust-belt town, turned out to be a pretty cool place. Finally, I told her about the arson story I was working on.

She glanced at me with a look I took as approving.

'I'm almost finished with this,' she said, motioning toward the poster. 'Give me a couple of minutes, look around the gallery, then we'll go to the backroom and I'll show you some of my serious work.'

Nothing could have been further from her slick seascapes than her rigorously executed multi-layered abstract oils. She pulled out half a dozen one by one, then set them up without comment against the walls of her backroom.

The backgrounds of these paintings were orderly and geometric, overlapping flat architectural shapes (squares, triangles, trapezoids, ovals and circles in muted hues), overlaid by rapidly drawn, brilliantly colored expressionist slashes which reminded me of calligraphy, but which Penny assured me were not.

'They're just marks,' she said. 'They have no meaning. People thought Franz Kline's black-and-white paintings were calligraphic. They didn't believe him when he insisted they weren't. I try to be patient when people ask whether I've been influenced by Zen. They shake their heads when I tell them the slashes are spontaneous marks. Do these paintings say something?' She shrugged. 'Your guess is as good as mine.' She paused. 'What do you see in them?'

'After what you just said, I'm timid about saying anything.'

'Hey, Joan, you write for the culture page, for Christ's sake!'

She was trying to provoke me. Perhaps she wanted to see if I was worthy to receive her confidences, but then she'd already confessed to participating in swap parties.

OK, I thought, *give it a shot.*

'I see paintings by an artist working toward disruption, imposing disorder on what she may regard as a falsely ordered universe. You build up a carefully balanced architectural world, then cut and slice at it hard. It's as if you're saying you want to rip away the fabric. These are no-bullshit pictures.'

I turned from the paintings, looked into her eyes and discovered she was gazing back at me. We stared at each other for several seconds, and then she nodded.

'Like I said,' she said, 'your guess is as good as mine.'

I think that was the moment when she decided to accept me, answer my queries as candidly as she could. Sitting side by side on her paint-spattered couch, I repeated what Kathy Zevin had told Tally – that she, Penny, worked inward from concepts, while Courtney worked outward from people's faces.

Penny said she liked that. 'Shrewd of Ms Z. I'm flattered she remembers us.'

I told her that Ms Zevin regarded the two of them as the most talented and interesting students she'd ever taught.

'So was it that way with the walls?' I asked. 'You thought up the idea, and then Courtney painted in the faces?'

She smiled. She said it was hard to remember exactly how they'd gotten started. Dr Ted had encouraged them to create something together, and had offered the attic walls as their canvas.

'He had them boarded up for us – windows too. He wanted us to really let loose on them, express our fears, our demons. We three discussed it for a while, then Courtney and I continued after he left us alone. I say "discussed," but you should know Courtney wasn't much of a talker. She listened to what people said, but rarely spoke herself. When she did, it was in short staccato whispers. I doubt, in all the time we spent together, she ever said more than a sentence at a time. But oh! – that girl could draw! Far, *far* better than me. She wasn't happy unless she was wielding a pencil, stick of charcoal, pastel, crayon or brush. She could have been a very successful caricaturist if she wanted.'

Penny said they believed Dr Ted was expecting them to execute violent action paintings, but once they were alone, they decided to create something rigorous.

'We were a couple of angry girls. I suggested that we not let loose like Doctor Ted seemed to want, but that we express our anger coolly. You know the phrase – "revenge is a dish best served cold."'

She also recalled being the one who came up with the idea of covering all four walls. She wanted, she said, to turn the room into what the Germans call *Gesamtkunstwerk*, a total work of art.

'I didn't know the word back then,' she said. 'I learned it at SFAI. But intuitively I understood the concept, and it struck me that the room was small enough that we'd be able to create something that would totally envelop us, something we couldn't escape. Which, I think, goes back to *No Exit* – turning that little room into a kind of hell.'

When they told Dr Ted their plan, he said he loved it and again urged them not to hold back.

'So the figures you two painted – were they your demons?'

'Some. Most of them were Court's. She had serious family issues. She thought her parents were arrogant and unfeeling. I had family issues too, so we sort of combined them. I think our being so much in sync is what made the project so exciting.'

She paused.

'You know, I think the Walls – or the Murals as you call them – was the most exciting project I've ever undertaken. Teens are like that – passionate and not afraid to throw themselves into something bigger than their trifling adolescent selves. Man, did we throw ourselves into it! Total commitment! There was nothing we weren't prepared to do to get those four walls covered. Nothing else mattered to us. We were in "the flow," as they say, caught up in our rage, which we somehow knew how to shape and discipline. The harder we worked, the more energized we felt. It was like we were on fire. We'd work for hours without a break. Just as you speak about discovering the power of investigative reporting, we were in the process of discovering the power of art. Not so much the power that art can have on viewers, but the power of being possessed by a vision, then striving to bring it to life. Pouring our confusion and angst into something totalizing and powerful. I often wish I could get back into that state of madness.' She paused. 'You see, Joan, we truly believed in the redemptive power of art, and that what we were painting on those walls . . . could be our redemption.'

She looked around at her paintings. 'Guess I still believe that, though not with the same intensity. These pieces – they're my attempts to say something I can't put into words. I think you may have been right about my trying to rip the fabric. I like that. It might even be true. Did you know there was an Italian painter, Lucio Fontana, who stabbed and slashed his paintings with a scalpel? We artists speak of "making marks." Fontana's cuts were the ultimate in mark-making. I think my paint slashes are my way of doing that. Whether there's any kind of redemption that goes beyond self-expression . . .' She threw up her hands. 'Who can say? All I know is that if I was restricted to the kind of work you see out in the gallery, I'd feel terrible about myself. These paintings, the ones in here – if I couldn't make them, I'm certain I'd fall apart.'

A bell tinkled. People had entered the gallery. Penny excused herself, went out to meet them. I heard the muffled sounds of conversation. After a while she popped her head back in.

'There's a couple interested in buying watercolors. This may take a while. Can you stay?'

'Of course!'

It took her a good half-hour to seal the deal, which, it turned out, led to her selling three of her seascapes. She was pleased.

'Nice folks,' she said, when she came back in. 'They bought good ones. Not bad for a Thursday morning. I'll paint more this weekend.'

As we settled back on the couch, I asked her about Courtney's issues.

'I know this is sensitive, and you may not want to answer,' I said, 'but I have to ask. What can you tell me about Courtney's problems with her family? And your own issues too, if you don't mind talking about them?'

She screwed up her features. 'I was physically and emotionally abused,' she said. 'My mom was an alcoholic. She took out all her frustrations on me, berating me and slapping me around. I doubt my father knew. She never did it when he was in the house. After I ran away, seems Mom felt remorse. When the cops raided A Caring House, they thought they were raiding a cult. They turned me over to this couple who'd worked at Synanon, who took me to their farm in New York State for so-called deprogramming. I kept telling them I hadn't been programmed, that the Schechtners hadn't been running a cult. But they were so into the cult concept that they didn't believe me.

'Think about that, the irony of it. I was taken from a refuge they claimed was a cult and planted smack-dab in the middle of a real one. Because that's what CIRS was. They had this horrible process they called "The Game" when everyone attacked you till you broke down and wept. Then they got all lovey-dovey and group-hugged you and wiped away your tears. After I played, or rather, suffered the Game, I persuaded Libby (she ran the place) to let me call home. When I got my dad on the line, I begged him to rescue me. I guess he heard the anguish in my voice, because the next day he drove all the way from Calista to the farm. On the way back he told me that Mom had started going to AA, that she felt terrible about the things she'd said and done to me, and she'd promised to turn over a new leaf. Seems my running off had really shaken her up.

'Anyway, I went back to high school, finished up, then applied to art schools. I chose SFAI because it was the farthest from home. After that, I only came back to Calista for quick visits. When Dad retired, he and Mom wanted to move down to Florida. They hated the Keys, thank God! They ended up in Sarasota. Occasionally, I go up there to see them. They never come down here. They like my watercolors, so when I visit, I always bring one as a gift. I've never shown them my personal work, 'cause I know they wouldn't get it.'

She was open, and her story made sense, but I noted that she avoided my question about Courtney's family. Also, whatever had gone on between her and her mother didn't seem like enough to cause her to run away. I asked her about that. She nodded as she tried to explain it. She'd had a boyfriend at school, they'd broken up – an experience she'd found devastating. She'd been depressed, but when she got to Red Raven that summer, things started looking up.

'Meeting Court was hugely important. We recognized one another right away. Kindred spirits. Turns out her home life was way worse than mine. We had these fantasies – we'd run away, take refuge at Doctor Ted's halfway house, then, once we both turned eighteen, move to Paris and start a new life there together as artists. Court was an heiress. She was due to come into money on her eighteenth birthday and a fortune on her twenty-first. We'd live on that, set ourselves up in a wonderful sky-lit studio. All we had to do was stay quiet and safe until we reached legal age.'

'Were you in love?' I asked.

She smiled. 'I guess so. Not physically, but our relationship

was intense. Kids at Red Raven complained to the counselors, said
we were cliquish. When they asked if we were lesbos, we'd gaze
at each other longingly and giggle. Believe me, being gay was no
big deal at Red Raven. About half the kids were into it. Frankly,
I think if I'd given Court any encouragement, we might have
experimented with that. But that wasn't my scene. It wasn't erotic
attraction that bound us. We had a powerful emotional bond that
had to do with seeing ourselves as serious artists superior to all
the dilettante kids at camp.'

'Liz Schechtner told us you were going to apply to become
liberated minors.'

'I remember that. But we were close enough to eighteen that it
didn't make sense. Not for me at least. Maybe for Court because
for her there was money at stake.'

'So what were her family issues?'

'Pretty bad,' Penny said. 'A lot more serious than mine.'

'Like what?'

She shook her head, signaling she didn't want to go into it.

'Let's just say bad,' she said. 'The worst part was that when
she tried to talk about it, no one in her family believed her. They
treated her like she was crazy. In a way, I guess she was. But I
believed her, and so did Doctor Ted. That's why he took us in
without informing her folks. He felt protective toward us, especially
Court. But then the Cobbs found out where we were, the cops
burst in, separated us, those people took us away, and I never saw
her or heard from her again.'

'And the people on the walls?'

'They were *the others*, the disbelievers, the ones who refused
to face the truth of what was happening before their eyes.' She
paused. 'They were our demons. We turned that little room into
our own special hell.'

'What about the little girl with the dog?'

She smiled. 'I painted her. My portrait of Court. She drew all
the other faces, and together we painted them in. I filled in her
drawings and painted the bodies. And then I drew and painted that
little girl.'

'Looking so wide-eyed and innocent.'

'Which is just how I wanted her to look,' Penny said.

Hannah Sachs

t wasn't hard to find Spencer Addams. He was living over on the West Side in a tract house on Badger Road. As Noah and I drove out to meet him, Noah filled me in.

'I saw him perform when I was at law school. He was admired for his summations and for daring moves such as putting a defendant on the stand, something a defense attorney rarely does. He was the kind of lawyer who liked taking on a hopeless cause, then exceeding expectations by pulling a victory out of thin air. That's what he did in the Decoite murder case, which made him famous. When my buddies heard he was going to deliver a summation, a bunch of us hurried over to the county courthouse to observe. The courtroom was jammed. We were lucky to get seats. When word went out that Addams was going to sum up, members of the criminal defense bar made a point of sitting in.

'He was good that day, incredibly persuasive. It was like watching an artist teach a master class. Words poured out of him like honey, grabbing and holding the jurors' attention. Some believed he mesmerized juries, won verdicts by employing diabolical powers of persuasion. In my view, he simply out-lawyered prosecutors and won his cases on the merits. There was a twinkle in his eye that day when he scanned the courtroom and noticed us. Recognizing us as law students, I think he started playing as much to us as to the jurors. Like he was saying "Hey guys, this is how it's done!"'

I was surprised when we pulled up in front of the house. It didn't look like the home of a famous barrister. Badger Road was full of potholes. The neighborhood was rundown. The property looked poorly kept, the siding peeling, the yard choked with weeds.

An unsmiling middle-aged woman with high cheekbones answered the door.

'I'm Carol Addams,' she said. 'You're here to see my dad.'

She led us through the house and then out the rear door to a patch of dry brown grass where Spencer Addams reclined in a plastic strap chair.

'Pardon me for not standing. I've got arthritis,' he said. He showed us a toothy grin. Although his face was marked by red lines and liver spots, there was something leonine about the man. He had piercing blue eyes, and long white hair woven into a pigtail in back. His voice was strong, despite his ruined face. He had, I thought, the deep compelling voice of a radio announcer.

'I live over there.' He gestured toward a decrepit mobile home mounted on cinder blocks across the dried-up lawn. 'Carol lets me park it here so long as I stay out of her way.' He turned to her. 'Ain't that right, darlin'?'

Carol sucked in her cheeks, turned and strode back into her house.

'We get along fine,' Addams assured us. 'As you may have gathered, I've seen better days. Used to live in a lovely view apartment on Keller Ridge. That was back in my salad years. If you're wondering how I've sunk to this debased state, I can't rightly explain it, except to say I spent too much on alcohol and women, made bad investments, forgot to file taxes – all the above. But you didn't come out here to hear my sob story. Not that I have one. I'm perfectly happy the way things are. I'm eighty-three, and I've been waiting a long, long time for someone to come around and ask me about the Schechtner matter.' He gazed into my eyes and then into Noah's. 'That's what you're here for, isn't it?'

'Yes, sir,' Noah said.

'Good, 'cause I got a story to tell and papers to back it up. It was a dirty business, that Schechtner thing, but then the Cobbs always played in the muck. I had a hunch someday someone'd come around asking how they happened to run my clients out of town.'

He was ready to tell us all about that 'dirty business,' but first he wanted us to tell him why we were interested. I told him most of it, and when he heard how Jase and I had flown out to New Mexico to see Liz Schechtner, he decided we were for real and deserved to hear what he had to tell.

The Schechtners got his name from the Public Defender's Office. An attorney there knew he despised wealthy people like the Cobbs. Spencer visited the Schechtners in jail, heard their story, was certain they'd been set up and that Walter Loetz was lying. The judge set bail so high that the Schechtners couldn't possibly raise it. That too made Spencer suspicious. His first step was to go into A Caring Place on Locust Street. He observed that there was no satanic material there except for the hastily spray-painted 666 on the living-room wall. As for the 'erotic murals' in the so-called attic 'orgy room,' he observed that they were not at all orgiastic and photographed them to show in court. Most important, he retrieved Ted Schechtner's case file on Courtney Cobb stuffed with notes on all the terrible and terrifying things she'd confided.

'That file was devastating. Soon as I read it, I knew I had them by their hairs. There were things in there that the Cobbs would never want known. So I had a little chat with their attorney, a dude name of Silver who dressed like a dandy. When I showed him a little bit of what I had, his mouth puckered like he'd been sucking on a lemon.

'"This is grave," he said. I liked that word. To me it meant I had stuff that, if exposed in open court, would follow his clients to their graves. I offered him a deal. Since A Caring Place was properly licensed, and there'd been no holding Courtney and her friend against their will, all criminal charges against the Schechtners were to be dropped and they were to be immediately released. I demanded complete exoneration, and a payment for damages to their names and reputations. Silver asked what sort of figure I had in mind. Quarter mil, I told him. He said that was too much, Horace Cobb would never pay it. It was extortion, pure and simple, he said. I knew he was bluffing, *knew* Cobb would pay. I told him so, and that he'd probably end up paying a helluva lot more if I got annoyed and into a real extortive mood. I told him this was very likely if I didn't get the quarter mil, and that he'd best get back to me by the end of the day; otherwise, I'd start feeding what I had to a *Times-Dispatch* reporter and then it would be too late to squeeze the ugly ooze back into the proverbial tube.

'He reappeared in my office at five p.m., panting and looking worried. He had a cashier's check for two hundred fifty thousand made out to my trustee account. But before he'd turn it over, he had some demands of his own. First, the Schechtners were to close up their practice and move out of state. Second, I was to turn over all their documents concerning Courtney Cobb. And, third, they were to sign a binding non-disclosure agreement he'd drawn up, regarding anything they knew or had heard regarding Courtney and her family, with severe financial penalties should they ever reveal any of it to anyone at any time.

'I read the agreement. I'll give Silver this much – it was well drawn. But I didn't like the requirement that the Schechtners pull up stakes. I told him that was not contemplated when I gave him my figure. He said he understood, and for that reason had a second check for seventy-five grand to cover their relocation expenses. I told him I'd speak to my clients and get back to him the following day. I remember the way he snickered, like he thought now he had the upper hand. "I'll give you till noon," he said.

'So, OK, it was a decent deal. The Schechtners didn't like it much, didn't like the notion of selling out the Cobb girl, but they understood they'd made a huge mistake not telling her parents where she was, and, worse, not passing on what Courtney had told Ted, which, being criminal, they were obliged to report to law enforcement. I pointed out that, far as I could tell, Courtney had been moved out of state and thus would likely be unavailable to testify, that basically there was nothing they could do to help her now, and that no matter what destruction they might wreak upon the Cobbs, that wouldn't get them out of the considerable trouble they were in. I looked around the jail attorney's conference room. It was pretty bleak. "No one wants you to sell anyone out," I told them, "but time's come to think about yourselves."

'They agreed to take the deal. I called Silver, told him to get them released. We'd meet again in my office at the end of the day where I would hand him the signed NDAs plus Ted Schechtner's notes in exchange for the two cashier's checks. He sounded relieved, and, frankly, so was I. It was a nasty business, but I'd served my clients' interests and felt pretty good about that.' He paused. 'And yet . . . I was so appalled by what I'd read in Ted's notes that I decided to photocopy them and keep them in my files just in case. *In case of what*, you're wondering.' He grinned. 'Well . . .'

'In case one day someone came around asking why the charges against the Schechtners were so suddenly dismissed,' I said.

Addams nodded. 'And now . . . here you are! Two of you, no less! And, yeah, I still have those old photocopies. I cleaned out most of my papers when I closed my practice. Spent days shredding documents. But there were some things I couldn't bring myself to shred – among them Ted's notes. Wanna see 'em?' He grinned. 'Sure you do!'

Ted Schechtner's notes were worse than devastating. They were sickening. They were also disjointed. But fortunately they were dated and arranged in sequence. Although the photocopies were on eight-by-ten sheets, the notes themselves came in a variety of sizes. Some were scrawled on small notepad paper, others were neatly handwritten on lined punch-holed stock, as if for inclusion in a three-ring binder, and still others were neatly typed. Based on the chaotic way he took notes on their sessions, Dr Ted came off as a hurried and harried scribe. I guessed he'd scribbled down his thoughts and notes as Courtney's words poured out of her.

Among his own notes were pithy phrases: 'deeply troubled,' 'heart goes out to her,' 'poor little rich girl!!!,' 'her voice so low I can barely make out her words.'

He wrote: 'serious abuse,' 'thinks no one cares,' 'for sure they know but they can't face the truth.'

He noted: 'so brave in the face of so much evil,' 'smiles when most anguished. When I ask why, she says "I don't feel so bad when I smile."' 'Says: "they hated me because I didn't fit in, didn't meet their expectations."' 'Says: "I was different, strange, always drawing pictures. People said I acted weird."'

And then perhaps the most poignant of all: 'She questions whether she imagined everything, whether it was, as her parents insisted, another of her weird distortions of reality.'

Ted leaves little doubt about what that 'everything' was. Her brothers sexually assaulted her. She tells Ted it started back when she was thirteen. Jack did it first. He came to her and, to groom her, said he needed her help, told her he had these urges because he was a boy and begged her to help him obtain relief. Would she please touch him in certain places? He came on sweet and vulnerable. He was her big brother, so of course she was willing to help him out.

She was intensely curious about these 'urges,' also amused by what he asked her to do and by his reactions when she did it. She knew about male genitalia and the role they played in reproduction, but she was surprised and amazed how when she touched Jack's organ, it would 'miraculously change shape.'

Afterwards Jack would thank her. He'd tell her how grateful he was for her understanding, and how embarrassing it was for him to plead for help. He also slyly suggested that if she let him touch her in certain places, he could make her feel good too.

For a while she demurred, but then one night told him she was willing to let him try. And so he did. The first time it didn't excite her much, but, yes, she admitted to Dr Ted, it was fun, and after a while that kind of intimate touching excited her quite a lot. She relished the fact that what they were doing was forbidden. There was a special excitement that came from breaking rules and crossing lines. Jack was pleased by her willingness to play. He was also excited by their transgressions. He told her it was a 'fun game' they were playing, and he was happy that she liked their game. He gave her little gifts to reward her for playing it – new charms for her charm bracelet, an antique scarab ring – and caresses, 'very sweet caresses,' that aroused her and made her feel loved.

This went on for over a year, then Jack introduced Kevin to their game.

They were her big brothers. They claimed they loved her. They told her that, being boys, they had their needs. Since she was their 'bestie,' their 'favorite girl in the whole world,' surely she'd want to help her loving brothers deal with their corporeal desires.

At first she helped Kevin the same way she helped Jack, and sometimes the three of them would lie together, she in the middle, her brothers on either side, and she would touch them both at the same time and the game became a contest as to which of the boys would spurt first.

Kevin was usually the winner, and the winner, they'd agreed, should receive a reward. There were different kinds of rewards. Usually, these consisted of her giving the winner additional satisfaction with her mouth. She didn't mind that. In fact, she kind of liked rewarding victorious Kevin in front of defeated Jack, because it made Jack jealous.

Things progressed. Would she like to try having sex? It would be good practice for all three of them. She'd be experienced when she started dating, and the boys she went out with would appreciate that.

It took considerable persuasion to convince her. They both kept asking, very nicely too, and finally she thought she owed it to herself to find out what it felt like. The first few times it hurt. When she'd told them so, they stopped and kissed her and said how sorry they were, how they never meant to hurt her, but sometimes they got so excited they couldn't help themselves. They hoped she understood.

Things changed after a while. One night they both came into her room and after Jack went into her, Kevin turned her over and thrust his thing into her rear. She didn't like that at all. She screamed and told him to stop. Kevin giggled and kept going. 'Sorry, too late, can't stop now,' he hissed into her ear. 'Gotta see it through.'

Kevin was so much bigger and stronger that she had no choice but to submit. Afterwards she showed them her anger. She told them both to get out of her room and not to come back because she wasn't going to let them touch her anymore.

Still, she admitted to Dr Ted, there was something interesting and intense about feeling so helpless, conquered and used. After a while she began to miss their attentions, and so agreed to resume the game. But with new rules. No hurting. No calling her names as Kevin liked to do when he went inside her – names like 'bitch' and 'whore.' They said OK, no more of that. They promised to make it sweet, like it was at the beginning, make it lovely for all three of them. And wasn't it fun, Jack asked her, that they were doing this, playing like this, and no one else in the whole wide world knew, and never would? This was their secret, their compact, their private game.

Jack always tried to make it fun. Kevin didn't bother. She gathered he didn't care if it was enjoyable for her as long as it was for him. At times he could be pretty nasty. He'd always had a mean streak. One time when the boys were lying on either side of her after sex, he asked Jack which of her holes Jack liked the best. Jack said he preferred her pussy. Kevin said it was more fun for him to fuck her in the ass because of the way that made her squeal. And, of course, they equally enjoyed thrusting themselves into her mouth. They agreed in future to divide her body up. Jack would insert his thing into her front and Kevin would stick his into her butt. Then they turned to her. What about her needs? What did she like best? She had no answer. 'I don't really like any of it,' she finally said. They laughed.

She was sixteen when she first tried to tell her mother.

Her mom cut her off, waved her hands in front of her face. 'Nonsense! I don't want to hear it. Your brothers are wonderful boys.' Her dad got really mad at her. 'Keep spouting that kind of filth and I'll send you away. Want to go to the insane asylum, Court?' She told him she didn't. 'Then stop your damn whining,' he said.

They must have confronted the boys because that night they came into her room, angry. 'This is our private business,' Jack said. 'It's just between the three of us. So stop tattling and keep your trap shut.' Then they forced her to suck them both off.

They fucked her in all three places. A few times they fucked her at the same time. She tried to enjoy it. They said that's what she should do. 'It's supposed to be fun,' Jack insisted. 'It doesn't mean anything. It's just a game.' Kevin told Jack he didn't give a shit whether she liked it or not. He was going to do what he wanted and he promised she'd be sorry if she ever tattled on them again.

This went on for a year, until Jack graduated from Richmond and went away to boarding school. The year alone with Kevin was the worst. He took to deliberately hurting her, pinching, slapping, squeezing her neck with his hands until she was on the verge of passing out. He explained that this was a new variation on their game, a variation he'd heard about and wanted to try. He told her he liked making her cry and liked it too when she tried not to. He liked seeing how long she could hold out, how far he could go before she broke down and wept. Always in the end, he promised her, 'You *will* cry because I won't stop until you do.'

It got to the point that Kevin told her he didn't enjoying fucking her unless she resisted and tried to fight him off. Her struggling, he told her, turned him on. Her resistance became a requirement.

She thought about killing herself. She would take the bus downtown, go to the Cobb Industries building, take the elevator up to her dad's office, tell him everything in great detail, then jump out the window right in front of him.

Then he'd *have* to believe her. Then he'd be sorry he hadn't listened. Then they'd *all* be sorry . . . at least for a while anyway.

She decided to try to enjoy what Kevin was doing to her. For a while that seemed to work. She admitted to Ted she sometimes liked being held down and forced. Kevin was thrilled when he discovered this. 'Yeah!' he said, 'I heard you bitches like it rough. Wow! Turns out to be true!'

When Jack came back on spring break, Kevin told him what he'd found out about her. 'Turns out little sis is a pain-lover.' Jack said he wasn't surprised. 'We trained you good, didn't we, Court?' She refused to answer, turned away and wept.

The next year Kevin joined Jack at St Paul's. When they both came home on Thanksgiving break, they told her how horny they were. 'Been looking forward to getting back in the saddle all fall,' Kevin said.

The incidents piled up. The abuse became increasingly depraved. One time, Miss Scott, the gym teacher at Ashley-Burnett, saw her dressing in the locker-room and asked her about some bruises on her thighs. Courtney turned beet-red and covered up. 'They're nothing,' she said. Miss Scott told her to finish getting dressed and come to her office. There Miss Scott asked her if there was anything she wanted to talk about. She said the bruises looked like Courtney may have been abused. Courtney said she'd just been 'messing around with a boy,' and it was none of Coach's business. Then she ran out.

The school called her parents. They confronted her when she got home. 'What's this about messing around with some boy?' her father demanded. 'Who've you been seeing?' She told them she hadn't been seeing anyone, that Jack and Kevin had been abusing her. They said that wasn't possible, the boys were away at school. Before she could explain that the bruises were two weeks old, that they'd hurt her during break, they accused her of being delusional. Her dad told her that if she kept saying stuff like that, he'd send her to a hospital where they'd put her in a straitjacket and give her shock treatments, and maybe that would finally straighten out her sick, evil mind.

It was difficult for me to keep reading Ted's notes. The narrative was disjointed. The abuse he described became monotonous. By recounting incident upon incident, it occurred to me that he'd been trying to build a case. This fit with Jase's and my suspicions, after we talked with Dr Liz in Abiquiú, that Ted had a plan to use his knowledge of Courtney's pain to extort money from the Cobbs.

Sometimes, Courtney told him, she reveled in what her brothers were doing to her and other times she despised it. She twice seriously considered suicide, even going so far as to stockpile pills.

She went to see her paternal grandmother with whom she'd always felt close. Grandma Flo, as they all called her, listened intently as Courtney tried to tell her what had been going on. She softened the story out of consideration for Grandma Flo, and also to spare herself embarrassment. She spoke very softly and shyly. She could barely bring herself to describe the abuse. When she was finished, Grandma Flo gazed at her lovingly. 'You always were a troubled child,' she finally said. 'You were always different. And so creative! Your drawing talent is just amazing. But these things you're telling me – I just can't believe them, dear. I know and love your brothers as much as I know and love you. I'm very sorry to tell you this, but what you're saying just doesn't seem possible.'

She dreaded when Jack and Kevin came home from school and from vacations. She was immensely relieved when her parents permitted her to spend the summer at Red Raven art camp. Not only did this get her out of the house, but she met someone there she really liked. Penny Dawson, she told Ted, was the best friend she'd ever had. She'd told Penny some of what had been going on, and Penny confided her own troubles at home. The best part of these exchanges was that each believed the other, and the similarity of their experiences proved to Courtney that the horrors she'd endured were not unique.

That autumn, while taking after-school art class, they made plans to run away. Penny said she knew a place where they could go. She told Courtney about Dr Ted and the house called A Caring Place in East Calista that he and his wife ran for runaway kids. And so they ran for it. Courtney began therapy with Dr Ted, and he kept notes on everything she told him.

In a final set of typed notes Ted wrote up his diagnosis and proposed prescription for Courtney's recovery:

> Patient suffers the after effects of repeated traumatic vicious sexual abuse by her two older brothers. Patient displays certain anti-social tendencies consistent with a diagnosis of Asperger Syndrome, including selective mutism, but is also a high-functioning visual artist of considerable talent. She should be encouraged to employ her talent to express her anguish and thereby work it through. This plus 2X per week psycho-therapy will hopefully in time relieve much of her pain. Prognosis uncertain. Full recovery may not be possible. As adulthood is imminent, patient should be encouraged to stay as far away as possible from her family. It is a wonder, considering so much inflicted abuse, that she is able to function at all. Without her art, it is questionable whether she can have a productive happy life.

Ted further describes how he tried to coax Courtney to draw the horrific scenes she'd described to him. When she resisted, he suggested that she devise her own art project, something that could lucidly express her feelings of anguish and betrayal. That's when she and Penny asked him to panel all four walls of the attic, including the windows, and then let them loose on the walls with brushes and paint. 'We have a plan,' they told him. Because he liked the gleam in their eyes when they said this, he gave their project his blessing. And thus the Locust Street Murals were born.

Noah and I didn't talk much on the drive back to the city. We were still absorbing, each in our own way, what we'd read that afternoon. It felt strange sitting in the car beside my loving brother after reading about the terrifying brothers-on-sister abuse Courtney had endured.

Noah must have been thinking the same thing. At one point he turned to me.

'We could never have done such things.'

'Never in a thousand years,' I agreed.

The sky was darkening as we neared Calista. Sirens were wailing and smoke from summer fires seeped into the car. Noah turned to me again.

'How're you feeling?'

'Horrified, heartbroken, sickened, depressed. How 'bout you?'

'Same. I know a tavern near here. I think we can both use a stiff drink.'

We went in, ordered. I peered at Noah. 'You look angry,' I told him. 'What're you thinking?'

'So much corruption! And the things people do within families – I know I shouldn't be surprised.'

I asked him what it was about the Cobb brothers that made him so detest them.

'Didn't we just read how detestable they are?'

'I mean, before we read Ted's notes. In your office, you told us you relished the opportunity to take them down. What's that about?'

'First, their politics. They're the worst kind of right-wing hypocrites. They talk a good game about being libertarians and go heavy on free will, "ethical self-interest" and the rest of the Ayn Rand crap. At the same time, they're major polluters. They've polluted the hell out of Watomi Lake, and if they had their way, they'd dump their industrial poison into the Calista River. Their smokestacks spew out noxious fumes. They've racked up hundreds of environmental infractions, been sued dozens of times. They fight back, counter-sue, dig up dirt on their enemies. They'll spend whatever it takes to keep doing what they're doing, all in the name of dynamic egoism, laissez-faire capitalism and their Darwinian economic survival-of-the-fittest beliefs. CI may be the biggest privately owned polluter in the country. If it was a public company, they'd never get away with it. Meantime, they finance academics who deny we're in the midst of climate change. I could go on. And then there's the personal stuff . . .'

'Such as?'

'Stuff consistent with what they did to Courtney. Rumors of sex parties with underage girls. I've heard tales like that for years. Then I hear people say, "How could that be possible? They're great humanists. Look at all the money they've donated to the museum. They fund free summer theater and dance performances. They paid for that new wing at the Calista Institute of Music. Maybe they have a few peccadilloes, but don't we all have our urges, our shames, our non-conforming desires? Surely such things can't annul all the good they do." You know the rap.'

He shook his head. 'Nate Silver could have told me about the Schechtner deal. So why'd he suggest I contact Spencer Addams? He had to know that if I found him, I'd get the story. He may even have guessed that Spencer had copies of Ted's notes.'

'Maybe he was sincerely trying to help you.'

Noah shrugged. 'Or frustrate me. I doubt a judge would allow Ted's notes to be read in court. Ted's dead and can't be cross-examined. The Cobbs' lawyers would designate them as "scurrilous hearsay." And even if Courtney's willing to come back and testify (a huge *if*), they'll attack her as a delusional schizophrenic. After what we read this afternoon, I'd truly love to go to war against the Cobbs. But Ted's notes aren't enough. I'm pretty sure Nate knew that when he suggested I look up Spencer. Probably didn't like the way I came on to him and didn't like that I turned down his invitation to play golf. So he decided to have some fun with me.'

'Is that really a lawyer's idea of fun? Strikes me as pathetic.'

'Yeah,' Noah agreed, 'and the worst part is that to guys like Nate something as awful as this is just a game.'

Noah was wrapped up in the legal aspects, while I was concerned by the huge emotional damage Courtney's brothers and parents had inflicted on her. I'd always felt, and Jase did too, that there was a secret history behind the murals, an engine that drove their creation. Now I knew what that dark energy was. The murals were about cold, two-faced people who refused to listen to Courtney and were incapable of understanding her pain. They were images of the resistance she'd met when she'd tried to tell her story. I thought her dolls were about the same thing: two-faced figures, genitals swelling beneath their garments, faces ravaged by being cut up and then sewn back together, the tears and stitches marking them for their malice, moral corruption and hypocrisy. As Penny Dawson told Joan, the murals were the girls' vision of hell.

We sat in the tavern in silence, lost in our respective thoughts.

'So what do you think?' Noah finally asked.

'Don't know. What about you?'

'I think it's urgent we find out what Courtney wants. Where her head is at and what, if anything, we can do for her.'

'Maybe we should just leave it alone.'

'I know you, Hannah. I don't believe for a second that's what you want.'

He was right, of course. It was too late to stop. We'd come this far. There was no turning back.

Thérèse Zellweger

I was thrilled when Hannah called me from New York and told me the plan: take Agnès on an outing for a covert meeting with her very close old friend, Penny. I went straight in to see Dr DeJ. I found him in a bright mood.

'Yes, my dear – what can I do for you today?' he said, speaking in the same unctuous tone he used back when he wanted to beguile me into bed.

I proposed taking Agnès and Johnny on an excursion along the coast, adding that I thought they could both use some relief from the clinic routine. They've become close friends, I told him, and would enjoy going out together. I, of course, would act as chaperone so as to preclude any *Gefummel*.

Dr DeJ smiled at that. 'The French call it *galipettes*, somersaults, but my favorite expression is the one the English use – "hanky-panky."'

I laughed.

'As you know,' he said, 'gay boys enjoy forging strong friend-ships with middle-aged women. And the women like it because they don't feel threatened.'

Such a brilliant insight! And straight from the Great Psychiatrist's mouth!

'Rather than a motor trip, take them out on the lake. Karl can run you around in the speedboat, then dock at one of the towns where you three can stroll to a café. What do you think?'

'Sounds excellent,' I assured him.

I emailed Hannah that I had permission to take Agnès and Johnny out for an excursion. She emailed back with a wet kiss emoji.

I thought it best not to upset Agnès by telling her in advance she'd be meeting her old friend. But I told Johnny after swearing him to secrecy. I explained that this was a delicate situation that could cost me my job, and that I was prepared for that as there were plenty of open positions at other clinics. But if anyone got wind of the plan, Dr DeJ would certainly cancel the outing. Then he might make trouble if we tried to bring Penny into the clinic.

'It's best,' I explained, 'for them to meet outside. You'll be there to keep her calm.'

Johnny loved the plan and said he was flattered that I asked him to be part of it.

'I'll do anything I can to help her,' he said.

Penny Dawson Ruiz

I recognized Court the moment I received the Ragdoll Artist photo. She looked just as I'd expect after twenty-five years. I immediately called Joan to confirm the ID.

'It's Court, no question,' I told her.

She told me there'd been some talk about sending me to see Court in Switzerland. Would I be up for that?

'You bet I would,' I said.

That evening she called back, then put Jason and Hannah on the line. They introduced themselves, then explained why they thought I was the best person to talk to Court, find out how she was doing, and then, if I thought it appropriate, subtly feel her out about leaving the clinic and returning to the US. They didn't want to upset her and so, for reasons of security, she wouldn't know in advance she'd be meeting me. She'd be accompanied by Thérèse, a trusted nurse from the clinic, and another patient, a nineteen-year-old gay kid named Johnny who was the only friend she'd made there in years. They said they knew this meeting would be emotional for us both, but because they weren't clear about Court's mental state, they thought it best to keep it low-key.

I told them I understood, and that I hoped that Courtney remembered me as warmly as I remembered her.

The next day Hannah emailed air tickets: Miami–Paris–Zurich with a departure in ten days. It was only then that I understood this was real. I was incredibly excited and eager to do my part.

Johnny Baldwin

t was a dazzling day. Lake Zurich was serene, the water flat and clear. The old man, Karl, who tended to the boats, laughed aloud as he buzzed us around the lake.

'Karl, please don't stir up such a wake,' Thérèse said.

Karl didn't care. He was having fun. The Cigarette boat purred like a fine automobile. It was Dr DeJ's favorite, the one he used to scoot around Zürichsee in the early evening with his girlfriends.

I thought Agnès would be scared by so much speed, but she surprised me. She loved it! She stood up so the wind caught her hair. Finally, Thérèse pulled her down. Then, to my astonishment, Agnès reached for my hand. She'd never done that before. She'd always kept her distance. If we happened to touch, it was only by accident. I wondered if she sensed that today would be different. She confirmed that when she whispered in my ear.

'Something's going to happen, isn't it?'

I nodded. 'Something nice, I think,' I whispered back.

Penny Dawson Ruiz

I arrived in Zurich jet-lagged. I hadn't managed to sleep much on the plane. It had been a long journey, my first outside of the States.

After I passed through immigration, I was grateful to find a man in a chauffeur's cap holding up a sign with my name. He took my bag, escorted me to his car. We drove south of the city to a luxury hotel, Beau Séjour au Lac, where I was to rest and spend the night before the long-anticipated meeting with Court the following afternoon.

I was nervous. Joan had handled the arrangements and so far things had gone well. But I felt foreboding. How well would Court remember me? What would she be like? I knew I'd changed a lot in the intervening years, and assumed she had, too. Yet it seemed she harbored the same obsession. Her ragdolls were clearly linked to the paintings we'd done in the attic of A Caring Place, renditions of duplicitous people who showed blank faces to the world while harboring malice behind their masks.

That evening the clinic nurse, Thérèse, visited me at the hotel. She was friendly, intense yet easy to talk to. Her blond hair was shag-cut like mine, and her blue eyes glowed with compassion.

I listened closely as she briefed me.

'Agnès, as we all call her at the clinic, has always struck me as lost in her own world. It's only in the last few months, when she made friends with a gay English boy, that she began to emerge from her shell. I'm not saying she's normal now. Far from it. You may find her distant. She doesn't bother much with the social graces. But I think she'll respond well to you, her only visitor as far as I know in many, many years. At the clinic we have the feeling her family has more or less forgotten about her. I wouldn't describe her as depressed. She's on a drug regimen and thus fairly stable. I believe it's her artwork that keeps her going. It seems to be the only thing that interests her. As she's told me many times, "My art is my life."'

'It always was,' I said.

Thérèse informed me she hadn't yet told 'Agnès' about my visit. She was saving that for the following day. She, Court and Johnny, the English boy, would arrive in town by motorboat. From the dock they'd walk to the tavern where we'd meet. En route, she'd tell Court I was waiting for her. She didn't believe Court would balk; if she did, Thérèse would come to tell me so. She promised she wouldn't leave me sitting there wondering what happened to them.

'I expect she'll be happy to see someone from her past, someone she was close to when she was young. I know about the murals you two painted. Hannah and Jason showed me photos. I found them amazing. But with someone in her condition, one can never be certain how she'll react.'

I asked how she would describe Court's condition.

She shrugged, admitting she couldn't define it. Agnès, she said, rarely spoke, and when she did, it was in barely more than a whisper. But her artwork showed great passion, suggesting strong emotions within.

'Sometimes I wonder if these dolls she makes are visions of how she views herself – placid and inscrutable on the outside, roiling and possessed beneath.'

I asked her about Johnny, the English boy – what was he like?

'A good kid. Very nice. He puts on this ironic front, referring to himself as a "perverted faggot," as if to forestall anyone calling him that. He's gentle with Agnès. No question they've been good for one another. They flirt in this cute, playful way.'

I was glad to have met Thérèse and been prepped by her for the meeting. She told me I could easily walk from the hotel to the pub, and drew me a little map to show me the route. At that time of day there'd be few customers. When I arrived, I should take a booth, order something to drink, then wait for them to show up.

Before she left, she told me that the meeting had not been authorized by the clinic director. It was likely he'd get angry if he found out about it. She wanted me to know this was a risk she was willing to take, that she cared a lot about Agnès and believed seeing me again would give her a lift.

'I've set this up, so it's totally my responsibility,' she said. 'If there's a bad outcome, it's on me.'

*   *   *

The next morning I took a walk along the lovely shore of Lake Zurich, thinking back to Court's and my days at Red Raven, the fun we'd had that summer messing around in the art studio, giggling, showing off our skills, hers being quite considerable. Word soon spread around camp that there was a girl who could draw your likeness in two minutes flat. Court loved doing caricatures. She drew several of camp staff, and a mean one of a haughty girl named Amanda whom we both disliked.

We played softball, canoed, swam, but spent most of our days making art. The air was hot and muggy, and there were lots of bugs. We were both bitten up pretty good. What I remember best was the feeling that, finally, I'd found a friend who shared my interests, and in whom I could confide. By the end of summer, to our surprise and delight, we discovered our periods were in sync.

At three p.m. I was seated in a booth at the Schwarze Katzenbar waiting for them to show up. The tavern was dark, and, as Thérèse predicted, there were barely any customers. I ordered a beer and looked around. The walls were covered with stuffed fish. Suddenly, the door opened, a shaft of light cut across the floor, and there stood Court, Thérèse on one side, Johnny on the other, the three of them blinking, their eyes adjusting to the gloom.

Court spotted me, stared and then her face broke into a smile.

'Pen!'

I stood. 'Court!'

She ran to me, hugged me. We held each other close. Her body felt thin. I could feel her shoulder blades beneath her blouse. We embraced the way we did twenty-five years before in that little attic room after we'd been working for hours on the walls. It was our ritual end-of-work embrace when we decided to break for the night. Feeling her in my arms, I remembered the last time we hugged, our ritual broken by a pair of burly cops who came charging up the ladder and then pulled us apart. I remember how we both screamed bloody murder. I remember punching and scratching the guy holding me, while I watched Court crying out and wriggling as the other one pulled her backwards down the ladder. Then the cop who had hold of me pulled me down too. Chaos! It was the end for us. And now here we were, in our forties, hugging it out in this strange dark pub in Switzerland, and it was as if no time had passed between.

We stood back, peered into each other's eyes. Hers looked clear, with crow's feet at the sides and a crease of concern in between.

'You look the same, just older,' I told her.

'We're both older,' she whispered. 'I think that's just fine.'

Once we settled down, I asked her how her life was going, while also telling her a little about mine. She looked distressed when I told her about losing my husband, and seemed fascinated by my description of Key West, the local art colony, my framing shop, how I went everywhere on a rusty old bike, and about my painted-to-sell watercolor seascapes and my personal work which was now totally abstract.

This is going well. She's relating, I thought.

'I never imagined I'd end up an abstract painter,' I told her. 'It just kinda happened. Making all those watercolors burned me out on representation. Just as well. I was never as good a draughtsman as you. You know you've become quite famous on account of your dolls. You're known as the Ragdoll Artist.'

She looked pleased. 'I'm glad people like them. I never sign them.'

'Do you know they sell for lots of money?'

She shrugged. 'That doesn't concern me. I have a story to tell. I've found a way of telling it with cloth and thread. That's all that matters to me. And if people like my story . . . well, that's fine too.' She paused, smiled. 'I sometimes think of myself as a one-trick pony,' she whispered.

I was surprised. *She doesn't seem to care that her dolls are being sold. Could her shrink be doing so on her behalf and not for his own account as Joan, Hannah and Jason believe? If so how many more of their other assumptions are wrong? And why doesn't she ask how I found out she's the Ragdoll Artist?*

'We didn't think you knew your dolls were being sold,' I said, without explaining who 'we' were.

She shook her head. 'I make them, then give them to Doctor DeJ. He's told me people like them. I don't care about that. I only care about them while I'm making them. Afterwards . . .' She shrugged again.

I told her that her dolls reminded me of the characters we'd painted on the walls.

'Yeah, I suppose,' she said.

I asked her if she remembered how hard we worked on those

walls, how passionately involved we were in that project. Then I asked if she ever wondered what had become of our work.

'No. I try never to think about the past,' she said, her voice flat. 'I try to live in the here and now, and carry on with my work.'

I told her our wall paintings were still there, that some people recently discovered them and were very impressed, even calling them a 'masterpiece.'

'Here, take a look.'

I brought out my phone, accessed photos of the walls, then pulled her close so we could look at them together. I watched her as she studied them. Immediately, I saw her eyes light up, gleam with recognition. For a few moments she seemed to revel in the memory. Then her eyes glistened and I thought she might start to cry. In a strange way, I was hoping that she would. But then just as quickly her interest flagged.

'Nice,' she said, turning away from my phone. 'But like I said, I only care about the here and now.'

I felt sad as I saw the excitement die out in her eyes.

In the hope of rekindling her interest, I told her I was planning to visit Calista to see them again up close.

'Would you like to come with me? I think it would be fun to see them together. Do you remember that we almost finished painting them? Do you think we could finish them now? Probably not, because we're so different. Or . . . maybe?'

'I am different,' she said, shaking her head. 'You go, Pen. Then come back and tell me about it.'

I was stunned into silence. She smiled at me, which I took as her way to show me she hadn't meant to offend. I had this strange feeling then – that she was with me there, and at the same time not, that in her head she was very much alone.

Suddenly, I started to weep.

'Now . . . now . . .' she said, comforting me. 'We're going to be fine. I believe that.'

Her kind words made me weep even more.

'I want to introduce you to my friends,' she said cheerfully, turning to the bar where the other two were waiting. She beckoned them to join us in the booth. After they slipped in beside us: 'This is my new friend, Johnny. This is my old friend, Pen. And this is Thérèse, my very kind nurse, who takes care of me and helps me get through the days.'

So strange, the way she introduced us, like an unschooled actress awkwardly reciting lines by rote.

The four of us chatted a few minutes. They asked how we met, I told them, and then, perhaps sensing we needed to speak privately again, they excused themselves and retreated back to the bar.

'So you're happy at the clinic?' I asked. She nodded vigorously. 'Any interest in traveling? You could stay with me in Key West, see it for yourself.'

She shook her head. 'This is my home – the clinic, the view of the lake. All my art materials are here. And my friends, Johnny and Thérèse.' She smiled. 'They call me "Agnès." I've gotten used to that. That's who I've become.'

'You don't want to go back to Calista, visit your family?'

'No,' she said, resuming the flat tone. I saw moisture in her eyes which told me her lack of affect was a mask. As I gazed at her, I saw her face start to fall. Then she smiled, just as she used to do whenever she felt bad and needed to cheer herself up.

'Your parents have passed away. Your brothers—'

'Please!' she hissed. She uttered the word with such passion, I took it as a signal I must stop mentioning them or Calista, that those were people and a place she could not bear to think about or discuss.

'Are you really content here?' I asked again.

'Very,' she said. 'I can't imagine living any place else.'

So, that was that, the end of any possibility she would return, confront her brothers or deal in any way with the issues that had driven her to run away. I wasn't at all convinced she was as content as she claimed, but there was no one there telling her what to say. Her family had buried her. She was receiving drugs that kept her stabilized and she was a productive artist. Perhaps, I thought, that was the best solution for her. What more did I or anyone else have to offer?

Deciding to drop my questions about her family and her feelings about staying or leaving, I asked her about sewing – how she'd happened to take it up.

'I don't remember you ever speaking of textile art,' I told her. 'I didn't even know you knew how to sew.'

'I didn't. I learned in OT,' she said, seemingly happy I'd changed the subject. 'For a long time I lost my sense of self. I knew that to get it back I needed to start making art again. Drawing, painting, sewing – when I do those things, I become this powerful person.

Anyway, I don't think of my doll-making as sewing. If you need to make art, does it matter what materials you use?'

This reminded me of our intense conversations back at Red Raven and A Caring Place. I was happy our dialogue had turned this way. This was the kind of thing we'd loved to talk about back then – art and what it meant to us.

'Do you remember Ms Zevin?' I asked.

'Of course! Our favorite teacher.'

'One of the people who saw our wall paintings went to see her. She remembered us both. She said she was always certain you'd become a famous artist.'

Court blushed. 'Really! Well, you too, I'm sure.'

'I'm not famous, but I'm pleased with what I make,' I told her.

She nodded gravely. 'Isn't that the only important thing?'

She looked at me then with the straight-on gaze of a person whose life is focused on only one thing, a gaze that conveyed a single-minded vision, or perhaps a successfully channeled form of madness.

We talked on for perhaps another hour, about art and how important it was to our lives. Then Thérèse came over and told us it was time for them to go back to the clinic.

'We have a motorboat waiting,' she explained.

We stood, embraced again. She said how happy she was to see me after so many years and how greatly she appreciated my visit.

'I hope you'll come again, Pen. Next time, come to the clinic and I'll show you what I'm working on. I have paints. We can work side by side. Wouldn't that be fun!'

I walked them to the door. Court and Thérèse slipped out, while Johnny lingered.

'How'd it go?' he whispered.

'Don't know,' I told him. 'She made it clear she's happy and settled here, and has no desire to leave, even for a visit.'

'I suspected as much,' he said. 'I don't believe she'll ever leave.'

'And you?'

'I hope to soon. I'll miss her when I do. Maybe I'll come visit you in Key West. I hear it's a great place for guys like me.'

I told him that if he came, I'd be happy to show him around and he could even stay with me if he liked. Then he too was gone. I watched him run to catch up with them, then the three as they moved down the street toward the docks.

*   *   *

Thinking back on the two hours I spent with Court, I have trouble reconciling the girl I'd known and the mature woman I met again. She was the same, and yet very different, more closed-off, more self-contained – perhaps less tormented, too. She seemed to have found a way of living that suited her, and the fact that her life was so closely circumscribed didn't seem to faze her. She was free to express what she felt about people, to create, make art out of her belief that human beings are duplicitous. She could express that again and again, as if always circling a controlling belief held deep within, trying over and over to create an ultimate expression of it, and yet always failing because her goal was by its nature unreachable, her conflicts unresolvable.

I emailed Joan as soon as I returned to the hotel: *Saw her. She doesn't want to leave.* Then I pulled the drapes and crawled into bed to catch up on sleep.

I was happy to have seen Court again, to find her in good health and relatively happy, but I felt that although she was seemingly more content, she was actually more disturbed than the girl I'd known years before. She was no longer that wide-eyed girl with the puppy I'd painted in a corner of one of the walls. That girl was troubled but alive with possibility. The woman I'd met with that afternoon had a far narrower vision. It was as if the world she lived in had contracted, and as fine and well made as her dolls were, there was something locked-in about them; my sense was that she was lost in a repetitive cycle with no possibility of breaking free.

I was glad I'd come. It was good to know she was alive and functioning as an artist. I also believed she was right about not going back to Calista to face her demons. She was far too brittle for that. I felt that if she left the clinic and went back, the experience could break her.

Her words haunted me: 'I have a story to tell and I've found a way to tell it with cloth and thread.' It was the same story that we had painted on the walls – You-Will-Be-Betrayed, You-Will-Not-Be-Believed. This was the story she was telling herself when we met, and had been telling herself ever since, again and again.

I also wondered if the paintings we made on those attic walls were her best expression of it, and, in fact, her greatest work.

Jason Poe

We were so naïve! Our fantasy that Courtney would be willing to come back to Calista, confront her brothers, reclaim her freedom and her fortune, then live something akin to a normal life . . . we should have known that was absurd.

She was too badly damaged, she'd spent a quarter of a century in a sanatorium, and considering all she'd been through, it was a wonder she could still make art.

Noah advised us that if she wouldn't come back and testify, there was no hope of reclaiming her life. Yes, Ted Schechtner's therapy notes were devastating, but would likely be inadmissible in a legal proceeding. Could Noah replace Nate Silver as Courtney's guardian *ad litem*? Possibly, but what would be the point? She was content where she was, her maintenance was being paid, and – it turned out, to our surprise – she was aware her shrink was selling her work. There was no real scandal aside from her brothers' abuse decades in the past. The only purpose in airing that would be to embarrass them, which would be useless. Those who would hate them already did so on account of their politics and environmental crimes.

'I wish there was something purposeful we could do for her,' Noah told us. 'Alas, I don't think there is.'

Hannah and I had several long discussions about this. We understood that Courtney's life was beyond our power to reclaim. Even so, we'd accomplished our primary goal: discovered the story and meaning behind the Locust Street Murals. Joan's interviews with Penny in Key West and Dr Ted's notes on his sessions with Courtney explained much of what had been mysterious about the murals. Now our remaining goal was to preserve and protect them.

A week or so after a lengthy FaceTime exchange with Penny, in which she described her meeting with Courtney in detail, I received an excited call from Cindy Broderick.

'We finally got half a mural out. It was tough. There was some minor chipping at the edges where the panels meet, but that can be easily restored. Three and a half murals to go.'

'Which half?' I asked.

'Two sections. Left side of the A wall.'

Terrific! That was the part that included Courtney and her puppy, Bonnie.

Cindy told me her biggest problem was getting the panels off the walls, then down the attic ladder.

'We considered loosening the gazebo, bringing in a crane to lift the whole thing off the roof, then setting it down on a flatbed truck. We decided that was too risky. The structure might fall apart. So we're carefully loosening the panels and bringing them out piecemeal. It'll take time and a lot of patience, but I'm convinced it can be done with minimal damage to the art.'

Hannah was frustrated. 'We know the story and Cindy is preserving the work. Why isn't that enough?'

It was a rhetorical question. We both knew it wasn't nearly enough. We had to do something about the brothers. Since it was clear that Courtney couldn't and wouldn't confront them, perhaps we owed it to her to do so on her behalf.

I got everyone together to discuss such a confrontation. Noah was the obvious choice, but he had a good reason not to take on the job.

'If I ask to meet with them, they'll refer me to their lawyers. Then what? For reasons I explained, without Courtney's participation this can't become a legal matter.'

'What kind of matter is it, then?' Hannah asked.

'Emotional. It's about satisfaction. You want to confront them with what you know and make them react.'

'They'll deny everything,' Hannah said.

'Of course! But it's *how* they deny that'll be telling,' Noah told her. 'Remember, they have no idea what you've been up to all these months, or even that the murals exist.'

'Vile as they are, they're a big piece of the story,' Joan said. 'At least we should try to hear their side of it.'

We all turned to her.

She shook her head. 'You guys want *me* to talk to them?'

'Why not? You're a journalist. Just ask for an interview,' I said.

Joan smiled. 'It would be an ambush interview.'

'All the better!' Hannah said. 'Are you up for it?'

'Yeah, I guess.'

'Be careful how you handle them,' Noah warned. 'Those guys play rough. Soon as you bring up Courtney's name, they'll probably throw you out.'

From the way Joan continued smiling, I had a hunch she was formulating a plan. My confidence in her was such that I was certain she could pull off such an interview. So far she'd done a terrific job for us: obtaining the police file on the raid; interviewing Loetz and Silver; getting Penny to open up, then recruiting her to go to Zurich and discover where Courtney's head was at. Meantime, she was writing an amazing series on the summer fires, chasing down leads from her arson investigator source. She'd already published three articles on the fires, each of which appeared on the front page of the *Times-Dispatch*. She was making a name for herself as an investigative journalist, just as I had once made my name as a conflict photographer. I was sure that if I hadn't gotten her involved, we would never have been able to put together the story behind the murals.

I went over to Locust Street to watch the conservators remove the final A-wall panels. I was impressed by the care they took bubble-wrapping the plywood panels, then lowering them to the third floor. After they took them down to their van, I went up to the attic to look around. With one wall now empty, the effect was different. There was no longer a sense of being overwhelmed. The paintings on the B, C and D walls were strong, but without the A wall the room felt incomplete. It was the four walls together that made the murals so powerful, the feeling that one was dead center inside a total work of art.

Driving back to the Capehart, I felt let down. The murals project was near its end, and I wasn't sure what I should do next. Finish up with *Leavings*, put together a show and accompanying book, then go back to full-time teaching in the fall – of course. But still I felt an emptiness. The murals had consumed me. I had come upon them on account of what some considered my great strength as a photographer, but which I had come to view as my great weakness: a love of taking risks. Just as I'd gone to Aleppo to be a witness, so I had entered the world of the murals with the intention of cracking their code. I had left Aleppo broken, and now was feeling pangs of withdrawal from the murals. I'd crawled into all those abandoned houses to document desperation and loss.

What I found was something both terrifying and magnificent, a work of art that had its roots in horrendous betrayal and abuse.

I understood again, driving back into the city, that my quest to comprehend and 'read' the murals had really been a quest to understand myself, the forces that drove me to take photographs of trauma and pain. It was upon that realization that I decided to go back to eye-contact photography. Images of the things people left behind could say a good deal about them, but the confusion and sorrow in their eyes would say far more. I was long done covering wars. But I wanted to go back to gazing at people as they gazed back at me, discovering the truth in their eyes.

What was it in my own life that drove me to identify with the agony in others? I had a hunch I would never plumb that mystery, but that was the road I was on and which I felt I had no choice but to follow.

Hannah Sachs

I was anxious to express my gratitude to Anna, tell her that her tip had been correct, that the Ragdoll Artist and the murals artist were one and the same. I phoned her a couple of times, left messages, was upset when she didn't return my calls.

Finally she sent an email: *Feeling awful. Not answering the phone. Please come see me when/if you can.*

I immediately emailed back. We made a date for me to come over to her place at six p.m. the following day.

She lived in the Windsor Arms, one of a pair of twin *Style Moderne* apartment houses just a block from Waverly Square. The Windsor Arms and the Cambridge Arms were two of the better buildings in the suburbs, streamlined with touches of nautical ornamentation, horizontal lines, rounded corners, and anomalous molded escutcheons set over their grand entranceways.

Anna didn't look well.

'I've been sleeping poorly,' she said as she fixed us drinks. 'Actually, I've been feeling like crap. Last week I even felt suicidal. Don't worry, that's over, but I'm still depressed.'

Her problem, she confided, was Anders Carlsen, who, she told me, was about to be fired from the CMA directorship.

'Turns out the museum board decided to get rid of him, not because of our affair, but for lying to Jack Cobb about it. I told you about the anonymous letter, and that Jack asked Anders if what it said was true. Anders shrugged it off, then tried to find out who wrote it. He called his curators into his office one at a time and interrogated them like a Grand Inquisitor. Several of them complained to the board, and then someone pointed out he'd never completed his PhD as he claimed. Did all the course work, but never handed in his dissertation. Yet he insisted everyone address him as "Doctor Carlsen."'

'Jesus!' I said. 'Aren't you glad you cut him loose?'

'Sure. But it's been painful. And really humiliating to find out everyone in the museum knew we were involved and gossiped about us at dinner parties. Now Anders insists he needs me. He keeps calling, leaving messages that because of me he's losing his job and his family, and begging me to take him back. "I'm being shit-canned at the museum and you're all I've got left. And now you don't return my calls."'

'He really said "shit-canned"?'

'At times he can be pretty crude. Thing is, I don't know how to react. I can't take the pressure. I'm tempted to see him if only out of pity. I've also thought about blocking his email address and his number, but I'm afraid that'll just enrage him.'

'Do it, Anna. And don't you dare even contemplate suicide. He's not worth it. No one is. Forget him. Move to New York. Become a private dealer there, like you planned. You were right – Courtney Cobb *is* the Ragdoll Artist. If it weren't for you and your terrific eye, we would never have made the connection.'

I told her the whole story, and that we had video of Courtney's shrink surreptitiously selling Courtney's dolls to Susanne Weber. I urged her to go to Zurich, talk to Courtney and then DeJonghe, use the video and photos of the pornographic doll as leverage to get herself appointed Courtney's US dealer. Then return to New York and start representing Courtney's work to collectors.

'As for Anders – he's damaged goods,' I reminded her. 'You'll be damaged too if you take him back.'

She gazed into my eyes. 'You're such a good friend.'

We talked for a while then about the murals, how they'd been created by two young people caught up in the passionate throes of art-making, who created an amazing work that most likely neither one of them could have produced on her own.

'And the terrifying part for me,' I said, 'is that if there had been no violation, no abuse, those murals would probably not exist. So was it worth it? Can art that good justify such terrible pain?'

'That,' Anna said, 'is always the great, horrible and unanswerable question.'

'Well,' I laughed, 'now that we've dealt with the fundamental issue of art-making, what say we go out to dinner? Maybe try that sushi bar "O" on the square. Get ourselves a couple flasks of really good sake and celebrate the start of your new life.'

I waited while she changed and touched up her face.

'Anders has a set of keys,' she told me as she locked her apartment door.

'You gotta get them back.'

'That would mean seeing him.'

'I'll see him. If he doesn't hand them over, change your locks.'

As we strolled out of the Windsor Arms, Anna suddenly stopped.

'*Shit!*' she hissed. 'Across the street. That guy in the doorway – it's him.'

I peered at a man wearing a fedora standing in the shadowed entrance of the Cambridge Arms, the twin of Anna's building. He was standing ominously still. He seemed to be gazing back at us. I couldn't make out his face, but then a car passed by, its headlights illuminating the doorway. For the fraction of a second that the man's face was lit, he raised his eyebrows in an ironic way and a tight half-smile curled his lips. No question, it was Anders.

'This is what I've been afraid of,' Anna whispered.

'Is he a stalker?'

'He told me in grad school he stalked an ex. He thought that was clever. "Got under her skin. Really freaked her out," he said.'

Jesus!

'I'm going to talk to him.'

She grasped my arm. 'No, Hannah! Please don't!'

'I'll be right back. I'm going to get your keys and warn him to stay away.'

I broke free and strode across the street.

'Anders?'

'Do I know you?' he asked.

'We've met. My name's Hannah Sachs. Stay away from Anna.

Stop this stalking bullshit, or you're going to be in a lot of trouble.'

'Who the hell are you to tell me what to do?'

I studied his face – strong jaw, intense blue eyes, dark blond mustache and goatee. Under other circumstances I'd probably consider him decent-looking. That night I viewed him as a creep. 'I'm Anna's friend,' I told him. 'My brother's a lawyer. Leave her alone or he'll serve you with a restraining order. How's that going to look along with your being fired from the museum for playing Torquemada with the curators, and lying to everyone about your doctorate?'

He sniffed. 'I see that's gotten around.'

'Yeah, it has.'

'I need to talk to her. Please tell her that.'

I shook my head. 'She doesn't want to talk. And she wants her keys back. Better hand them over now.'

As he stared at me, I saw madness in his eyes, the look of a cornered animal deciding whether to lash out or retreat.

'Don't do anything stupid,' I warned him. 'You're in enough trouble as it is.'

'Yeah. Because the bitch ruined my life.' He turned to where Anna was standing. 'Hear that, cunt?' he yelled. Then he reached into his pocket, threw a set of keys at my feet. 'Take 'em! Tell her we're done. Tell her I've got no use for her.' And with that he huffed, spat at the spot where he'd thrown the keys, tipped his hat, huffed again, turned his back, then walked off with the swagger of a man under the delusion that he was making a dignified retreat.

When I got back to Anna, I found her looking strong.

'I heard the whole thing,' she said.

'Still want to go out?'

'Oh, yeah!' she said, taking my arm. 'Let's go get that sake.'

Joan Nguyen

I spent a week prepping for the interview. I read every article I could find on the Cobb brothers, then contacted the public relations office at Cobb Industries. I spoke with a Ms Evelyn Maw who told me in an efficient tone that she handled all interview requests.

'The guys rarely grant interviews,' she told me briskly. 'They've been burned too many times.'

'I've no intention of burning them,' I assured her. 'My piece will be about the Cobb family's commitment to the arts.'

'Sounds innocuous enough. What about politics?'

'I don't write about politics, never have.'

'I've read your articles about the fires. Not bad.'

'Actually, most of my writing's about art.'

'Well and good,' Evelyn said. 'Send over a file of all your articles from the last two years. I'll look them over, and if I think an interview will be worth their time, I'll pass it along with my recommendation. The final decision will be theirs.'

I sent over the file as requested. Three days later she called me back.

'They're up for it, so long as there's no discussion of politics or environmental issues. Confine yourself to the arts, and you'll be fine. They'll give you half an hour.'

'That's all?'

'They're busy. But if they get interested, they'll probably extend.'

'They'll be on the record, right?'

'They will. If they want to go off, they'll tell you so.'

'Sounds fair.'

'We always play fair, Joan,' she told me. 'Just be sure you play fair with us.'

'Understood.'

'Good. We'll meet you in the company conference room. Tuesday, two p.m. sharp. I'll leave your name at reception.'

The Cobb Industries building is an impressive structure, designed by Nils Lindstrøm, the Swedish-American architect who designed Calista's heroic twin structures, Tower of the Great Lakes and Tower of the Great Plains. It was a bold brutalist-style multistoried building made of raw reinforced concrete, signifying strength and power. There were similar signifiers on the lobby floor, a large mural that couldn't have been more different from the murals in the cupola on Locust. It depicted workers mining ore and forging steel, attending to huge turbines and dams, against backgrounds of factories and mills belching smoke. This was a leftover from the company's early days when it was known as Cobb Steel. I winced when I saw it, for it struck me as an in-your-face retort to those who accused CI of environmental crimes.

Staring at it, I had a thought: Gallagher had mentioned that two homes had been torched in Danzig Heights, the connection being that both home-owners were environmental activists. Hmmm . . . could the Cobbs have used the summer fires as a cover to punish their enemies? That, I decided, might well be worth looking into.

A sign directed visitors to a security desk where my name was checked against a list. A uniformed guy with sidearm and shoulder patch instructed me to stand still and gaze at a lens. My picture was snapped and seconds later a computer spat out a visitor's ID card which he attached to a necklace.

'Wear this at all times while you're in the building,' he ordered. 'It expires at the close of business. Turn it in when you leave. It's not a souvenir.'

He grinned as he hung it around my neck. 'Very becoming,' he said.

The elevator bank was outlined in stainless steel. Since I was ascending to the executive floor, I was required to take a car with a uniformed attendant. He was also armed and wore the same shoulder patch as the man at the lobby desk.

'Security here's pretty tight,' I commented as the door closed.

'Has to be,' he said. 'Lotsa flakes come in here to make trouble.'

'What kind of trouble?' I asked, as the elevator picked up speed.

'One came in last week, yelled and splashed around a bucket of animal blood.' He bared his teeth. 'We know how to handle folks like that.'

Folks! 'Rough them up?'

He shrugged. 'Folks want to make trouble, then trouble's what they're going to get. And once their biometric data's stored, they never get in this building again.'

The elevator came to a hushed stop. A quiet disembodied female voice announced, 'Penthouse floor. Please check in at reception.'

Evelyn Maw had the lined face of an aging model who'd spent too much time in the sun. I figured her for late forties. Her dyed blond hair was precision-cut and her cheekbones were sharp, but the flesh of her neck and the skin around her eyes showed signs of distress. She was short and perhaps as compensation wore

stiletto heels. Her most prominent feature was a pair of dark eyes
that cut at mine like lasers.

'Hi, I'm Evelyn,' she said, extending her hand. 'Thanks for
being prompt.'

'I strive to be obedient,' I said lightly.

She was not amused.

'I'm sure I needn't remind you of the ground rules,' she said
as she walked me down a hushed corridor, her heels clicking on
the terrazzo floor. 'You may record only while we're on the record.
If we go off, you're to turn off your device. Another thing – we're
informal here. Address the guys as Jack and Kevin. They hate
being called "sir."'

'Got it.'

She led me to a glassed-in conference room at the end of the
hall. There was a wide wooden table with steel edges and perfectly
aligned molded metal chairs. Aside from a huge etching of the CI
logo, there was no art on the walls.

Evelyn pointed to the ceiling. 'Camera,' she explained.
'Everything in here is video-recorded. Of course, you'll be making
your own recording.' She gestured to a chair. 'Can I get you
something? Water, soda, coffee?' I told her no thanks. 'I'll be back
shortly with the guys.' She left me alone.

I peered up at the ceiling camera, winced slightly, then pulled
out a *New Yorker* magazine from my bag. Figuring I was being
watched, I hoped to make it clear I was not intimidated.

I saw them approach through the glass wall. They were talking
and gesturing, but I couldn't hear a word. The conference room
was soundproof.

Suddenly, they were there, the much-feared Cobb brothers,
sporting nearly identical preppy-style haircuts and matching
painted-on smiles. They were dressed informally – no suits or ties,
just really well-tailored sports jackets, black loafers and mottled
designer jeans. The message was clear: *We're real nice guys.*

'Thanks for coming,' Jack told me, his voice whispery, just as
Nate Silver had described. 'Evelyn thinks highly of your work.
It'll be a pleasure to talk about art for a change.'

'Not what journalists usually ask us about,' Kevin added. His
manner was more aggressive than his brother's. 'Everyone thinks
we're ogres.' He made a mock-scary face and bugged out his eyes.

'You know – "The Cobb Brothers, those right-wing nuts despoiling our pristine environment."' He grinned. 'In truth, we're just a couple of average guys trying to make an honest buck.'

Oh, the irony!

After we all had a good chuckle, Evelyn glanced at her watch, then at me. 'So, shall we get down to it?'

I watched them closely as I tossed out a series of innocuous questions about their family and its generations-long support of the fine arts: How did that start? Was there much talk of art around the family dinner table? Any particular art works in the house they remember from the time when they were growing up? I noted that their grandfather, Alfred Cobb, gave the CMA several important old master paintings, while their parents gave works by the impressionists. What kind of art were they interested in? And were their own kids interested in carrying on the family philanthropic tradition?

I could see they were bored. This was my intention, to lull them with blandness before I pounced. They were polite, affable, feigned enthusiasm, but their responses were robotic. As they were similar in appearance, I looked for ways to differentiate them. Both had athletic builds. Jack was stouter than his brother, and his hair was starting to gray. Kevin was lean and struck me as edgy. They both displayed a country-club bonhomie.

Evelyn, I noticed, sat very still, in a posture of obsequious obedience, her lipsticked mouth a thin red slash across her face. But as we talked, her eyes darted from brother to brother, and then to me. I got the impression the men frightened her, not because she feared they'd say something impolitic, but because of how they might reproach her after I left.

'We have so much respect for artists,' Jack was saying. 'We always wonder at their ability to create such remarkable works. Where do they get their insights? We love the ways they show us how to *see*.'

'For us it's all about the *seeing*,' Kevin added. 'We're business guys. We view the world a certain way. Artists have their own angles on things. You might say our support of artists is a way to bask in their reflected glory. We BIRG, as they say.' He smiled, 'And, I should add, we also CORF.'

'Excuse me. I'm not sure . . .'

Evelyn broke in. 'BIRG means bask-in-reflected-glory and CORF means cut-off-reflected-failure.'

'Does that mean you cut off artists whose work no longer interests you?'

'We like winners. Doesn't everyone?' Kevin snapped.

This rejoinder was the first break in their feigned joviality. *Time now to rattle them. Go get 'em, girl!*

'Actually, there's quite an accomplished artist in your family,' I said casually.

They showed me blank looks.

'Your sister, Courtney. Her ragdolls, as I'm sure you know, sell for tens of thousands of dollars. But I don't believe the CMA has so far acquired any of her work.'

'What the hell are you talking about?' Kevin demanded.

Evelyn, I noticed, immediately tensed up.

'Courtney Cobb. She's quite secretive, but people I know have identified her as the famous Ragdoll Artist.'

'We do have a sister named Courtney,' Jack said. He enunciated slowly, trying to keep his whisper steady. 'She's been institutionalized for many years. It's a great sadness in our family, something painful we don't really like to talk about. Frankly, I'm surprised you'd bring up her name.'

'Well, I didn't mean to tread into forbidden territory. I only mention her because she's an important contemporary artist. And this interview is about your family's long-standing connection to art.'

'Perhaps—' Evelyn, leaning forward, clearly wanted to call a halt to the interview. But Kevin hushed her with a wave of his hand.

'What is this?' he demanded. 'Court's a sick woman. Mentally ill. We don't know anything about some "ragdoll artist." I think you'd better explain yourself.'

'I believe it's getting time—' Again Evelyn tried to intervene.

'Shut up, Evelyn!' Kevin snapped. 'We'll handle this.'

'I don't know what you mean by "explain myself,"' I said. 'I know for a fact that your sister is the Ragdoll Artist. Images of her work are all over the internet. If you don't want to talk about her – fine, I understand. Why don't you tell me more about your BIRGing and CORFing? Who, for example, have you CORFed of late?'

'You're here under false pretenses. Who put you up to this?'

'I'm here to talk about art. Your sister's an important artist, something of which you seem unaware.' I glanced over at Evelyn, busy now working her iPhone. I guessed she was accessing images of Courtney's ragdolls, because she went over to Jack, knelt beside him and showed him her screen.

'You're claiming our sister made these?' Jack demanded.

'Let me see!' Kevin said, snatching the phone out of his brother's hand. He gave a quick glance to the screen, then handed the phone back to Jack. Sweat had broken out on his forehead. He gave me a hard stare. 'What is this shit?'

'Are you saying you don't think much of it?' I asked.

'Calm down, Kev.' Jack turned to me. 'You're telling us Court made these?'

I nodded. 'She's in residence at the Privatklinik DeJonghe in Switzerland. Dr DeJonghe sells her dolls through Galerie Susanne Weber in Lucerne. Her old friend, Penny Dawson, recently visited her there. She found your sister in good spirits.'

'Why don't we know about this?' Jack asked Kevin.

'Because someone isn't keeping us fucking informed,' Kevin said.

Jack turned back to me. 'Why are you so sure our sister made these dolls?'

'You know art. You've got a good eye. All you have to do is look at them, then compare them to the murals she and Penny painted twenty-five years ago in A Caring Place on Locust Street.'

'Caring Place – what the fuck is that?' Kevin demanded.

'It's that East Calista shithouse where she holed up after she ran,' Jack explained.

'Actually, it was a licensed refuge for runaway teens. Cops busted it the night they took your sister away.'

'There're paintings there?'

'Powerful ones. I've seen them. I hoped to ask you about them. Because they include portraits of both of you. Your parents and grandparents, too. And they're done in the same two-faced style as the ragdolls, but with similar, shall we say, "expressive" faces hovering above. Quite extraordinary really.'

They went silent, stared at me, gaped, then nodded at one another.

'Evelyn, please show this person out,' Jack said. 'Then come right back.'

Evelyn nodded, turned to me. 'Come along,' she said.

I rose. 'It's been a pleasure.' As I moved toward the brothers, they turned away as if repulsed even by the notion of shaking my hand.

* * *

'What the hell did you think you were doing in there?' Evelyn demanded, as she briskly walked me to the elevator, stiletto heels stabbing at the terrazzo.

'Just what I said I would do – conducting an interview. I'm sorry if the guys got upset.'

'They were furious. You misrepresented yourself. They'll never forgive you for that, and neither will I.'

'Believe me, Evelyn, I don't need anyone's forgiveness.'

She glared at me. 'Don't you dare quote anything they said.'

'No one said anything about going off the record. Everything they said is usable. You know that, too.'

We stopped at the elevator. Her eyes steamed with hate. 'You used me for a fool.'

'Oh, really, Evelyn! Please!'

'Is that true about their sister? I didn't even know they had a sister.'

'It's true. And it's an awful story. You should ask them about it.'

'I wouldn't dare.' She shook her head. 'They'll probably fire me for letting you in.'

'It was their decision, wasn't it?'

She sniffed. 'I doubt they'll remember it that way.'

'I hope you don't lose your job over this.'

'*Thanks, sweetie!* So kind of you to say so!' The elevator door opened. 'Turn in your badge at the desk. And don't try coming in here again. You won't be welcome.'

Holy shit!

Somehow in the conference room I'd managed to stay calm. Now, walking away from the building, I began to shake. I paused on a corner, leaned against a store front, held out my trembling hands. I took some deep breaths to steady myself, then went into a bookstore, walked around looking at books on meditation, all the while telling myself I was out and safe and had no reason to be scared.

Good for you, girl! You brought it off! All of it recorded, too!

I walked back to the *Times-Dispatch*, went up to the newsroom, hurried to my cubicle, sat back in my chair, closed my eyes, took some more deep breaths and tried to regain my calm.

I phoned Gallagher, left him a message: 'Want to talk to you about those environmental guys, the ones whose houses were torched. Please get back to me on this, Nick. It's important.'

Then I phoned Jason, left a message on his voicemail: 'Just left the Cobbs. I'll be over at six to play my recording. So, Jase – I know you're wondering how it went? Let's just say it wasn't pretty.'

When I arrived at the Capehart, Hannah and Tally were waiting in Jase's loft. We sat down at his dining table, I turned on my phone, then we all listened to the interview.

'Oh, you rattled them!' Tally said when it was finished. 'You've got some kind of balls, girl.'

I took that as a high compliment.

Jason gazed at me with admiration. 'Soon as you mentioned Courtney, they knew they were being ambushed. Then they totally lost it. Couldn't help themselves. You, on the other hand, kept your cool. Terrific job!'

I have to admit I was impressed myself. I liked my meek start, so different from the approaches I'd taken with Walter Loetz and Nate Silver.

'They won't take this lightly,' Hannah said.

'What can they do?' Tally asked.

'Call the clinic. Check out your story. I hope they don't take it out on Courtney.'

'They could pull her out of there. If they do, maybe Noah can make a case for guardianship. More likely they'd give DeJonghe hell for letting Penny in to see her.'

'Which he didn't do.'

'Yeah, so DeJonghe'll take it out on the nurse.'

Jase shook his head. 'If I were them, I'd take pride in the fact that my little sister has become such an important artist.'

'Thank God you're not them, Jase,' I told him. 'Those guys are real slimeballs. It was awful to sit with them. They wore these smug smiles, faking modesty while reeking of entitlement and self-importance.' I shook my head. 'Poor Evelyn probably got fired, escorted out of the building by a pair of swarthy security guys, humiliated in front of her co-workers, carrying her personal stuff in a crappy cardboard box.'

'They won't let this go, I'm sure of that,' Hannah said again.

Gallagher got back to me that evening.

'I was planning to call you even before I got your message.

You're free to go with the firebug zero story. Norm Hicks will be indicted tomorrow afternoon.'

'Great!'

I told him I'd been over at the Cobb Industries building to interview the Cobbs, and was struck by the murals in the lobby. 'There're images of smokestacks belching smoke, like a big "Fuck you!" to CI's detractors. I was thinking about that, and the fire at Watomi Lake, then I remembered the environmentalists whose houses were torched. Could there be a connection?'

'You mean the environmentalists started the lake fire, and Cobb Industries retaliated by burning down their homes?'

'No, Nick, that's *not* what I was thinking. More like, CI took advantage of the "random" fires, to do a couple of things at once: burn out the lakeside neighborhood to expand their paint complex, as we discussed, and also punish a couple of their enemies.'

There was a long pause before he replied. When he did, it was in a respectful tone. 'You're not only good, Joan. You're *very* good. That's all I can tell you now. Off the record, we're closing in. Can't reveal the target yet, but I'm sure you can figure it out. When we're ready to go for the kill, you'll be the first to know.'

I put down the phone, pumped my fist. Everything was coming together.

Late that night, trying to sleep, I suddenly had a fearsome thought: *Why had I told the Cobbs that they and their parents were depicted in the Locust Street Murals?*

Thérèse Zellweger

had just arrived at work when Berthe, DeJ's secretary, told me the Great Psychiatrist wanted to see me in his office.

'Why are you glaring at me?' I asked.

'You'll find out soon enough.'

'Am I in trouble?'

She sniffed.

'I'll put on my uniform, then come down.'

'I wouldn't bother with the uniform,' she said, turning her back and stalking off.

Berthe and I had never gotten along. She had worked at the clinic for many years, was in charge of the office when I first arrived. I found out later she'd had an affair with DeJ, one of many as he worked his way through the administrative and nursing staffs. She hated all the women DeJ slept with after he was finished with her, and we all hated her as well. Still, we all put on false fronts and pretended to get along. Today she didn't bother to conceal her pleasure that DeJ was displeased and I was about to be subjected to one of his tongue-lashings.

All right, I thought, if he's going to bawl me out, I might as well go to his office and get it over with.

'What is this about Agnès meeting a visitor?' he demanded, the moment I appeared at his door. His face was red. I could see he was furious. Somehow he'd found out about our meeting with Penny in Meilen.

There was no point denying it. 'She met an old friend at the café there.'

'So your little motorboat jaunt was a pretext.'

'It was you who suggested it.'

He ignored that. 'This meeting was prearranged?'

'It was perfectly innocent, Herr Doktor. I wanted to help her. Johnny did, too. I didn't see the harm.'

'You didn't tell me!' His fury was mounting. Droplets of spittle were shooting out of his mouth.

'As I said, it was innocent. I didn't think you'd mind. It was up to Agnès to tell you if she wanted to. I didn't think she needed permission—'

'I've discussed this with Agnès. She tells me she didn't know about the meeting before you arrived in Meilen. Someone got to you, didn't they? I want to know who and what you've been up to behind my back.'

'There was an American couple. They were tracking the Ragdoll Artist.'

He glared at me. 'And you didn't think you were obligated to report this?'

'It wasn't about clinic business. I did what I thought was best for the patient.'

'You don't make those kinds of decisions. That's not your role.

You betrayed me and you betrayed the clinic. You acted unprofessionally and, worse, betrayed one of our most troubled patients. I'm terminating you. You have one hour to pack up your stuff and get out. And don't expect a recommendation. If anyone asks, I won't hesitate to say I sacked you for dishonesty.'

We stared at one another for a full twenty seconds. I could see him savoring my distress.

'I'd like to say goodbye to my patients.'

'I forbid it.'

I moved closer to him, got right in his face. 'How dare you deny me that!'

'I'm in charge here. I make the rules.'

I stared into his eyes. 'I've known for a long time that you're a cruel, controlling man. Everyone on the lake knows about your affairs with staff. Some even know you've been selling Agnès's dolls on the sly to a gallery in Lucerne, no doubt pocketing the money for yourself. Maybe the canton police would like to hear about that. Maybe family members who pay enormous fees to maintain their relatives here will be hearing about it too. Not to mention your dismissal from the Jung Institute for unwelcome touching and gross improprieties. Oh, yes! And your dispensing of unauthorized compounded drugs. Should I go on?'

He looked stricken. 'What exactly do you want, Thérèse?'

'Permission to say goodbye to my patients and a favorable letter of recommendation. I have no wish to destroy your reputation, Herr Doktor, and I expect you to refrain from harming mine.'

He nodded, retreated to the window and stared out at the lake. That was it. There was nothing more to be said. I gathered my things, then went around the clinic saying my goodbyes, wishing everyone well. Johnny wept when I told him I was leaving. We sobbed together as I held him in my arms.

When I told Agnès, she shook her head. 'I know why you're going,' she said. 'You did a special thing for me and I'm very grateful to you for it. I had to tell Doctor DeJ. He threatened to take away my art materials if I didn't.' She paused. 'I'll miss you terribly, Thérèse,' she whispered as she hugged me close.

I found out later from Hannah that Agnès's brothers heard about the meeting, phoned DeJ in a rage, demanded that Agnès not be permitted any further meetings with anyone, and that any dolls she made in the future were not to appear on the market, or they'd yank her out of his clinic and install her someplace else.

The following week I was hired to work at the Canton Psychiatric Clinic in Zurich. I was happy to begin a new phase of my life.

I still go back on occasional Saturday evenings to see my old friends at Schwarze Katzenbar. We laugh and sing and they pass on tidbits of gossip about the goings-on at the clinic, and, amidst much mutual laughter, I commiserate with them for still having to work in such a hellhole.

I still think often of Johnny and Agnès.

Tally Vaughan

'll never forget that night. Oscar called me at two a.m. We'd stayed in touch since I called out to him the day after Jason discovered the murals. Every so often I'd stop by the observatory with a six-pack. We'd sit out on the terrace in his Adirondack chairs, drink and shoot the breeze. I enjoyed talking to him. He wasn't the kind of guy you'd expect to find working as a watchman. He liked his job and loved the rundown neighborhood, proud he knew everything going on. He particularly liked observing through his state-of-the-art night-vision goggles. As he liked to put it, 'Since this here's an observatory, I figure my job here's to *observe*.'

He was not at all relaxed when he called me that night. He was panicked.

'Tally! Something bad's going down at the house. Van pulls up, two guys get out with gas cans, walk around sprinkling liquid. Then they break in through the back. I already called Ms Broderick and the cops. I think they're going to torch the place.'

Jesus!

I told him I'd be right over, pulled on some clothes, grabbed my camera and phone, ran down to my car and started toward East Calista, calling Jason en route.

'I know. Cindy called me. Hannah and I are on our way.'

I don't like to drive fast, especially at night. Cops see a black man driving an old car like mine, they're likely to pull me over.

That night was different. This was an emergency, so I stepped on it, hit the interstate and drove to East Calista like a demon. As I neared Locust, I heard the sirens – CPD and CFD. Then as I swerved around the corner and caught sight of the observatory, I saw the flames dancing up the walls of the house. Two big fire trucks were parked on Locust. Firemen were wrestling hoses. The cops stopped me half a block away. I pulled over, slung my camera around my neck and started firing off shots as I ran toward the blaze.

It was a hot night. The smoke was acrid and there was a scent of gasoline in the air. Immediately, the adrenaline kicked in. I went on auto-pilot, racing toward the fire, moving as close as I could, then circling the house, shooting from different angles, heart pounding, totally focused as I worked. The rush I felt was like the rush Jase used to talk about when he described going into a combat situation: nothing else mattered but the task – it seizes you and doesn't let you go. I'd never felt that before, certainly not covering weddings. Later, coming down from the high, I realized how seductive that kind of shoot is – when nothing else has meaning except capturing images of the event, and it doesn't matter what you have to do and what risks you have to take to nail them.

My passion rose as the flames began licking at the gazebo. I couldn't think of anything except that I had to work fast to document what would be the last moments of the murals' existence before they were consumed. This was a once-in-a-lifetime event. It was occurring in real time. I was there with a camera. There'd be no second chance to get it right.

There came a point, within minutes of my arrival, when the flames totally engulfed the gazebo. A sudden burst of wind fanned the fire, showering red embers into the air. The flames rose high above the gazebo, feasting on the wood, biting into it, swallowing it, turning the attic room into a torch. Then, as if in slow motion, the roof collapsed beneath, and the flaming shell of the gazebo sank into the inferno below.

I moved closer while firing off multiple frames. I thought I caught a glimpse of a panel from the murals, paint bubbling off its surface, then the bubbles bursting, then being devoured by flames. I moved as close as I could without getting burned, focusing on the charred beams glowing orange, crashing, smashing against one another, seeming to melt together into the pile of flaming wood that had been the house. Feeling the heat searing my skin, I dropped back.

Choking on smoke, I gasped for air. My shirt was soaked. My throat felt scorched. Was it the smell of burning acrylic that was turning my nostrils raw, the harsh smell of the murals burning up? It happened very fast then, the fire reducing the house to a blazing heap. I stood back, let my camera fall loose and simply gazed, spellbound, at the conflagration as the timbers roasted in a pile, and listened to the hiss as water from the hoses hit the smoldering ruins.

I found Oscar standing in a gray T-shirt just outside the main gate of the observatory. He was slowly shaking his head. I caught a glimmer of moisture in the old guy's eyes.

'They asked me if anyone was inside,' he said. 'I told 'em no.' He glanced at me. 'That part where the art was – it's gone. Good thing you got the art out of there.'

I didn't have the heart to tell him then that we'd only gotten some of it out, that the rest had burned up.

Cindy came over. Oscar introduced us. 'Heard about you,' she said. She turned to Oscar. 'Disaster.' She said the word several times. 'Oh, Oscar, my Caring Place – gone now. All gone . . .'

As she started to weep, Oscar took her in his arms.

An arson investigator came over. I listened as Oscar told him what he'd seen. No question, he said, the men had targeted the house. No, he'd never seen them before. They came in a light-colored VW van. He'd noted down the plate number.

The investigator stared at him. 'What made you do that?'

'I'm the watchman here,' Oscar said.

I found Jase and Hannah sitting on the ground, gazing at the smoking ruins. I was surprised to discover Jase hadn't brought along his camera.

He looked at me. 'Forgot it in the rush. You got the fire?'

I told him I'd shot the hell out of it.

'Good!' he said, then turned to Hannah who had started to weep. He put his arm around her. 'At least we got some of it out,' he told her. 'But not enough.'

'The Cobbs did this,' Hannah said.

'We mustn't blame Joan for telling them about the murals.'

'I don't blame her. Noah warned us. Now we know what "nasty" really means.'

*   *   *

I remember well the moment at dawn when our despair turned into hope. We'd been sitting out there all night on the front steps of the observatory – Jason, Hannah, Cynthia, me, and Joan who'd driven over soon as she heard. We were all bemoaning the lost murals. Just out of habit I started taking pictures of their faces etched with grief and loss, lit by the flickering light of the dying fire.

Hannah was going on about how people who deliberately set out to destroy art are the worst, most barbarous people in the world.

'It's the fascist mentality,' she said. 'That's what the Cobbs are. Fascists, polluters, destroyers.'

'They didn't do this themselves,' I said. 'They got some goons to do it for them.'

'Where do you find people like that?' Hannah asked.

'I saw people like that working security in their building,' Joan said.

'At least we still have the A wall and the B,' Cindy said.

'Half,' Hannah said. 'That's something, I guess.'

'Doesn't work unless you have all four walls,' Jase said.

'You have your photos,' I reminded him.

'Yeah. Maybe . . .'

And then, suddenly, the idea struck – not just to one of us but to all five of us, it seemed, and all at once. Like lightning, Joan said later. Jason said it reminded him of the old comic book image of light bulbs appearing above people's heads.

Then, as we grasped the thought – though no one had so far put it into words – Cindy looked at us, from one to the other, and announced, 'It's certainly possible. Yeah, we could do it. For sure we could. There're several ways it could be done.'

'We're all thinking the same thing, right?' Joan asked.

'Reconstruction. Combine what we have of the original with Jase's photos,' Hannah told her. 'That *is* what we're talking about, right, everybody?'

'You got it, babe,' Jase said.

'Hey, there's the sun!' Joan said, pointing.

We all looked. It was rising fast, a great orb showing red through the smoke.

'A blood sun,' Jase said. 'Calista'll be broiling in an hour.'

Joan turned back to us. 'The sunrise, a new start. That'll be part of the story – how you found the Locust Street Murals, Jase; how we discovered who made them and why; how we tried to save them; the fire that destroyed most of them; and then the reconstruction.'

'It could be a fabulous story,' Jase said.

'It will be!' Joan said. 'I'm going to write it.'

She did write it. And the images I took that night, the ones of the fire and of our faces afterwards – they were incorporated into it. Those images changed my life. They set me on my career. People who saw them saw something in them. Jase said what they saw was my compassion. And that, he said, could not be taught. You either have it or you don't, he said. And then he added that maybe the murals brought out that quality in all of us.

Joan Nguyen

The time has come to reveal, as promised, what I imagine most readers have already figured out – that I am the editor of this text, the person who conducted the interviews, rendered the testimonies of the participants into story form by presenting recalled conversations as dialogue, and utilized other methods of the non-fiction novel to create a coherent narrative.

It's been eighteen months since the Locust Street house caught fire. In that time I've worked with the participants whose testimonies are collected here, assisting them as they distilled their memories, then submitting their edited statements back to them for approval.

In this regard I want especially to thank Cynthia Broderick for granting permission to include Hannah Sachs's summary of her 'confession,' originally made on a promise of confidentiality. Without that account of Cindy's role, the story of the Locust Street Murals would be incomplete. If she did anything improper at the age of sixteen, she has more than made up for it by her close supervision of the reconstruction. As Cynthia recently put it, 'I can't get over the thought that while I was plotting against Courtney and Penny, they were creating a masterpiece in the attic above the very room where I slept.'

Several people mentioned in these testimonies declined to

participate. This was their right and I respect it. Even without their participation, I believe the story is fully told herein.

The Arson Investigation: I'm grateful to Nick Gallagher for the following information regarding his investigation.

As mentioned, Oscar took down the plate number of the van used by the arsonists, a van stolen earlier that evening and found the next day by the police, abandoned in the parking lot of the Walmart store on Ansel Road.

It stank of gasoline, but Gallagher's men could find no forensic evidence inside that would lead them to the arsonists. However, after they contacted the van owner and learned where it was last parked, they found footage from a camera mounted in front of a pharmacy down the street that showed it being stolen. The men who stole it could not be identified from this footage, but the plate number on the car that dropped them off was clear.

Police located the driver, a guy named Hal Castle, who, it turned out, worked as a corporate security contractor. Under interrogation, he spat out the names of the two arsonists, who were arrested the following afternoon. Each confessed to the Locust Street arson and also to torching two houses in Danzig Heights belonging to environmental activists. The arsonists had received $2,000 cash apiece for each job. Castle, the security contractor, told Gallagher he'd received $10,000 per job, out of which he'd paid the arsonists.

He was vague about who hired him, saying only that it was a woman he knew casually as 'Marge,' whom he'd met a couple of times at a West Side bar. When informed that the only way he could avoid a lengthy prison sentence was to find this 'Marge' and give her up, he agreed, was fitted out with a wire, then returned to the bar where he and Marge were regulars.

When, after three nights, Marge appeared, the contractor engaged her in conversation, saying he was eager for more jobs if Marge was satisfied with his work. When Marge confided that she was highly satisfied, he told her that next time he'd need more money, thus initiating a negotiation regarding future arsons. As soon as Marge clearly admitted she'd paid him to start the three fires, Gallagher's men arrested her. Her full name was Margaret Evans, a manager in the security division at Cobb Industries.

She denied hiring Castle, and even after her DNA was found on the cash, declined to turn state's evidence. The case went to trial. Ms Evans was represented by experienced, high-priced attorneys paid for by CI, who were able to raise reasonable doubt in one juror, resulting in a mistrial.

When the City Attorney informed Ms Evans that he would bring her to trial a second time, she hired new attorneys who worked out a plea agreement. In exchange for a light sentence, she implicated Kevin Cobb, who, she stated under oath, had ordered her to have the three houses torched. Kevin Cobb was then arrested and is currently out on bail awaiting trial.

Meantime, Noah Sachs, representing Cindy Broderick, filed a civil suit against Margaret Evans, the Cobb brothers and Cobb Industries for malicious destruction of her property. The case will likely come to court within two years.

But Gallagher isn't finished with the Cobbs. His team has put together a case against them for the Watomi Lake conflagration. Between the three cases, two criminal and one civil, the Cobbs are in a world of hurt.

The Reconstruction of the Locust Street Murals: Cindy and Jase together located an empty two-story industrial space, formerly a welding shop, in East Calista. With funds provided half by Hannah and the remainder raised on the crowd-funding website Kickstarter, they were able to take a long-term lease on the building. They then contracted for the construction of a gazebo the exact dimensions of the original which they had mounted on a platform which could be visited by viewers via a pull-down ladder similar to the pull-down in the Locust Street house.

Art conservators then connected the two salvaged walls of the original murals to Jason's photographs of the burned half, blown up to exactly the same size. The original and the photos were fitted seamlessly together and installed on the interior walls of the reconstructed gazebo. (Care was taken to differentiate the original paintings from the photographs by printing the photographs in a slightly different set of tones.)

Those of us who had seen the originals visited the reconstruction every day as it was mounted. Every effort was made to recreate the experience of the original. When work was near completion, Penny Dawson Ruiz came up from Key West to take a look. She wholeheartedly approved the reconstruction. She also wept when she saw it.

Once the reconstruction was done, Cindy held an opening party. Artists, art critics and local art collectors were invited, as were critics and gallerists from New York and LA. Press coverage was extensive and soon people were talking about the murals.

A website has been set up (www.TheMurals.net) where people can make reservations for quarter-hour-long visits. The cost of admission is twelve dollars per person, all of which goes toward the maintenance of the project, including twenty-four-hour security protection lest anyone again attempts to destroy the artwork. The only rule is that no more than four people may go up the ladder and stand in the reconstructed gazebo at one time. Since the opening, reservations have been booked three months in advance.

The Visitors' Book: There's a Visitors' Book available in the exhibition space in which visitors are encouraged to jot down their thoughts after visiting the murals. A sampling of some recent comments:

'Was deeply moved! Mysterious and overpowering.'

'Don't really get it, but they definitely set a mood.'

'Felt like I was being squeezed by those people. Who were they?'

'Tremendous experience. I won't forget those murals.'

'They're saying something very deep. Not sure what it is.'

'I felt like I was in the middle of someone else's nightmare.'

'Scary!'

'Eerie!'

'It's like you're surrounded and there's no escape. Kind of like life if you look at it a certain way.'

'The most evil people I've ever seen. They'll haunt me.'

'What screwballs painted this and why?'

'Crazy, compelling, irresistible.'

'Like being in the middle of a war between four tribes. Couldn't stay too long. Afraid I'd be crushed.'

'Dark, dark, dark. Want to come back and see them again.'

'Felt a lot of pain in those paintings. You could call them *pain*-tings.'

'Inspiring. Makes me want to paint on walls.'

'Maybe I'll understand them better after I read the book.'

'Felt anguished. Felt the artists' hurt.'

'This is what things are like these days – people cornering you, closing in on you. No matter which way you turn, you're being oppressed.'

'Nothing happy up there. Need relief. Going over now to the CMA to bathe in the warm glow of Monet.'

'If this is how the world is, I want to stick my head in an oven.'

'Impressive accomplishment by immensely talented young artists. You can tell they really felt it . . . whatever "it" was.'

'Haunting, so haunting.'

'These murals make me want to rethink my life.'

The Current Status of Courtney Cobb and Others: Courtney still resides at Privatklinik DeJonghe where she continues to create her ragdolls. Anna von Arx is now the exclusive representative for her artwork throughout the world. Courtney occasionally receives visitors, and has been visited by Penny Ruiz several times. Prior to publication, she read through the text of this book. Although she has chosen not to comment about it, nor to grant it her imprimatur, she has not voiced objections to any of its content or its dissemination.

Johnny Baldwin has left the clinic and now lives in Amsterdam. Since settling there, he has visited Courtney several times. He intends to continue doing so.

Shortly before this text was published, lawyers for Jack and Kevin Cobb threatened to sue me for defamation. So far no such suit has been filed. If it is, Noah Sachs will represent me and the publisher pro bono.

What do the Locust Street Murals Mean to Us? Finally, I asked each of us (including myself) to write a line or two in answer to the question 'Looking back, what do the Locust Street Murals mean to you?'

Jason: To me the murals are about seeing and being seen. The people in them appear to be gazing at us, undressing us. For me they're all about the *eyes!*

Hannah: For me the murals are about the healing and redemptive power of art.

Tally: For me the murals are about the role of chance – looking for one thing, then finding another.

Me: Our quest for the meaning of the murals became the story of the murals. If I learned one thing from this experience, it's that the backstory is *always* the story.

Acknowledgements

The author wishes to thank the following for advice and suggestions during the writing and editing of this novel: my very supportive agent, George Lucas; Kate Lyall Grant, Carl Smith, Natasha Bell and the gang at Severn House; Carrie Tillie and Eugenia Martino for their helpful early critiques; Bob Butler for boosting my morale, especially during the difficult period following the California Wine Country fires; and to my family, Paula, Nick and Leila for their support and confidence throughout. I couldn't have done it without you guys.

French artist Anne-Valérie Dupond's marvellous textile sculptures inspired the face-stitching technique employed by my fictional Ragdoll Artist.

11/19